THE
RAYDEN VALKYRIE
TALES
VOLUME I

Also by Stephen Zimmer

The Rising Dawn Saga
The Exodus Gate
The Storm Guardians
The Seventh Throne
The Undying Light

The Fires in Eden Series
Crown of Vengeance
Dream of Legends
Spirit of Fire

The Faraway Saga
Dream of the Navigator

Hellscapes
Hellscapes, Volume 1
Hellscapes, Volume II

Chronicles of Ave
Chronicles of Ave, Volume 1

The Ragnar Stormbringer Tales (eBook only)
Depths of Night
When the Cold Breathes

The Rayden Valkyrie Tales (eBook only)
Blood of a Queen
Winds of War
The Sun's Caress
Across Desert Plains

THE
RAYDEN VALKYRIE
TALES
VOLUME I

Stephen Zimmer

 SEVENTH STAR PRESS

Cover art: Olivia Pro Design
Cover art in this book copyright © 2018 Olivia Pro Design & Seventh Star
Press, LLC.

Editor: Holly Marie Phillippe
Published by Seventh Star Press, LLC.

ISBN Number: 978-1-948042-64-2

Seventh Star Press
www.seventhstarpress.com
info@seventhstarpress.com

Publisher's Note:
The Rayden Valkyrie Tales, Volume I is a work of fiction. All names,
characters, and places are the product of the author's imagination, used
in fictitious manner. Any resemblances to actual persons, places, locales,
events, etc. are purely coincidental.

Printed in the United States of America

First Edition

ACKNOWLEDGEMENTS

I would like to thank all of my readers, who are the ones that make all of the work and sacrifice involved in the writing process worth enduring. Your encouragement and support mean the world to me. You are the reason why I moved forward with writing projects like the Rayden Valkyrie Tales, as I want my readers to always have new and exciting adventures to look forward to! Enjoy the tales here in Volume I, as there is so much more ahead!

I deeply appreciate the time and effort that Holly Marie Phillippe applied to these novellas as an editor. Knowing my voice, the characters, and my vision very clearly, she has done a wonderful job in identifying the things that needed to be done to strengthen the text. A good editor watches your back, and she definitely has done exactly that for these tales.

Olivia, of Olivia Pro Design, has my heartfelt gratitude for the outstanding cover designs she has done on these tales for their eBook releases and for this print compendium. She has given them a consistent look that captures the tone of each story so well.

Thank you to my family, both those of blood, like my sister Courtney, and those who have become family, whether of a human nature like Martin and Mindy Roberts, and Eric and Kylie Jude, or of a four-legged nature like our dear cat Dubious!

Finally, I would like to thank those who I consider to be part of my tribe, including friends, fellow authors in the writing community, and other professionals whose encouragement and support helps me travel my road. There are too many to list in a small space like this, but you know who you are!

Enjoy your adventures in the Rayden Valkyrie Tales! Each one tells a little more of her greater story! Onward and Upward!

ACKNOWLEDGMENTS

DEDICATION

To the One Who is the Beacon of Light in the darkest of times.

To my mother and father, for each of them being genuine examples of living a life with honor.

To my beloved Holly, for showing me that loyalty still exists in this world

To my sister, for showing resilience in the face of adversity.

BLOOD
OF A
QUEEN

A RAYDEN VALKYRIE TALE

STEPHEN ZIMMER

BLOOD OF A QUEEN

"Best for you to stay inside, until dawn," the narrow-faced innkeeper told Rayden. "You can handle yourself well-enough, but the streets of Terith-Ka are no place to roam when the sorcery of Rastapur plagues us. What stalks the night is not human. Many have gained glimpses of it. Thieves and cutthroats alike huddle in their lairs and refuse to venture out when dark falls."

Grim-faced, Rayden nodded in response, concealing her intentions. "I have found sorcery to be a plague more often than not in my journeys."

"It is something I do not understand," the innkeeper replied, frowning. "It is also something I do not wish to understand."

"You are a wise man," Rayden said. Reaching into the small leather pouch attached to her belt, she took out a couple of silver coins and gave them over to the innkeeper.

"What is this for?" he asked, dark eyebrows converging in an expression of puzzlement. "You have paid me for your room. There is nothing you owe."

"For your troubles, earlier this evening," Rayden said.

"I should be the one giving you coins. Those two dregs deserved a lesson, and you proved to be an excellent teacher," the innkeeper replied, giving her a smile. "I wish more louts like them could receive such thorough instruction. The girls that work for

1

me have to put up with too much, and I cannot be everywhere at once to put a stop to it when it happens."

The hint of a grin played about Rayden's lips at the praise. Both of the uncouth vagabonds had been dragged unconscious from the inn by their friends, after having attempted to grope Rayden under the influence of lust emboldened by far too much wine consumed.

She had ignored their bawdy comments and looks, but she could never tolerate them trying to lay their hands on her. One would awaken with a broken wrist and missing teeth, while the other would greet the morning with a blackened eye, aching groin, and smashed nose.

Having witnessed Rayden's stark demonstration of speed and power, the tavern's remaining patrons had chosen to leave her alone during the rest of her meal. Even the two serving girls were treated more respectfully than they had been earlier, an observation that brought Rayden a little cheer.

"You have been a good host to me the past couple of days, and things like what happened last night are still troublesome for you, whether justified or not," Rayden said. "You have a tavern to run, and a living that you work hard to earn."

"I imagine the men of the lands you are from behave themselves much better, with women such as you around them," the innkeeper said, a smile manifesting within his thick, dark beard. He then shook his head, and the smile faded, his next words sounding contrite. "You must think the men of this city to be pigs, with what you have experienced, observed, and listened to in here at night."

"Most men behave well-enough, wherever I have gone," Rayden said. "There are always a few in every land who choose to be less than swine, but it is important never to condemn all men for the actions of a few scum. Neither should all women be condemned for the actions of a few. Each should be held to account for their own actions."

"You speak wisely ... and I should have better sense, and not be keeping you from a good night's rest any longer," the innkeeper replied. "I have a few matters to attend to myself before I turn in for the night, which has already grown late."

"It was good speaking with you," Rayden said, giving him a smile. "I will see you when dawn breaks.".

"May Ahuran-Maz bless you with a restful sleep," the innkeeper said, mentioning the god of light that many people of the region worshipped.

Rayden gave the innkeeper a nod and walked past him. Making her way from the common room of the tavern, she proceeded into an enclosed courtyard, which had several doors facing the open space.

A pensive stillness pervaded the shadows. A chill clung to the midnight air, but no breeze stirred.

Walking over to the door of the small chamber that served as her quarters, Rayden cast a glance about the courtyard. Satisfied that no eyes were upon her, she leaped up, grabbing the edge of the flat roof.

Pulling herself up, and careful to make no sounds, she crouched low on the rooftop a few moments later.

From the higher vantage, Rayden gained a broad view of the labyrinthine maze of alleys, paths, and buildings spread before the high walls of the queen's towering citadel. Moonlight and scattered torches provided a limited amount of illumination, but for the most part the city remained shrouded in darkness.

After spending several days in Terith-Ka, Rayden had found its people awash in fear; fear of enemies, their own queen, and a night-born plague of terror that had come upon them not long ago.

Her curiosity piqued, Rayden had gleaned quite a few things about recent events affecting Terith-Ka's populace from the innkeeper and others she had spoken with.

A widespread drought causing an abysmal harvest had ignited a simmering restlessness in the populace. The growing hunger soon resulted in mass riots and talk of revolt.

The riots had been suppressed with great ferocity at the order of the queen, and many had been executed in horrific ways. The brutal displays cowed the people, but they did nothing to assuage their gnawing resentment.

Not long after, an outbreak of gruesome murders had begun in the shadows of the night. Claiming a wide array of victims, the savage killings were attributed to the workings of dark sorcery.

Witnesses spoke of seeing terrifying wraiths roving through the streets in the depths of night. Living shadows that left death in their wake, the entities were said to be the work of Rastapur, a city deemed to be a main rival to Terith-Ka in the lands of the east.

In little time, the streets of Terith-Ka grew barren with the falling of night. Only the most courageous or foolhardy braved the alleyways and paths of the sprawling city when the moon traveled across the skies.

Several men said to be spies from Rastapur had then been discovered in Terith-Ka. After being whisked off to the queen's citadel, it was announced to the people that they had confessed the sorcery behind the killings on the streets.

Even more angering to the people of Terith-Ka, it was announced that the drought had also been a working of Rastapurian sorcery. In an instant, all indignation harbored toward the queen evaporated, and the people's ire turned toward Rastapur.

Now, a starving populace endured higher taxation and prepared for a looming war against Rastapur. Despite the onerous burdens placed on a suffering populace, it stood clear that all thoughts of revolt against the queen had been abandoned.

Every instinct within Rayden cried out that something was greatly amiss about the situation. Knowing she could not ease her mind until she found some answers, Rayden had decided to extend her stay in Terith-Ka.

Keeping a moonlit vigil on the rooftop, she waited. Her gaze well-honed to pick up any hint of motion in the scene before her, Rayden listened for the slightest sounds, remaining poised for any disturbance in her surroundings.

The night crawling onward, her great discipline maintained an unwavering state of alertness. Her breathing remained steady, taking in the cool night air. Shifting her position a little from time to time, she kept limber and ready to move at a moment's notice.

Finally, at the edge of her vision, distinct movement in the skies drew her eyes upward.

Outlined against the clear, starry horizon, and approaching from the direction of the citadel, a dark, winged shape glided through the air. Far larger than any natural denizen of the skies around Terith-Ka, the entity looked to be humanoid in shape, with a broad pair of membranous wings spreading from its back.

Descending out of the sky, the creature alighted on a rooftop located a far distance from where Rayden watched. Folding its wings, the entity took a few strides forward, before pausing and then dropping out of view.

Looking back up, Rayden took account of another of the thing's ilk flying through the air, and then a third, both also coming from the vicinity of the queen's citadel.

The second entity took to a rooftop not far from the first, while the third glided onward, drawing ever closer to Rayden. Just before it drifted over her position, the entity swooped downward and landed a couple of rooftops away from her.

Wings outstretched, the creature remained upright for a couple of heartbeats. At first, Rayden thought her eyes to be deceiving her. The outline of the citadel visible beyond its body, it appeared as if she could see through the creature, but a few moments later the thing appeared solid enough.

Blinking her eyes, Rayden kept her focus on the entity.

Its attention appeared focused on something below it. Lowering into a crouch, it crept toward the edge of the roof and hunched down further. To Rayden's eyes, the entity had the air of a serpent coiled to strike.

Her assessment proved accurate. Springing from its position, the entity fell upon something beneath it. Human in nature, and brimming with fear, a sharp cry penetrated the night before abruptly going silent.

Rayden moved over to the edge of the roof closest to the area where the entity had leaped down. Hearing no immediate sounds, she turned her body, grasped the edge, and lowered herself to the ground, keeping her footfall soft.

Advancing along the side of an alleyway, Rayden worked her way closer to the place where she estimated the entity to be. Immersed in shadows, she slid her weapons out.

Stalking forward without a sound, Rayden held her weapons at the ready, prepared to strike at any sudden movements. Drawing to a stop, she leaned forward and looked around the corner of an alley to the right.

Seeing nothing, Rayden crossed the open space and proceeded onward.

Nearing the corner of another alleyway, Rayden paused. Her ears picked up a faint series of noises; slurping, sucking, and tearing sounds that sent a chill racing through her blood.

The dreadful sounds came from a short distance down the side alley. Rayden braced herself, steeling her mind for whatever the night was about to reveal. Taking another couple of steps forward, she halted at the edge of the alley.

Peering around the corner, Rayden saw the winged entity

stooped over the body of a human. From a closer vantage, she gained a solid perspective of the creature's great size in comparison to the body underneath it.

No signs of life came from the figure on the ground.

Rearing up, the creature looked around, its eyes glowing like flaring embers. The entity had a flatter facial structure, with two prominent slits for nostrils atop a wide set of jaws, the latter teeming with spiky teeth of exceptional lengths.

The creature had long limbs, and its elongated hands ended in curving talons.

Sniffing at the air, the entity's nostrils flared wide.

Rising to a towering height, the creature stood up, several drops of its victim's blood falling from its jaws, along with a gobbet of flesh. A sibilant hiss passing through its arsenal of teeth, the entity stared in the direction of Rayden.

Spreading its wings, the entity's form filled the narrow alley with ease. Continuing its hissing, the creature took a step in Rayden's direction.

Knowing the entity to be aware of her, Rayden stepped out from the shadows and took up a balanced combat stance in the center of the alley's entrance.

At her appearance, the fiery light within the deep sockets of the creature's eyes flared brighter. Spreading its jaws wider, a loud, rasping sound erupted from the depths of the creature's throat.

"Hell spawn, you will not find me such easy prey," Rayden declared to the entity, bringing her weapons up a little higher.

Her defiance appeared to provoke the creature. Leaning forward, the creature left its quarry behind and rushed down the alley toward her. Maw opening wide, the entity loosed a guttural, hellish roar.

Shifting quickly to the right, Rayden abandoned the mouth of the alley. Turning to her left and squaring her body, she lowered into a crouch.

Thumping on the alley's surface, the heavy, pounding strides of the creature grew louder.

Loosing another sonorous roar, the creature burst out of the alley a moment later. Whipping about in Rayden's direction, the beast surged forward and reached for her with its talons.

For an instant of time, before the creature's broad mass enveloped her body, Rayden had one chance to strike.

Lunging forward, and dodging inside the creature's outstretched talons, Rayden thrust her sword deep into its exposed abdomen. Continuing the attack with full force, she chopped down hard with her axe, burying the head between the beast's left shoulder and neck.

The two blades drove into a solid, flesh-like substance at first, eliciting a piercing cry from the entity. A moment later, the tension holding the two blades firm in place released its grip upon them, the weapons passing through the creature's body as if it were no longer there.

The creature remained in place, but Rayden could now see down the alley, through its body.

Releasing a cry of anger and frustration, Rayden slashed and hacked with her blades, the weapons continuing to meet no resistance, passing right through the translucent form.

Drifting just above the ground instead of taking steps, the beast drew back several paces from Rayden. Facing toward her, the creature made no move to attack.

Rayden stayed her ground and did not press her own attack. Knowing it to be folly to run, she also realized her weapons could not harm the entity in the incorporeal state it had taken.

Hovering in place, the creature's form solidified once more, until Rayden could no longer see the depths of the alleyway through its body. When the beast had attained a full, physical presence, it stood upon the ground.

Gripping her weapons tight, Rayden absorbed a troubling revelation. Focusing on the places where her weapons had struck the beast, she could see no signs of any wounds.

Casting a baleful gaze toward Rayden, the creature opened its jaws wide, a grating, sonorous cry erupting from within.

Springing forward, the beast launched itself toward Rayden.

Dropping low and tumbling forward, Rayden tucked and rolled over her right shoulder. The move took her beneath the oncoming beast's left wing.

The instant she came up, Rayden rotated to her left and slashed through with her axe, cutting the beast deep across the back of its leg, just beneath the knee. Screeching, the creature stumbled forward, unable to bear weight upon the injured leg.

Rayden gained her feet and oriented toward the beast. Once again, she could see the alley beyond through its body, the latter now floating just off the ground.

Taking a solid appearance again, the beast stepped toward her, putting its full weight upon the leg that she had seemingly crippled. Baring its teeth at her, the creature growled, its fiery eyes blazing even brighter.

Shifting between states, the beast could restore itself from any wounds suffered while in a physical form. A terrible dilemma loomed before Rayden. Unless she could somehow land a killing blow when the creature took a corporeal form, it could sustain an attack all night, wearing her down bit by bit.

She had no time to ponder the vexing situation further. Continuing forward, the beast crouched down, closing off any maneuver like the one she had executed moments before.

Pushing off her left foot, Rayden hurtled toward the beast and launched a forward kick with her right foot that landed squarely in its face, snapping its head back.

Striking down on both sides of its wide neck, she embedded her axe and sword deep. Yanking hard, she tore the weapons free.

The creature shrieked, swinging its arms wildly. A left backhand caught Rayden, batting her aside and knocking the air from her lungs. Careening off the wall of the alley, she fell to the ground.

The beast did not follow up on the blow. Retreating, it shifted states again, seeking to heal the latest wounds Rayden had inflicted.

Dazed slightly from the impact on the wall, Rayden shook her head, and got up to her feet. Moving back to the center of the alley, she awaited the next assault.

Then, a strange development occurred. The creature attained a physical form again, but, after just a few moments, fell back into its translucent state.

Again, it tried to shift into a physical state. Like before, transition lasted only a few moments.

The failure to sustain a corporeal state appeared to enrage the beast. Gnashing its teeth and glowering, the beast roared, but Rayden could still see through it.

With an eerie, guttural cry, the half-transparent entity then leapt upward. Taking to the sky, it climbed into the heights with wings spread wide.

"You bastard, I had the best of you!" Rayden said in a growling tone, through clenched teeth, eyeing the creature ascending into the star-filled night.

Frustration boiling inside, she looked at her blades. No blood marring their gleaming surfaces, she returned the weapons back to the sheath and loop at her waist.

Turning, she jumped and grabbed onto the roof of the edifice behind her. Pulling herself up a heartbeat later, and swinging her legs around to gain purchase, she climbed onto the roof and stood up.

It took a few moments to find the creature against the night skies, but with the aid of the moon she espied it in the distance, heading fast in the direction of the citadel.

"At least I know where you came from," Rayden muttered to herself, watching the creature diminish in size, until it reached the main tower of the citadel and disappeared from view. "And it was not from Rastapur."

She kept her vigil for a little while longer and witnessed the other two winged entities returning to the citadel. The sight reinforced her conviction.

The citadel had to be investigated.

***

Returning to the inn shortly before the approach of dawn, Rayden had a fitful time gaining sleep. A host of thoughts ran through her mind, not the least of which was the fact that the malignant sorcery being loosed upon the populace of Terith-Ka came from inside the citadel.

Later during the following day, Rayden headed from the inn and scouted the area around the citadel. She took careful account of the various approaches to the towering complex of structures, and the nature of the walls surrounding it.

While robust and formed of massive stone blocks, the walls had been built centuries before. Time and weather had worked upon the facing for ages, creating an abundance of handholds for a climber of even modest experience.

Rayden eyed the towering figures carved in relief on the walls near the front gates of the citadel. Bearing spears and attired in ceremonial garments, the bearded warriors depicted kept an unwavering vigil; unlike the living guards patrolling the walls, whose patterns were easy enough to ascertain.

When she finally left the area around the citadel, Rayden harbored no worries about getting inside the walls.

The late afternoon sun cast lengthy shadows through the city by the time she returned to the inn. Finding an unoccupied corner of the tavern, Rayden ordered up a meal from one of the serving girls.

Rayden spent a little extra to partake of a better fare than usual, treating herself to some tender mutton prepared with spices, bread softened with olive oil, figs, and honeyed dates. Instead of wine, she chose a lighter drink common to the area made from pomegranate and water.

When she had finished, the serving girl collected the tray and bowls used for the meal. Stomach full, and feeling replenished, Rayden sipped at her cup and relaxed.

When twilight loomed, the tavern began filling with patrons. Remaining in the corner, Rayden watched the growing activity with a casual eye.

In light of her recent encounter in the tavern with lust-driven men, Rayden paid closer attention to a pair of attractive young women who sauntered in and began flitting about the tables. Basking in the attention given to them, the women did not have to pay for their cups of wine. More than one man offered to cover their cost, whenever one of them wanted another cup.

Readily indulging the generosity of the tavern patrons, the women quaffed wine, bantered, and jested with their benefactors.

After having consumed too much wine, in a short time, the pair began to lose their balance, tumbling into the arms of seated patrons more than once. The women's obvious drunkenness emboldened several of the men catching them. Whether slipping a hand onto a breast or fondling buttocks while helping one of the women back upright, the more lascivious within the crowd took advantage of the situation.

Rayden glared at the brazen transgressors, and a part of her desired to pummel them outright, but they did not represent the greatest danger in the room to the young women.

It had not taken long for Rayden to glean the most concerning predators within the raucous throng. Three men sitting together on the opposite side of the room had grown increasingly quiet after the women began losing control of their faculties.

Upper lips and heads shaved bare, all three had dense, longer beards. Clad in flowing tunics of lighter hues that descended to the lower part of their legs, the men wore narrow black headbands that marked them as followers of the moon god Suenanna, a deity whose worshippers believed to be supreme over all other gods and goddesses.

Rayden knew enough about the cult of Suenanna to understand that its followers viewed those who did not follow their god to be inferior, lesser beings, little more than dumb herd animals. While controlling and protective of their own women, men who followed Suenanna had a very different attitude toward women who were not of their faith. Even when forcing a non-believing woman against her will, using one to satisfy carnal desires did not constitute an affront to their god.

Such arrogant and wicked beliefs gave rise to the scenario taking shape before Rayden's eyes.

Casting furtive glances between each other, the trio had begun casting intent looks at the women. Whispering in one another's ears, all the while keeping their attention fixed on the young women, they had the air of beasts stalking prey.

When night fell, the tavern began emptying out. While the murders taking place in Terith-Ka occurred late in the night, few desired to chance fate, so most of the patrons wasted little time in taking leave of their comrades and making their way home.

The two young women still remained within the tavern's main room, continuing to flirt and chat with those foolhardy or courageous enough to risk a little more time.

Waiting and watching, the three men that Rayden had identified maintained their vigil.

Laughing together, and arm in arm, the two women finally broke away from a pair of older men they had been chatting with and staggered toward the exit of the tavern. Once outside, they lurched to the right, starting down the street.

Without delay, the three men watching them got up and crossed the room, following after the women.

Knowing what they intended, Rayden got to her feet and set her near-empty cup down. Her investigation of the citadel would have to wait for just a little while longer.

She took a couple of steps in the direction of the doorway leading onto the street when a tall, broad-shouldered man stepped in front of her. The front of his tunic damp with wine, the large man carried a hostile look on his face. A glaze across his eyes showed that not all of the wine had been spilled on his tunic.

"You the wench who hurt my lads last night?" he asked in a deep voice, his breath reeking of garlic.

"If they were the ones that put their hands on me uninvited, then yes," Rayden responded in a firm manner. "And I think you should step aside."

"You think you are so tough?" the man responded, giving her a toothy grin. A low belch escaped his lips.

"Leave her be," the innkeeper interjected in a sharp tone, from where he had been collecting a few drinking vessels left behind by patrons.

Looking agitated toward the interruption, the big man put up a hand and told the innkeeper, "Do not get in my way. This wench needs a good lesson."

"I told you to step out of my way, I do not have time," Rayden told the man, fast growing impatient.

"Wench, I will tell you when you can ..." the man started to say, reaching out to grab Rayden.

With a circular move of her right hand, Rayden swept his arm aside. Whipping her back leg around, she delivered a solid kick to the side of his right knee.

Howling in pain, the large man dropped to the floor, bracing on his left knee.

Sliding forward and to the man's right, Rayden sent a hard right hook crashing straight into his jaws. The punch snapping his head back, the man fell in a heap onto the floor, dazed and taken out of the fight.

"I will take care of this later," Rayden said to the innkeeper.

Hurrying across the room, she did not wait for a response.

Exiting the tavern and looking to the right, Rayden saw that the two women and the men heading after them had proceeded far down the street.

Oblivious to the three men pursuing them, the young women laughed and continued in their spirited repartee. Turning from the street, the women entered the mouth of an alleyway.

Increasing their gait, the men hastened after them, disappearing into the alleyway just a few paces behind.

Seeing the hunters closing in upon their quarry, Rayden broke into a run. Muffled cries broke out from the depths of the alleyway a couple moments later, followed by an outburst of laughter.

Turning from the street, Rayden took up her weapons and stormed down the narrow passageway.

Jeering and laughing at the sobbing, terrified women gripped in their hands, the cruel trio mocked their victims. Rage filled Rayden at the horrific sight just ahead of her, sealing three death sentences in her mind.

Holding one of the women's arms from behind, the first man Rayden came upon had no hint of her approach until she delivered a kick full force between his legs from behind. With a deep gasp of air, he crumpled to the ground, releasing his hold on the young woman.

Rayden did not pause for an instant. Advancing past the fallen rogue, she drew up behind his comrade a couple paces away.

Kneeling between the legs of the second woman, his tunic hoisted up, the malignant cur had been readying to violate her. With a vicious, underhanded swing of her axe, Rayden brought the blade up fast between his legs. The sharp edge tore through his groin and continued up the flesh of his backside, following the split of his rear and cleaving deep.

With a savage jerk, Rayden tore her blade free. Blood poured from the grisly wound.

Using her right fist, closed around the hilt of her sword, Rayden shoved the man aside. Falling to the ground, he shook all over, his life ebbing fast through the blood gushing out.

Turning her wrist and arm, Rayden thrust the blade straight into the mouth of the last predator, who had been holding the second woman down for his comrade. The tip fragmented teeth and drove through flesh and bone.

Laughing just a few moments before, the man gurgled and gagged, a look of shock splayed on his face. Honed iron skewering his head, the end of the sword protruded out the back of his ruined skull.

Rayden lifted her right foot up, set it firm against the chest of the third man, and pushed outward, pulling her blade free and sending him toppling back into the side of the alley. Turning around, she set her weapons down, knowing that neither of the two men now at her feet would rise to threaten her, or anyone else.

She oriented toward the first of the miscreants, who had begun to stumble down the alleyway, whimpering in great throes of pain from the crushing blow delivered to his groin. Having abandoned the woman he had been terrorizing, he sought to escape the blade-wielding tempest who had just slain his comrades in brutal fashion.

Chasing him down in moments, Rayden hurled the man to the ground and spun him over. Straddling his torso and pinning his arms with her knees, she rained a torrent of hard fists into his face, shattering teeth, breaking his nose and jaws, and continuing until no sign of life remained within him.

Glaring down at the dead scoundrel, it took Rayden a few moments to unclench her blood-covered fists. The execution consummated, her fury abated.

Getting up, she went over to the second woman, who remained on the ground. Her companion now kneeled at her side and cradled her head. Both of the women looked to Rayden, their eyes wide in fright.

"You are safe ... those three beasts will threaten you no longer," Rayden told them in a low, calm voice. "Their actions condemned them."

Saying nothing in response, the women continued to glance toward the still forms of their attackers.

"Do you think you can stand up?" Rayden asked the woman on the ground.

Tears continuing to run down her cheeks, the woman looked to Rayden after a moment and nodded.

"Help her up," Rayden instructed her kneeling companion. Then, in a firmer tone of voice, she directed her next words toward both of the women. "Go back to your homes, without delay. Take more care in places where both beasts and men gather. Those that sought to harm you tonight made their intent plain, but other beasts can disguise their nature well, and even appear honorable. Do not let recklessness see you become their prey."

Gathering up her weapons and cleaning them off on the tunic of the man she had driven her sword through, Rayden took her time and let the young women collect themselves.

After helping her friend up to her feet, the first woman turned to look at Rayden.

"I do not know who you are, but thank you," she said, in a voice laden with emotion.

"Yes, thank you ... with all my heart," her friend added, looking a little unsteady.

"I only did what any of us should do," Rayden said. Pausing, she looked each of the women in the eyes. "We live in an unforgiving, harsh world. You must learn to rely upon yourselves, and to look out for each other, from this night onward."

"We will," the first said after a few heartbeats. "I will not forget you."

Letting her gaze linger for a moment upon Rayden, she turned and curled an arm about her friend's waist. Taking slow steps, she began to guide her companion down the alleyway, heading in the direction they had been going when overtaken by the three men.

Rayden watched the pair heading away through the shadows, until they reached the end of the alley and disappeared around the corner to the right.

Taking a deep breath, Rayden started down the passageway in the other direction, stepping over the body of the body of the man she had beaten to death with her fists.

Other kinds of murderous beasts still needed to be hunted down, and the time had come to take a closer look around the citadel.

***

Oil-burning lamps hanging from chains cast a reddish light across the marble flooring and broad, soaring columns running the length of the capacious hall. Rayden eyed the pools of shadow throughout the large space for several heartbeats before continuing forward.

Moving swift and silent, Rayden made use of the columns. Bounding from one to another, and pausing whenever servants or guards manifested, she made her way to the far end of the hall.

From the great hall, she proceeded through a few more

halls, passed chambers and doorways, strode down the length of galleries, and climbed up staircases.

Open to the stars, courtyards harboring glistening pools of clear water, fountains, and foliage in abundance graced the palace environs. Sweet floral scents wafted along the night breezes, a stark contrast to the aromas of sweat, dung, animals, and other refuse pervading the streets beyond the citadel's walls.

Rayden found the ornate, tranquil atmosphere to be like another world, shielded from the congestion, trials, and suffering that the mass populace faced on a daily basis.

Delving deeper into the palace, Rayden evaded guards with ease. Their voices and footsteps echoed far in the spacious chambers and halls, giving her ample warning to conceal herself.

Clad in knee-length black tunics, trousers, leather boots and short hoods, the latter containing lappets to cover the lower half of their faces, the guards displayed a uniform appearance. Rayden suspected they held an elite status within the queen's forces, selected for loyalty and discipline.

The guards had short, dark beards, styled into ringlets matching the fashion of their hair, the length of which descended to the upper part of their necks. All of them carried long spears, which featured distinctive, golden spheres at the base.

Rayden also came across more servants, both male and female. Most of the servants were attired in brown tunics, but a few wore white garments. Noticing the cleaner appearance, softer-looking skin, and better grooming on the servants attired in white, Rayden guessed them to be the ones given the more intimate household tasks.

Continuing further through the palace complex, the furnishings became more opulent, from clusters of low couches arranged so an intimate group could converse, to elaborately woven carpets, to exquisite tapestries adorning the walls. The frequency of guards and white-garbed servants also increased

Taking account of the changes, Rayden knew she was drawing closer to the area she sought, where answers to the flying monstrosities would be found.

Working her way upward, along a wide, circular staircase, Rayden heard voices coming from above. Springing from one step to the next, Rayden reached the top in swift fashion.

Crossing through an antechamber, and avoiding another pair of guards, she eyed a broad, open doorway that let into a much larger chamber beyond. With soundless steps, she continued forward, entering the chamber and moving along the wall to the right.

Melting into the curtains and shadows, Rayden surveyed the grand chamber.

A woman in exquisite robes of white and gold reclined upon the cushions of a lavish couch crafted of a darker wood, with finely-carved vines and flowers running down its legs and single, raised end. A resplendent golden circlet encompassed her head. Long earrings of gold fitted with gleaming jewels dangled down each side of her angular face, the bright ornamentation a vivid contrast with the deep black of her hair.

Displaying a luxuriant sheen, her curly locks tumbled about her shoulders, the ends brushing against the mid-point of her chest. Intricately crafted bracelets and anklets of gold decorated her ankles and wrists.

Dark, piercing eyes and soft, full lips highlighted a face both beautiful and stern. While not a young woman, she displayed no tarnishing from the advance of time, which had not left its first marks upon her silken skin. If anything, she looked to be a woman in the heights of her physical prime.

Rayden knew, without a doubt, that she gazed upon Queen Annukeyen, the ruler of Terith-Ka.

Near to the queen, another woman stood.

Dark robes flowed to the tops of her sandaled feet. Her

beauty rivaled that of the woman on the couch, the only blemish in her smooth, olive-hued skin a distinctive scar running down the side of her face; beginning from just below her left eye and continuing to the base of her jaw line.

Rayden tensed at the sight of the pronounced scar, recognizing the mark at once; Belphaal's Caress.

Worshipped in the shadows by many in the lands east of Griaca, the ancient demonic entity was said to trace a single claw down the face of those receiving the secrets of its dark mysteries and arts. The lengthy scar served both as an acclamation and warning. It confirmed the high rank of the one bearing it, but it also stood as a reminder to the marked individual of what would come should they ever betray or fail the dark god.

The presence of a sorceress bearing Belphaal's Caress surprised and troubled Rayden. Those who carried the mark led hidden, guarded lives, wielding their powers under cloaks of darkness and sending others to do their public bidding.

Seeing the queen holding a direct audience with such an enigmatic figure, Rayden knew that she stood on the cusp of unraveling the mystery to the winged nightmares preying upon the streets of Terith-Ka.

"Anger grows with every passing day toward Rastapur," Queen Annukeyen said, taking a sip from a golden cup. "It is already to where the people ask for war."

"How long do you intend to wait for the war? Will it begin soon?" the sorceress asked, a hint of impatience in her face.

"Soon enough, Urian-Na" the queen replied. "Another turning of the moon, and my army will march upon them. I assure you."

"It is good to know that the wait is almost over," Urian-Na replied. A grin touched her lips. "Great queen, I will see that you are well-aided."

The queen smiled back. "What more could you possibly

do? You brought great hunger over all the land and followed it with terror in the streets. You lured some men from Rastapur, gave me their whereabouts to seize them, and then counseled me on how I could use them in proclaiming to the people the source of their suffering and fear. Now, all eyes have turned to Rastapur. It will soon be delivered into my hands.

"You have guided me in all of this. I promise you, Urian-Na, when Rastapur falls under my dominion, you will then be able to build a temple to Belphaal and none will dare object. For the first time in ages, the servants of Belphaal will no longer have to abide in the shadows. The worship of Belphaal will return to the open."

"Know, great queen, that the worship of Belphaal in the open once more will bring great power to your rule," Urian-Na said, giving the queen a slight bow. "Belphaal will reward those who bring his worship out from the shadows. It has been far too long since His altars received sacrifice in the open, in front of all eyes."

Listening to the conversation, disgust and ire filled Rayden's heart. She had suspected something amiss under the surface of everything plaguing the people of Terith-Ka. A great ruse had been played upon them, serving to harden their hearts and gain their assent for war against Rastapur.

So many had died in the terrible famine, and many others had perished in the city streets at night. All of it had been done at the command of the queen herself, in close alliance with a sorceress of Belphaal.

Rayden's hands slipped down to her weapons, readying to draw them out and bring an immediate end to the grand deception. Her eyes narrowing, and letting her mind clear for the pending attack, she kept her gaze fixed upon the queen and sorceress.

Urian-Na then paused, and looked away, staring toward

an opening leading onto a wide balcony on the other side of the chamber.

"It seems that our time together is at an end for tonight, as the hunters have returned," Urian-Na declared.

Turning her gaze to the balcony, the queen smiled and sat upright. "Then let us greet them. They advance our purpose every time they fly out."

A deep, icy chill taking hold of the air, and revealing her breaths to her eyes, Rayden held back from her intended attack. Looking over to the balcony, she witnessed a pair of large, dark forms standing within the portal.

Moving into the firelight, the creatures were of the same kind as the one Rayden encountered in the alleyway. Indicating an incorporeal state, both had a slight translucence to their bodies.

Drifting just above the floor, through the power of some unseen force, the towering pair of entities approached the sorceress. Drawing near to Urian-Na, they took up positions on either side of her.

"Wine!" the queen called out.

A young serving girl, no more than fourteen or fifteen years of age, strode into view. Blanching, she came to a sudden halt, her eyes reflecting terror at the sight of the sorceress' otherworldly companions.

"You are a new one," the queen remarked, glaring at the young girl.

The girl gave a bow to the queen, but she did not advance any further. Her gaze remained locked on the creatures.

"They serve at our pleasure, as do you," the queen told her with a dismissive, impatient air. "I will not be delayed. Come here now. They will not interfere with you filling my cup."

The young serving girl stepped forward, though she cast nervous glances in the direction of the creatures. When she reached the queen, the girl raised the pitcher, tilting it such that the reddish contents within tumbled into the gold vessel held forth by Queen Annukeyen.

The girl cast another anxiety-ridden glance toward the winged entities. Her body trembled, causing her hands to shake the pitcher.

A few drops of wine escaped the pitcher and fell, spattering upon the couch.

Freezing in place, the serving girl's eyes spread even wider.

"I have allowed you to serve me in my personal chambers, and you cannot even fill a single cup of wine?" the queen asked in an even tone, her expression darkening.

"I ... I am sorry, great queen," the serving girl replied, bowing and lowering her eyes.

The queen pointed down to the floor. "Set the pitcher upon the floor. On your knees and keep your eyes down."

Out of the girl's view, the queen cast a grin toward Urian-Na.

The girl set the pitcher down and dropped to the floor at once, huddling up with her legs tucked beneath her. Continuing to tremble, she pressed her face to the marble surface.

The queen raised her right hand. At the gesture, a hulking figure stepped into sight from where his form had been hidden behind a column on the far side of the chamber.

Powerfully-built, his face set in a grim countenance, the huge man had a shaved head, save for one thick lock sprouting from the top and running to the middle of his back in a tight braid.

Dressed only in a white loincloth and high-strapped sandals, the giant held a long, curving blade that glinted in the firelight.

Showing no change of expression, the massive figure stepped behind the serving girl and looked to the queen. After a moment, the queen gestured. Gripping the hilt of his blade with two hands, the giant raised his blade up high.

She hated what they were doing to the girl. Many times in the past, Rayden had witnessed such repugnant displays, meant to intimidate and frighten the powerless, while providing amusement for those holding power.

"Kneel up straight, and look at me," the queen commanded the girl.

Cautious and shaking in her fear, the girl did as the queen dictated.

The queen smiled, looking directly into the terrified girl's eyes.

"Well, Urian-Na, whatever should I do?" the queen said, with a tone of amusement. Her gaze flicked upward, toward the gleaming sword poised above the girl in the hands of her enormous guardian.

"She should be made to contemplate what spilling from a vessel is like, I believe," the sorceress replied, her eyes and face showing that she took great pleasure in the proceedings.

"I agree, Urian-Na" the queen said. "A lesson that will be unforgettable, I imagine."

Keeping her eyes on the serving girl, she made a downward gesture with her right hand.

The broad blade descended fast, severing the girl's head clear off her body. Her headless torso remained upright for another couple of moments, before falling forward, onto the marble surface.

The head rolled to the base of the queen's couch and came to a stop. Lifeless eyes stared upward. Staring into the dead girl's face, the queen's smile grew broader, looking even more gratified.

Stunned, Rayden looked upon the body of the poor serving girl. She had thought the queen intended only to make a servant cower at her feet and endure a little humiliation for the infraction of spilling a few drops of wine. Now, Rayden realized that a much crueler, more malicious spirit reigned within the corrupted heart of Terith-Ka's sovereign.

"Perhaps I should have given her over to you, for your purposes, but I needed some amusement tonight," the queen said to Urian-Na, in a lighthearted air.

"I share your pleasure at sights like this, great queen," the sorceress replied, looking upon the girl's body.

Body close to shaking with the rage churning within her, Rayden cast a baleful glare at the three remaining figures. She held back from attacking them, knowing to strike at that moment would be sheer folly with the two supernatural creatures in the chamber.

Vengeance would have to wait.

Making a vow to herself, Rayden marked the three for death; a queen, her personal bodyguard, and a powerful sorceress of Belphaal. She swore in the silence of her heart that she would not leave the city until all three had answered for the serving girl's life.

"With your leave, they can slake their thirst and hunger," Urian-Na said with a suggestive air, looking to the entities standing by her. She turned back to the queen. "A true thirst for blood can never be quenched, entirely."

Grinning, the queen nodded to Urian-Na.

Urian-Na looked to the two dark entities and gestured toward the corpse of the serving girl.

With great speed, both of the monstrous things fell upon the girl's head and body, while also lapping up the blood spreading on the floor. The two creatures looked to be ravenous, their long, narrow tongues licking with great vigor at every last drop that they could find.

When at last they returned to the side of Urian-Na, the body and head left behind were desiccated and withered. The creatures' own bodies had shifted, returning to a solid appearance.

Her face brimming with elation, the queen gazed upon the two creatures.

"Such magnificent, extraordinary beings," the queen said. "Who could wage war against us, with them fighting at our side?"

"It takes blood to sustain them when they are in this world, great queen," Urian-Na replied. "To hold a solid form, they must draw even more upon the life essence taken from blood. Then, there is the blood sacrifice needed to bring them across the veil between worlds."

A mild look of disappointment crossed the face of the queen. "I would provide you with rivers of blood if I were able."

"One day may there be oceans of blood, and Belphaal enthroned in this world," Urian-Na replied. "But that time is not yet here."

"Sometimes I grow impatient thinking of what could be," the queen said, standing up from the couch.

"It is no easy thing to endure a great hunger," Urian-Na said.

"No, it is not," the queen said. Pausing, she looked at the winged entities. "I know they must return, and the hour is growing late."

Urian-Na nodded. "It is best that they return, and that I go to my own chamber. Dawn is not far off."

"You can sense the approach of dawn?" the queen asked.

"Yes, like a looming pestilence, and I dream of the day that Belphaal blackens the sun, forevermore," Urian-Na said.

"A world shrouded in unending night," the queen said. "I would not mind that at all."

A smile crept across the lips of Urian-Na. "You would find it a world filled with new wonders."

"I will dream of it then ... but for now, let us adjourn for what remains of the night," Annukeyen said, starting across the chamber. The queen's huge guardian fell in behind her. The queen paused, and looked back to Urian-Na. "Take heart, Urian-Na, the day will pass soon enough."

Urian-Na smiled and gave a low bow to the queen, who then continued forward. Straightening back up, the sorceress followed a couple strides after the guardian.

After resuming a translucent form, the two creatures drifted across the floor in the wake of the black-garbed sorceress who had called them into the world from another dimension.

Rayden watched the wicked procession exit the chamber. Stirring the flames within several lamps, a light breeze rippled through the curtains.

Before leaving the chamber, Rayden took a few moments to gaze upon the ill-fated serving girl's remains. In the eyes of the queen, the girl's life did not matter. Rayden found it hard to imagine how any human could become so callous and treat a creature of their own kind like chattel to be used and discarded at will. Yet the queen was far from the first ruler who held such a view.

At another time, in another place, a mother had cradled a newborn daughter. That infant had grown into a child, a little girl playing and dreaming without the burden of knowing the ways of the world.

Over time, the innocence had been stripped away and the bonds of servitude had been placed upon that girl, beginning a sorrowful path leading to her final moments; kneeling, terrified and crying, before a malevolent queen.

It did not matter what the queen thought of the serving girl's life. Her life mattered to Rayden.

Heading out of the chamber, Rayden found her way to a place on the citadel's wall where she descended with little trouble to the ground. The streets beyond lay quiet and empty.

With morning's light drawing near, Rayden picked up her gait, carrying an objective within her heart that had become even more personal in nature.

***

Returning to her room at the inn, Rayden got a little rest before the first golden rays of morning arrived. Outside, the noise of the streets began to swell as a city awoke from its slumber.

After washing her hands and face, using a pitcher of water and small bowl set near her cotton-stuffed mattress, she made her way to the tavern. Inside the main room, she found the innkeeper, sitting by himself honing a few knives.

Rayden walked over to where he sat. Before she could say a word to him, he took up a small pouch and handed it over to her. Holding it in her palm, she could feel a considerable number of coins within.

"I was hoping I would see you this morning," the innkeeper said. "You have done many a good and needed favor. Accept the pouch as a sign of our gratitude."

"There are oafish louts like that in most all taverns I have been to," Rayden said, thinking of the big man she had knocked to the ground the previous evening.

"Not him ... the three who would have ravaged the young women," the innkeeper said, a knowing gaze within his dark eyes. "Word came that they were found dead, and not in the manner of the things stalking the streets at night."

"Certain crimes bring a swift death, when I come across them," Rayden said, her tone firm and a cold, dispassionate look nestled within her eyes.

"All three of those rabid curs were followers of this crazed moon god cult growing fast in these regions," the innkeeper replied, a rueful expression coming to his face. "Travelers who come here speak of temples to Suenanna going up in many cities. It bodes ill for the rest of us. The men who follow Suenanna believe women to be created only for their service, and women not of their beliefs to be fodder for their amusement."

"The curs found out they could not have been more wrong,"

Rayden said, a glint in her eyes.

"Too many religions swirling in the kingdoms of these lands," the innkeeper said. "It brings some that carry a lot of danger within them."

Rayden thought of the queen promising Urian-Na the restoration of the worship of Belphaal. "Including many that should never take root."

The innkeeper nodded. "These lands have seen the thrones of dark gods in ancient times. Some fools believe the tales of those ages of blood and fire to be nothing more than myths. I know how fortunate we are that those days did not last."

"I would say that the stain of such gods has not yet been cleansed," Rayden said, a grim undercurrent to her voice.

"It is why I wish more would seek the path of Ahuran-Maz," the innkeeper said. "A god who calls us to compassion, charity, and light."

"I fear the stain of dark gods will not never be removed from the world, entirely," Rayden said. "Power is seductive and there are hearts among men and women who take pleasure in wickedness."

The innkeeper smiled. "And that is why it is good there are those such as you, Rayden."

Rayden smiled back. "I had better let you get back to your preparations. I have a few things to ponder and am going to take a walk in the streets."

"Head to the market," the innkeeper said. "I heard of some caravans arriving outside the city's walls. There should be much to look at."

"I believe I will do that," Rayden said. She held up the pouch. "Thank you for this."

The innkeeper gave her a slight bow. "It is the least we can do. You spared us from rabid dogs."

Rayden nodded back and strode from the tavern into the

light of a new day.

***

Voices filled the air. Buyers haggled, sellers proclaimed their wares, and others just visited and shared conversation.

Pungent and pleasant aromas intertwined. The musk of animals and their leavings contended with flowery perfumes.

Rayden made her way down the path running between lines of market stalls. Ignoring the calls of merchants seeking to draw her to their stalls, she lingered at couple of places, admiring the metalwork of one artisan, and the leatherwork of another.

Armed guards were most prevalent in the areas where foodstuffs were being sold. Rayden heard more than one curse-laden rant toward a merchant from those unhappy with the high prices of the most common grains. The offerings of fishmongers and others looked meager, yet still attracted steady interest.

It pained Rayden to see hungry-looking children in plain garments of rough spun wool eyeing the contents of the food sellers. Buying a few ripe dates from one stall, she tossed them to a cluster of such urchins, eliciting squeals of glee that brought a smile to Rayden's face.

She attracted a little extra attention herself. More than a few in the crowd, merchants and buyers alike, eyed the blond-haired figure with the paler hue of skin. Well used to such curiosity, Rayden ignored the attention and continued browsing the stalls.

A little while afterward, Rayden came upon a sickly-looking beggar, leaning against the side of an artisan's shop, in a pool of shade close to the rows of market stalls. A gnarled wooden staff lay propped against the wall next to him. A small, empty bowl of clay rested in his hands.

Tattered and smudged with dirt, the beggar's loose tunic echoed the weathered, creased look of his angular face. A scraggly beard of silvery gray dropped down to his mid chest.

His left leg withered, whether from affliction or injury, the man could not labor and earn his own bread. The haunted look in his eyes alone told Rayden that he was no indolent oaf, of a kind found often in larger cities who became the source for a criminal population. The man before Rayden carried a heavy burden; desperation having wounded his pride to the point where he had taken on the yoke of a beggar, sitting in filth and enduring derision each day, just to survive from one until the next.

Few would recognize the great strength in the crippled, weary-looking man, but Rayden's eyes perceived things that not many others did.

Reaching into the pouch given to her by the innkeeper, she took out several coins.

"Do not give a single crumb to that groveling rat," a well-dressed man in flowing, colorful robes told her in a petulant tone of voice. Curled into ringlets, his hair carried a lustrous sheen from the oils used upon it. A sweet-scented perfume wafted from his body. "It only encourages these dregs to infest our market area."

"You fool!" Rayden exclaimed, glaring at the haughty figure.

Looking taken aback, the man's eyes widened. "Fool? Humor me and tell me how I am a fool."

"Do you not realize how fragile the world is?" Rayden responded. "Do you think yourself untouchable? You are one war, one pestilence, one disease, one revolution, or one movement of religious fanatics away from losing all you have. Who are you to condemn this man, for things not of his control?"

Having looked shocked toward her response at first, the wealthy man regained his composure quickly. His eyes narrowed, and his voice took an indignant edge. "There is no defending such useless wretches. May this one vanish from the streets, like so many others of his filthy kind in recent weeks."

"It is a cruel thing to wish murder on another" Rayden

said in a slow, deeper timbre. Her right hand balled into a fist at her side, but she restrained from the urge to show the man how fragile he really was.

"Some are murdered. Some vanish, either way, they are gotten rid of for the betterment of all," the man replied in a nonchalant air, an ice-cold look set in his eyes. "Maybe you will share their fate, since you are so fond of them, foreigner."

Without another word, the man walked onward, his precious silks swishing with his measured strides. Rayden took a deep breath, letting her anger simmer down.

She looked back to the beggar, who had listened to the entire exchange.

Stepping forward and leaning over, Rayden dropped the coins in her hand into the small bowl the beggar cradled in the palms of his hands. His eyes widened for a moment at the sight of silver.

"Thank you, kind heart," the beggar said after a moment, in a voice that had a scratchy edge to it. "I would not have thought ill of you to be swayed by such a man of wealth."

"I am sorry you had to listen to that witless fool," Rayden responded, her voice softening. "Wealth blinds many to the great sickness inside them. One day he will find that his wealth avails him nothing. It is a lesson taught to all such as him, by time itself."

"What he says is still true," the beggar replied, looking even more downcast. "Each night I do not know whether I will be killed, or if I will disappear."

"I did not know of these vanishings," Rayden said, disquieted at the talk of disappearances in addition to murders.

"More are concerned with the murders, because they strike rich and poor alike," the man said. "Many like that man celebrate the disappearances, as they claim only those such as myself, who are at the mercy of the streets. We have no other course. There is no one to fight for us."

"Another thing to bring a swift end to," Rayden replied, in a growling timbre. "If only I could find some guidance about this city, and the things of it."

"For guidance, seek the priest at the temple of Ahuran-Maz, not far down that street," the beggar answered her, pointing toward a street to the right. "He has never wavered in looking after those on the streets. He is a wise man, whose eyes have witnessed the things of this city for well over eighty years. Go to him. I hope he has the guidance you seek."

"But I do not follow Ahuran-Maz," Rayden said. "I follow none of the gods worshipped in this city."

"It will not matter with him," the beggar said. "He is not like the priests of the great temples. He is only interested in the nature of a person's spirit. Nothing more."

Rayden reached into her pouch and pulled out a couple more silver coins. "Thank you for this information. Accept this as an expression of my gratitude for your help."

"Thank you for seeing that I am here," the old man told her. "Not a beggar. But a man who chooses to live. Few have been willing to do that."

Rayden gave the man a smile, though sorrow clenched her heart at his words. Reaching forward with her right hand, she clasped his shoulder.

"I will do what I can to bring an end to the plague on the streets," Rayden whispered.

"Then may Ahuran-Maz's light shine strong from within you," the beggar said.

Rayden gave the old man a gentle squeeze on the shoulder. She looked him in the eyes. "I am honored to receive such a wish from you. Know that I will be fighting for you, and the others on the streets."

Standing up, Rayden turned to the right and started

forward, passing down a long line of market stalls before entering the street indicated by the beggar.

About midway down the street, Rayden came across an elongated stone building set within a patch of open ground. A low wooden fence surrounded the entire area.

A square piece of carved stone displaying an image of the sun had been set into the facing of the building, just above the entryway. While the edifice was far from ornate, Rayden knew it to be a temple. The sun symbol of Ahuran-Maz left no doubt that she had found the place that the beggar had spoken of.

Rayden turned from the street at an open gate and entered the grounds. Crossing through the yard, she stepped through the entryway of the temple and continued inside the building.

Halting, she let her eyes adjust to the dimmer ambience.

The small rectangular room had none of the opulence of the grander temples in Terith-Ka. Daylight streaming in through three narrow windows on each of the lengthier sides illuminated the interior, revealing a hard-packed dirt floor, an altar of rough-hewn stones, a few oil lamps, and a wood-carved symbol, of a radiant sun representing Ahuran-Maz, hanging on the far wall.

"You have traveled far to get here," a gentle voice addressed Rayden. Turning her head at the sound, she saw that the voice belonged to an old, white-bearded man in long, brown robes and a low turban. He smiled, and then continued. "I doubt you came to Terith-Ka to visit a humble place of worship."

"A humble place of worship is likely the only place I stand a chance of finding what I need," Rayden said.

"Well said, in many ways of looking at it," the old priest replied. "Do you follow Ahuran-Maz?"

Rayden shook her head. "I follow no gods. It does not mean I never will. It is just that I have come across too many who are cruel, are less than they boast to be, or who likely do not exist."

A somber look came to the priest's face. "The world is a

confusing and deceiving place. In Terith-Ka alone there are many gods venerated ... some openly, in grand temples and places like this ... and others in the shadows."

"It may be that I am seeking help to confront the power of one of those in the shadows," Rayden said, watching the priest's face with great scrutiny.

"Help?" the priest responded, his demeanor unchanged at her words. "I have little to offer other than my blessing and prayers if you pursue a righteous cause. I do what I can from this place for the downtrodden and poor in the streets of Terith-Ka. They have suffered more than anyone during this time of trial. Not only have many been slain, by the wicked things roving the streets in the night, but many others have vanished."

"I heard something of the vanishings in the market," Rayden said. "From more than one person."

"Many good men and women who I have tended to for years have been taken," the old man said, in a voice laden with sadness. "I have no doubt these disappearances are part of a vile, wicked purpose."

"It may be part of what I am seeking to bring an end to," Rayden said.

"It falls to someone from another land to desire to protect the most vulnerable in our city," the old priest said. "What a plague of indifference has spread through these streets. I wish I were a younger man who could take a greater stand. Alas, I am at the sunset of my years."

"Many are frightened," Rayden said. "I have seen what stalks them in the night and their fear is understandable."

She then proceeded to tell the priest about everything that she had witnessed in the citadel. From the conversation between Queen Annukeyen and Urian-Na about bringing the worship of Belphaal back into the open, to the return of the hell-spawned creatures, to the slaying of the servant girl, Rayden related everything that she could think of.

The priest listened to her account with a somber, attentive countenance, and did not interrupt her a single time.

"Let me ask you a question, traveler," the priest said, a few moments after she had finished.

Rayden nodded

"If you had to ask Ahuran-Maz for something ... and it had to be for yourself, and yourself alone, what would you ask for?" the priest asked.

Rayden thought about the question for a moment. Looking the priest in the eyes, she answered him in a low, measured voice. "I would ask for the wisdom to know what the right path of action should be, when a choice of action is put before me ... and the resolve and strength to see that action through, to whatever end might come."

The priest's expression did not change in the slightest. He stared at Rayden for several moments, though what his dark eyes looked for she could not say.

"There is great wisdom in what you would ask," the priest said, breaking the long impasse. "Growing in wisdom, resolve, and strength, you become a greater light for others. Your wish for yourself becomes a wish for the well-being of others."

"I have one life, and I seek to live it as best as I can, in a way that honors those I hold in my heart," Rayden said. "I am not in control of what may come after this world. I am only in control of the choices I make now. Why would I not ask for such a thing?"

"I believe with all my heart that Ahuran-Maz would smile upon such a request," the priest said. "I will pray that He grants this to you, whether you choose to follow Him or not."

"Thank you," Rayden said, in a tone of respect. Though she did not believe in the priest's god, Rayden admired the fervent devotion and compassion she saw in the old man.

"What the strong and powerful could do, if they turned

their hearts to a kinder purpose," the priest lamented.

"What they could do, indeed," Rayden said, in full agreement with him.

She thought of the vast riches that she had witnessed during her journeys; heaps of gold, silver, and jewels that would persist long after mortals possessing them had gone to dust. Even a fraction of such wealth could alleviate a tremendous amount of suffering in the world.

Yet the wealth remained in chests, coffers, and vaults, guarded and hoarded, and the great suffering in the world persisted.

"In a world so filled with fear and hate, it is not easy to kindle a love for one another," the priest said.

"Nor is it easy to avoid becoming hardened when your eyes have witnessed great cruelty and mercilessness," Rayden said, a distinct trace of weariness coursing through her words.

"I imagine the path you have taken has been far from easy," the priest said. Stepping forward, he gave Rayden a light pat on her right shoulder. "Yet you are not of a hardened heart."

"My heart yearns for a destination that is hidden from my mind," Rayden said. "Such is the nature of my journey."

"You will find your way home, one day," the old priest told her, a little firmer in voice and looking her direct in the eyes. "Trust to your heart to guide you."

The priest straightened up a moment later.

"Wait here," the priest said. "I will return soon, with something that may be of help to you."

Departing through a door to the right of the altar, the priest left Rayden standing alone in the temple.

Rayden walked over and sat down on the floor, cross-legged, at the back of the sanctuary. She contemplated everything that the priest had told her, and then thought of the sun symbol of Ahuran-Maz.

In a way, the image of the sun testified to the power of light against darkness. In the absence of the sun, the world lay shrouded in darkness. In a similar manner, evil shrouded the world in the absence of those willing to take a stand against wickedness.

Rayden tried not to think of how few lights there were in the world, and how much wickedness existed.

The priest returned a short while later, bearing a small wooden box in his hands. Crossing the floor with shuffling, slow steps, he carried it with a reverend air. Rayden got to her feet and stepped forward to meet him in the center of the sanctuary.

Opening the box, the priest carefully took out a lock of dark brown hair that had been tied into a braid.

"This is a lock of hair taken from the head of a prophet and miracle worker who lived in Terith-Ka long before I was born," the priest said. "Manduan stood against the things of the dark often ... including powerful evils that no others dared to challenge. We believe he had the favor of Ahuran-Maz, as he exercised great powers of light more than once. Take this relic of Manduan with you. Wear it upon your body. It is the only true relic of him that is in our possession. Perhaps it retains something of Manduan, that can still affect the things of the abyss."

With both of her hands together, palms facing up, Rayden accepted the braid of hair.

"Where shall I wear this?" Rayden asked, looking upon the relic.

"Tie it about a wrist you will use to strike at the things of the abyss," the priest replied. "Perhaps the hand that holds the sword I see at your side."

Rayden nodded. "Would you tie it there for me?"

The priest took the braid into his hands again. Holding her right hand up, Rayden let the priest assist her, tying the length of hair about her wrist.

"This night, I will go to find this sorceress, and put an end to the power she wields over Terith-Ka," Rayden stated. "Maybe that will bring an end to the coming war against Rastapur, too."

Looking Rayden in the eyes, the priest reached out and gripped her forearm with his right hand. "I have an important thing to tell you ... if you should come across the servant of Belphaal and the place where she conducts her wickedness. It is a warning. One you must take to heart."

Keeping his gaze connected to hers, the priest fell silent for a moment. Rayden said nothing in reply, waiting in patience for him to proceed.

"Wicked gods will not be denied a sacrifice," the priest continued, in a lower tone of voice that conveyed tremendous importance to the warning being given. "If you happen to disrupt a sacrifice, another will be expected to take the place of the one not completed. It is a hunger so great that it drives dark gods to manifest in this world. Be careful, lest you become an offering to darkness."

"I promise that I shall remember your warning," Rayden said, her voice and eyes carrying the sincerity of her response.

"I wish to see you again," the priest said, giving her arm a gentle squeeze, before releasing his hold upon her.

"Unless I have fallen, I will return this sacred relic to you," Rayden told the priest. "You have my gratitude."

"May Ahuran-Maz watch over you," the old priest responded, a glisten in his eyes. "Always."

***

The last vestiges of twilight finding Rayden across the walls of the citadel and deep into the labyrinthine palace, night descended at last upon Terith-Ka.

From the time she had left the temple of Ahuran-Maz, time had crawled by for the rest of the afternoon. A light meal and short rest back at the inn had refreshed her body, but far too much swirled within Rayden's mind.

When lengthening shadows heralded the approach of dusk, Rayden had not delayed a moment in setting out for the citadel.

Rayden eyed the male servant in the white tunic a few paces ahead of her. Carrying a jug in his hands, he walked toward the glittering square pool occupying most of the small chamber.

Learning over, he poured the contents of the jug into the water. Setting the vessel to the side for a moment, he regarded the pool as a sweet aroma began filling the room. His eyes snapped wide, a shimmering reflection of a blond-haired woman manifesting in the water over his shoulder.

Her right hand clamped hard over his mouth, and left arm wrapped about him under the left shoulder, Rayden yanked the servant back from the water's edge.

"Keep your silence if you wish to live," Rayden whispered into the man's ear, dragging him from the chamber and behind a column in a larger hall beyond. Once concealed, she pulled him down to the floor.

He struggled in her grasp, prompting Rayden to tighten her own hold upon him.

"I do not wish to harm or kill you," Rayden continued. "I wish only to know where Urian-Na works her sorcery ... the same Urian-Na that laughs at the deaths of servants like you. You have a chance to help stop her."

Rayden kept the hold locked on the servant and waited until he eased in his resistance.

"You just have to show me where Urian-Na goes, nothing more," Rayden said. "Understand?"

After a few heartbeats, the servant nodded.

Rayden took out a strip of rough wool she had brought along for the purpose, and then gagged the servant. Then, she took another long strip and bound his hands together, behind his back.

"You will have to trust that I wish to do you no harm, but if you cause me any trouble, you will regret it," she said, in a firm tone.

Knowing how servants talked amongst each other in private, she had no doubts that all of the servants in the white tunics knew of the monstrosities conjured by Urian-Na. She counted on the young male to fear the creatures conjured by the sorceress.

"I have witnessed a serving girl clad in white like you, given over to Urian-Na's creatures, to feed them with her blood until she was left a husk," Rayden continued. "Do you bear any love for Urian-Na?"

The young man hesitated, but then shook his head.

"Neither do I, and I seek to put an end to this nightmare," Rayden told him. "I am going to help you get to your feet. Lead me to the place where Urian-Na works her dark arts. I will do the rest."

Rayden helped the young man up, and after giving him a moment to gain his full equilibrium she let him take the lead. Pulling him back from time to time, she ducked into shadows and hid behind columns whenever they encountered guards or other servants.

The young man took Rayden through doors leading to lower levels, until they reached an area where the passages had been cut out of the rock beneath the citadel. Oil lamps had been set at regular intervals, providing enough light to see by within the shadowy, narrow environs.

Breathing in the damp, musty air, Rayden knew that they would not be going much farther.

After traversing a long corridor, the servant came to a stop at the mouth of an offshoot passage. He gestured with his head toward an iron-banded timber door set in the rock at the far end.

Rayden turned toward the servant. "I cannot have you run

off and raise an alarm. I will free you when I am finished."

Taking him to the ground, she bound his ankles with another strip of cloth. Immobilized, the young man looked at her with plaintive eyes.

"If I do not survive this, they will find you soon enough," she said. "Discovering you bound like this, they will let you live."

Turning away from the servant, Rayden walked down the passage and approached the small wooden door. Unlocked, the door swung inward.

Opening the door just enough to slip inside the chamber beyond, Rayden took great care not to make a sound. Once inside, she guided the door shut behind her, maintaining her silence with a soft touch.

A low altar of dark stone stood near the far end of the rock-hewn chamber. Her back to Rayden, Urian-Na swayed in the throes of a rhythmic, haunting chant.

Arms outstretched, the sorceress held onto some kind of object in her blood-covered right hand.

Tethered from the wrists and ankles to narrow posts at each corner, a naked young woman lying on her back had been secured to the altar's surface. Eyes with no spark of life within them stared upward, casting the sightless gaze of the dead.

The woman's chest had been cut open in a savage fashion; the single-edged, ceremonial blade used in the act resting by the sacrificial victim's head.

Blood dripped in a steady course from the edge of the altar, pattering onto the floor.

Rayden then took account of five bound, gagged figures lying on the ground a few strides into the chamber. Four men and a woman, they all looked toward Rayden, terror reflecting in their eyes.

Sensing a tingle in the air, Rayden glanced back toward Urian-Na, who continued to sway back and forth in her trance.

The firelight from the lamps about the chamber cast distorted shadows across the walls, adding to the brooding atmosphere.

Rayden took out her axe and shortened her grip on the haft. Creeping forward at a low crouch, she kneeled by the five figures.

Gesturing to each of them to remain silent, Rayden cut the bonds on the arms and legs of the men and the woman. As a precaution, she left their gags in place.

A short distance away, Urian-Na continued to chant, facing the altar and far wall.

The freed captives cast fearful glances toward Urian-Na. From their dirty, rough garments and haggard physical condition, Rayden suspected all of them came from a world similar to that of the old beggar she had encountered by the market. The purpose for the disappearances in the streets no longer remained a mystery.

Using her strength, Rayden propped the weakened figures up and helped them from the chamber, one by one. When the last of the five had gone through the door, Rayden closed it after them and turned back toward Urian-Na.

Without making a sound, Rayden took up her weapons.

Casting a glance down to the lock of hair tied about her right wrist, Rayden took a deep breath. She started forward, intent to kill a sorceress, but came to a sudden halt.

The temperature within the chamber plummeted, and the far wall darkened before Rayden's eyes. For a moment, the face of the wall held the appearance of a dark pool, shimmering in the firelight from the braziers.

Then, the darkness deepened even more, becoming an impenetrable maw that swallowed all light.

The chants of Urian-Na swelling louder, Rayden could not take her eyes off the numinous, mesmerizing blackness beckoning to her.

Staring into the abyss' limitless depths, Rayden blinked her eyes in rapid succession, contending with surging wave of dizziness and nausea that threatened to overwhelm her faculties.

A remote, fading part of her realizing the cause of her instability, and calling upon every shred of willpower that she could muster, Rayden tore her gaze away from the newly-manifested portal. Fixing her eyes toward the floor, she focused on her breathing, recovering her equilibrium in swift fashion.

When she brought her eyes up once more, Rayden remained careful not to let her gaze linger upon the caliginous depths beyond the portal. The temperature in the chamber continued dropping until her breaths became visible; each exhalation forming a dissipating puff of light gray.

Urian-Na's chant reached a peak, the last words shouted with the air of a command, before the sorceress fell into silence and became still. Seeing movements from within the portal, Rayden stayed rooted in place, and stopped herself from assailing Urian-Na

Wraith-like entities began emerging from the abyssal darkness, one after another, until five of the winged creatures had entered the chamber. After drifting forward a few paces, they came to an abrupt halt, loosing a torrent of sepulchral cries.

Reacting to their extreme agitation, Urian-Na straightened up and turned about. A look of disbelief filled her eyes when her gaze took in the sight of Rayden, standing alone the middle of the chamber; where five victims had been only moments before.

"What have you done!" cried Urian-Na, her expression brimming with madness and rage. "Belphaal's servants are not to be denied! You will replace them!"

With a grating cry, the sorceress strode toward Rayden, reaching forward.

Urian-Na's skin then changed hue, becoming corpse gray. Her fingers elongated, ending in sharp talons, and when the sorceress opened her mouth she exhibited a pair of pronounced, snake-like fangs.

The sorceress' eyes blackened over, turning into small pools that reflected the essence of the darkness in the portal looming beyond her.

Rayden took a step to meet the advance of her would-be assailant. Her discipline offset her shock at the fast-shifting form of the sorceress.

The sorceress' hands lashed out with incredible speed, grabbing onto her wrists. Urian-Na exhibited a tremendous strength that took Rayden by surprise, forcing her to drop her weapons.

Shrieking, the sorceress abruptly released her grip and backed up, stymied from pressing her advantage. Where she had touched Manduan's lock of hair with her left hand, Urian-Na's skin had been singed to black.

Rayden brought her arm up and brandished the relic before the eyes of the five wraiths. Looking upon the braid of Manduan, they recoiled, shielding their eyes with great quickness, as if confronted by a blinding light.

Urian-Na lunged fast toward Rayden, just as she had anticipated. A swift forward kick bringing her high-sandaled foot slamming hard into the belly of the sorceress, Rayden sent Urian-Na toppling back toward the far end of the chamber. The sorceress came to a stop a few paces from the stone altar.

The five wraith-entities hissed and shrieked, turning baleful, glowing eyes toward Rayden. Behind them, the sorceress regained her feet.

Rayden could see that the relic upon her wrist gave the entities pause. But without the blood sacrifice of the five bound victims that Rayden had freed, the infernal creatures had nothing to draw upon, and could not yet manifest into a full, physical state.

An eerie, primal sound began rising from the ebon miasma, a swelling roar that could not be attributed to anything of the living world. The winged entities began edging away from

Rayden, moving toward the dark maw at the rear of the chamber.

A look of distress unfurling on the sorceress' face, Urian-Na turned her head away from Rayden.

The cacophony growing in volume, the entities hastened from the chamber, gliding fast through the air before disappearing into the blackness from which they had come. Rayden had no illusions that anything other than raw fear had spurred their unexpected flight, after having drawn so close to their quarry.

A horned monstrosity with eyes of burning flame, and an enormous maw filled with jagged, sharp teeth, emerged out of the deep blackness. Her body shaking in terror, Urian-Na fell to the floor, groveling before the fearsome entity looming above her.

"You have invoked my servants with a promise of sacrifice ... and a sacrifice will be made!" the massive creature declared in an unnatural, harsh voice, one that sounded like a blend of screeches, growls, and roars.

Urian-Na loosed a pitiful wail as the enormous being reached beyond the altar with a giant, clawed hand. Gripping her about her mid-section, the demon lifted her up from the floor and pulled her back into the frigid darkness.

The sorceress' wail faded into the distance of a nightmare realm.

The cold permeating the chamber dissipated a moment later, and the darkness filling the back wall faded back into the gray stone that had been there when Rayden had first entered.

Heart beating fast, Rayden moved forward with great caution. Grabbing up her weapons, she made her way out of the chamber, keeping an eye on the wall beyond the altar.

Once outside, she closed the door. Returning down the passage, Rayden found the servant where she had left him.

She cut the binding on his legs, leaving the others in place. He looked toward her with an expression blending fear and curiosity.

"Urian-Na is gone and will plague Terith-Ka no more," she told him. "But I have not finished what I have come to do. You have seen that I have kept my word to you, and that all in this palace are free of Urian-Na. Now, I need to find my way to the queen's chambers, by the quickest route."

The servant nodded. Rayden helped him back up to his feet.

"One more thing," she said.

Hearing hushed voices coming from a short distance away, she headed down the corridor to the right.

Rayden caught up with the five she had liberated, finding them milling about within the passageway not far down from the offshoot to Urian-Na's chamber. Knowing that any palace guards encountering them would treat the group as escaped captives, Rayden instructed the five to come with her and the servant.

She admonished them to maintain silence and follow her lead. All assented, without argument.

Once she reached the queen's chamber, Rayden determined to leave the servant in their care, until everything had been resolved.

The small group of seven proceeded onward, working their way up from the subterranean level, and into the main body of the place. The five freed prisoners huddled close, keeping up with Rayden and the servant.

The servant guided them through a series of smaller passages and rooms. They came upon one pair of guards, but neither of the startled men got so much as a single cry out before Rayden struck them down with swift blows.

Rayden barely took notice of the beautiful trappings of the rooms and smaller chambers that they passed through.

Her mind fixed upon one thought; fulfilling the rest of her vow.

***

Rayden found the second of the three that she had condemned outside the doors of the queen's private chamber. Stepping out from the stairwell with sword and axe out, she glared at the giant of a man, and took up a combat stance in the large open space of the antechamber.

Anger filling his face at the sight of her, the eunuch guardian advanced, slashing at Rayden with his long, well-honed blade.

Shifting to the left and right, nimble and quick, Rayden evaded a few strikes, while blocking others using her sword. The clash of metal echoed off the walls of the antechamber.

The queen's guardian bellowed in frustration, turning and launching wide, vicious sweeps of his blade. Rayden stayed clear of the powerful strikes, watching for a chance to get inside his broad attacks.

Poised, Rayden sprang forward when the guardian missed her with a back slash of his weapon. Drawing within range, she swung her axe at the giant's head.

Her axe blade passing within a finger-length of his wide chin, the huge warrior reared back just in time. In his haste to lean away from the axe blow, the guardian shuffled back and straightened his legs, striving to keep his balance.

Bringing her left foot up, Rayden sent a hard kick barreling into the front of the brute's right knee. Connecting solidly, the impact elicited a loud snap as the leg buckled. Shrieking in pain, the huge warrior grimaced.

Before Rayden could continue the assault, he lurched forward, bracing upon his left leg. Sweeping his left arm in a hooking motion, the guardian snatched Rayden up with ease, crushing her tight against his body.

Rayden gasped, emptied of air and unable to draw breath.

The guardian began lifting his right arm, his blade gripped firm and oriented toward Rayden, positioned to be driven into the exposed, left side of her head.

At the same instant, Rayden let the haft slide down in her left hand until she gripped her axe near the base of its head. Whipping her hand back across, she brought the sharp edge along the top of the axe blade raking across the warrior's eyes and the bridge of his nose.

With a loud cry, bleeding and blinded, the guardian let go of Rayden, dropping her to the ground in the throes of his sudden agony.

Feet hitting the floor, Rayden took in a big gulp of breath and did not hesitate for an instant, knowing she had to disarm her opponent at once. Shifting her body, she chopped down hard with her sword, cleaving the guardian's hand off at the wrist, and sending the large blade clattering to the floor with the warrior's massive fingers still wrapped about the hilt.

Rayden brought her axe back through, slashing hard along a horizontal course that cut deep across the throat of her enemy. Blood gushed out of the laceration and ran down his chest.

Gurgling and sputtering, the guardian fell heavily to the ground, like a sacrificial bull, his life and vitality ebbing fast in the blood pouring from the gaping wound. His body went still a few moments later.

Rayden stepped over the guardian's body and walked toward the chamber doors. She pushed them open and entered, making no attempt at stealth.

Dressed in the same manner as when Rayden had last been in the palace, the queen stood in the center of the chamber. Facing the doors, she held a long dagger in her right hand.

Her posture remained confident, but a look of unease dwelled in her eyes at the sight of Rayden. Her expression betrayed that she had expected to see the eunuch guardian, not the blond-headed foreigner.

"Who are you?" the queen asked in an even tone. "Where

is my guard?"

"Your guard is dead, lying in his own blood just outside these doors," Rayden said. "You will be joining him very soon."

"I am the Queen of Terith-Ka!" the queen responded, flaring in anger at Rayden's brazen manner. "How dare you speak to me in this way!"

"My weapons make no distinction between those I wield them against," Rayden stated, keeping her voice measured, and taking a step toward the queen.

The queen took a step back. The confidence that had returned to her face dampened.

"Why are you doing this?" Queen Annukeyen asked.

"For the servant girl you had beheaded ... for the poor taken from the streets to feed the sacrifices of your sorceress, who is now suffering torments in the abyss," Rayden said. "I watched her vile god take her into the darkness with my own eyes, in the chamber far below."

The queen's eyes widened at Rayden's pronouncement. She spoke in a low, guarded voice. "Urian-Na ... is gone?"

"As you will be," Rayden said, glaring at the queen, and taking another step forward.

"I can take you now to a vault where a mere handful of the jewels kept there could buy you a palace," the queen said. "Leave Terith-Ka ... and go live in luxury."

Eyes like blue flame, Rayden gaze pierced into the queen's eyes. "Do you think an entire vault of your ill-gotten baubles can sway me?"

A new look arose in the queen's eyes, likely one that the longtime ruler of Terith-Ka had not exhibited in a long time; that of raw fear.

Images of everything she had witnessed during her time in Terith-Ka passed through Rayden's mind; starving children living in squalor, crying mothers seeing their sons conscripted to fight wars desired by others, and old, weak beggars beaten and mocked.

Her weapons up, Rayden strode toward the queen, ready to bring the tyrant's wicked rule to an end.

The queen swung her dagger at Rayden, who batted aside the clumsy attempt with ease, knocking the weapon out of her hand. Panic filling her face, Queen Annukeyen backed up further.

Rayden advanced forward.

The queen tripped on her long, luxuriant garments and fell to the floor. Rayden moved fast, standing over the queen a moment later.

"Get up!" Rayden shouted at the prostrate queen, the thoughts of the suffering and defenseless swirling through her mind and spiraling her rage. She returned her axe to the loop at her belt.

Rayden let the queen get up to her knees.

"A queen kneels before me," Rayden declared, in an icy, humorless tone. "But do not lower your eyes."

Looking to Rayden, Queen Annukeyen had a puzzled expression on her face.

Rayden's left fist cracked across the Queen's jaw, sending a couple of her pearl-white teeth flying, and bloodying the wicked ruler's mouth. Falling aside to the ground, dazed and sputtering out blood, Queen Annukayen lay sprawled out at Rayden's feet.

"Get up!" Rayden thundered, reaching down and dragging Queen Annuyaken up to her knees.

The queen looked to her with glazed eyes and a teetering consciousness. A hint of defiance rising in her face, she blubbered, blood oozing over broken teeth. "I am the Queen of Terith-Ka!"

"My blade has sipped the blood of kings," Rayden addressed the queen. "But today, for the first time, it shall quench its thirst upon the blood of a queen!"

Thinking of the serving girl, who had her life taken from her for the cruel amusement of the dark-hearted queen now before her, Rayden brought her sword into a vicious, downward slash, cutting through hair, flesh, bone, sinew, and muscle alike.

Her face displaying an expression of sheer disbelief, the queen's head went flying across the marble floor.

A gasp from behind caused Rayden to spin about, sword at the ready and axe drawn out a moment later. A servant girl in white stood at the entrance to the chamber, a look of shock splayed across her face.

She looked to be of the same age as the one Rayden had just avenged.

"The queen is dead," Rayden said, in a calm, measured tone. "And don't think about raising an alarm, if you want to live."

"The queen is dead?" the girl finally replied, a look of fear welling up. "We will all be killed!"

"On who's authority?" Rayden asked the girl.

"If not the queen, then Urian-Na," the girl answered, showing even more fear on her face at the mention of the sorceress.

"Who has been taken into the abyss, by the wicked things that she served," Rayden said.

"The sorceress is dead?" the girl asked, in a tone of astonishment.

"Right now, she probably wishes she could die," Rayden said, thinking of the monstrous demon that had pulled her screaming into the darkness.

"The queen's soldiers will never let us leave," the girl said.

"I will get you out of here," Rayden said. 'You are now free."

The girl turned her eyes to the body of the queen and stared. "They will surely hunt us down."

"Who is the queen's successor?" Rayden asked. "I have heard of no heirs since I have been here."

The girl shook her head. "There is no heir."

"Then who holds the greatest authority in this palace?"

Rayden asked.

"One of the queen's generals ... but who I cannot say," the girl said. "It would have been Nassa-Di, but he is held in confinement now.".

"Why?" Rayden asked.

"He spoke against war with Rastapur, and spoke against Urian-Na," the serving girl said. "He told the queen he did not think the creatures to be the doing of any in Rastapur."

"And he was her general of highest rank?" Rayden asked.

"Yes," the serving girl nodded. "Well-loved by the soldiers."

"How was he to those like you, servants of the palace?" Rayden asked. "Was he cruel?"

The girl shook her head. "Not at all. He was always fair with us, and even kind at times. He was a man much different than some of the others."

A thought formed fast in Rayden's mind. "Can you take me to this general?"

The girl nodded.

"Do you know of a place where there are vaults? Like those to hold treasure?"

Again, the girl nodded.

A grin spread on Rayden's face.

***

With the servant girl's help, Rayden found the vault mentioned by the queen, filling one sack with the coins of Terith-Ka, and another with a sack of glinting jewels. The servant girl gawked at the piles of treasure within the room, whether stored in chests, coffers, sacks, or loose heaps.

"Now, I need to find where the queen's old general is being held," Rayden told the girl. "This Nassa-Di that you spoke of."

"It is not far from here," the girl answered. "But there will be a guard, or two."

"Carry this," Rayden said, extending the sack of jewels to the girl. "I need to keep one weapon in hand."

A sack of coins gripped in her left hand, and sword clasped in her right, Rayden followed the serving girl down the passage outside the vault, leaving a realm's fortune behind.

***

A guard lay unconscious several paces behind Rayden. She doubted he would be waking up anytime soon, having caught a hammering punch from her flush on his jaws.

The serving girl stood near to the guard, eyeing him and poised to alert Rayden if there were any signs of him regaining consciousness.

Peering through the iron bars, Rayden fitted the key to the lock and turned, the welcome sounds of metallic clicks meeting her effort. Creaking on its hinges, the door to the cell swung open.

Clad in filthy, ragged clothes, the old general lay curled up on the hard stone floor. Roused awake at her entrance, he looked toward Rayden with an alarmed expression. Dragging a chain attached to a shackle on his right ankle, he scrabbled toward the back of the chamber.

Sleeplessness and hunger had left their marks upon the man, from sunken eyes to a drawn, emaciated appearance. His gray hair stringy and greasy, the man had a dense, unkempt beard.

Staring at Rayden, he remained quiet.

"Nassa-Di ... I am not here to harm or kill you," Rayden said, keeping her timbre low and calm.

"Then ... who are you, and what have you come here for?" the general asked her after a slight pause, in a hoarse tone of voice that testified further to the severity of his confinement. "I see that you are a foreigner."

"My name is Rayden, I am from lands far to the west," she replied.

"I have come to tell you that the sorceress, Urian-Na, is no more. No longer will your streets be plagued by her creatures at night." The general gazed at her, but he made no reply.

"I know that you believed the creatures were not the doing of any sorcerer of Rastapur," Rayden said. "You were right. Your opposition to Urian-Na, and war with Rastapur, is what got you locked in here."

"Curse her name, that vile snake," General Nassa-Di said, his expression hardening.

"She has received her reward," Rayden said. "She has been taken into the darkness beyond this world."

"May she rot and burn in the Abyss," the general responded, ire flowing through his words.

"Our concern is no longer with her, but making certain a war is stopped, and that chaos does not bring more suffering to the people of Terith-Ka," Rayden said. "You can walk from this dungeon now and spare the people from all of this wickedness."

"It was not Urian-Na who placed me in here, it was the queen," the old general said.

"The queen is also no more," Rayden said, gazing into his eyes.

Nassa-Di looked stunned at her pronouncement. "The queen is dead?"

Rayden nodded. "I took her head off with my sword."

"Who are you?" Nassa-Di said, his eyes narrowing.

"Just one who does not suffer wickedness, wherever I encounter it," Rayden said.

"Are you taking the throne of Terith-Ka?" he asked.

"I have no desire to rule over others,": Rayden said. "But order is needed, with the queen having no heirs. I am told that you held the greatest authority in Terith-Ka after the queen, not that long ago."

"What you say is true ... I held the highest rank in her army,"

Nassa-Di said.

"Do others of high rank remain loyal to you?" Rayden asked.

The old general nodded. "There are many who I guided myself and became like a father to. Only fear of Urian-Na and the queen stayed their hand when I was seized and imprisoned."

"I desire only to prevent bloodshed and chaos in the streets," Rayden said. "It is too large of a city to have a sudden collapse of all order. But some changes must be made."

"What would those be?" Nassa-Di asked.

Rayden turned and walked out of the cell, returning a few moments later with the sack of coins that she had taken from the vault. Bringing the sack over, she set it down by the general, leaving it closed.

Taking out her axe, Rayden gripped it near the head and crouched down. Setting the blade at the throat of the general, she locked her eyes with his.

He did not cower, nor did his gaze waver. The reaction encouraged her that the general's imprisonment had not extinguished his inner strength.

"Strengthen the loyalty of those serving you with gold and silver if you must, but you must promise me that Terith-Ka will not march upon Rastapur," Rayden told the general, her eyes carrying a look colder than the sharp blade set at his throat. "Return the sons taken to fight the queen's war against Rastapur back to their homes. Do you understand this?"

The general nodded, looking her direct in the eyes. "There will be no war against Rastapur, and the army shall be what it was before. Any taken from their homes by the queen will be returned to their families."

"I will know if you deceive me," Rayden told him in a firm, low tone. "If you do, I will find you, and your blood will water the ground."

The old man nodded again. Rayden took her axe blade

from his throat and slid the weapon back into the loop at her waist. She turned and picked up the sack that she had brought into the cell.

"Open it," she instructed the general, putting the sack into his hands.

Glancing between her and the sack, he lifted his hands and carefully opened the sack His pronounced intake of breath told Rayden that the general realized the nature of the sack's contents.

"Secure loyalty, then secure the vault with the queen's treasure, and then see to the needs of the palace and city," Rayden said.

She took up another key and inserted it into the lock on his shackle. Opening it, she freed the general's leg.

Rayden helped Nassa-Di up to his feet. She looked him in the eyes one more time.

"You have witnessed a tyrant and know what it is to suffer under one," Rayden said. "Bring a new spirit to Terith-Ka and become a ruler who will be remembered in hearts, and not just minds."

The old general held her eyes, and she could see no trace of deceit in the depths of his gaze.

"Will this be the last time I see you?" the general asked her.

"Perhaps not," Rayden said. "Who knows what the world will bring? But be sure that the next time we meet, that we meet in friendship."

***

Slipping out of the palace, Rayden kept to the shadows and made it back to the inn with no difficulty. Not even the most reckless cutthroat or thief yet knew that the menace stalking the streets of Terith-Ka had been overcome.

Neither did any outside the citadel's walls know that the queen's reign had come to an end.

***

Over the next several days, Rayden waited and watched.

Rumors of fighting at the palace spread across the city, followed by the pronouncement that the queen's former general, Nassa-Di, had emerged victorious. Proclaiming himself Satrap, and possessing the loyalty of the army behind him, the general asserted order across Terith-Ka.

The public execution of the queen's last primary general and several others of high-rank convinced Rayden that the old general had truly prevailed.

No major chaos broke out in the aftermath of the queen's fall. Instead, jubilation filled the streets when a great many young men, and quite a few older men, were released from service in the army and returned back to their homes, in the city and surrounding villages.

It was also announced that the queen had been in league with a dark sorceress, and that Rastapur had not been behind the famine and terror in the night. Many greeted the news with skepticism, but when no more deaths or disappearances transpired within the streets of Terith-Ka at night, more and more of the populace softened their view of Rastapur.

Rayden could only hope that Nassa-Di stayed true to the early course that he had set, but everything that she observed heartened her. Satisfied that the queen's former general had not deceived her, Rayden deemed that she no longer needed to remain in Terith-Ka.

***

"You wished to see me again," Rayden said, smiling at the old priest, who had just entered the sanctuary of the temple. "I have returned to see that wish fulfilled."

The old priest's eyes sparkled with merriment, and a joyous

look beamed from his face. "I did indeed wish to see you again, and it gladdens my heart that you have returned. It has been many days."

Rayden walked toward him. She extended her hand, displaying the braid of Manduan that the priest had given to her, to help against Urian-Na.

"I am glad to say that I can return this sacred relic to you, unharmed," Rayden said.

"I trust that it was of help to you?" the priest asked, working carefully to untie it from her wrist.

"Yes, and a great evil has been overcome," she replied.

"The word spread fast in the streets about the queen's death," the priest said.

The loop untied, he held the braid in his hands. Walking over to the altar, he lay the braid gently atop it.

"Her old general has stepped forward from his imprisonment and kept good order," the priest continued. "It is said there will be no war against Rastapur, and many men, both young and old, taken to fight against Rastapur, have been given back to their homes."

"Nassa-Di looks to be a good man, from what I have seen," Rayden said. "It is my hope that he remains so."

"No more terror stalking in the night, for many days now," the priest said.

"The sorceress behind it is no longer in this world," Rayden said. "The streets are freed, unless something else comes."

"Belphaal claimed her, I am guessing," the priest said, looking into Rayden's eyes.

"Yes," Rayden said. "A sight that will not be easy for me to forget."

"I imagine not," the priest said. "The things of darkness are haunting to any who witness them."

"She showed another face before the monstrosity took her

into darkness," Rayden said, recalling the nightmarish, final moments.

"Another face?" the old priest asked, a curious expression forming.

"Just a shape shifting power, like others using sorcery can do at times," Rayden said. "It gave her unnatural speed and strength."

The priest appeared deeply concerned at her words. "Tell me of this."

"Her skin turned a pale gray, all over, and she grew long fangs," Rayden said. "Her hands extended and formed claws, and her eyes became black as the darkest night."

A troubled look spread across the priest's face. "Now we know where she came from. Urian-Na was one of the Sharir-Mord, creatures from Sereth-Naga. It means an even greater danger exists beyond the queen's ambitions here in Terith-Ka."

"What are the Sharir-Mord?" Rayden asked, with a look of curiosity. "What is Sereth-Naga?"

"Creatures who cannot be worn down by time or disease," the old priest said. "The Sharir-Mord can no longer suffer the light of day. They slake their thirst on blood taken from living beings, and they are anything but human.

"As for Sereth-Naga, it is a great den filled with those vipers, steeped in dark arts and atrocities. The Sharir-Mord have a city held in thrall on the edges of the vast desert wastes, farther to the east. To hear that they were beginning to grow roots in Terith-Ka is a dire thing indeed. It means they are bold enough to seek to expand their power."

"These things have a city?" Rayden asked.

"Not a large city like Terith-Ka, but it has enough of a human population to serve their every whim and provide an abundant source of blood," the priest said. He then shook his head, a rueful look upon his face. "You spoke of things that shift shape. A race of such creatures has helped to keep the Sharir-Mord in Sereth-

Naga for long ages ... though I know little of them."

"Then what does it mean, that Urian-Na was here, working sorcery in alliance with Queen Annuyaken?" Rayden asked.

"It means the Sharir-Mord are seeking to go farther into the world and are no longer held at bay," the old priest said. "They are creatures who deem themselves fated to rule all others. Humans are their slaves and cattle."

Rayden frowned. "Not a thing I would like to see unleashed upon the world."

"Nor I," the old priest said.

"I may have to see this city for myself," Rayden said, a simmering look emerging within her eyes.

Rayden would never forget the faces of the bound victims in Urian-Na's altar chamber. The thought of an entire city held hostage to others like Urian-Na repulsed her to the core of her being.

"Do not go there, not without an army," the priest said.

"Then who will go to see what the state of things are in Sereth-Naga?" Rayden asked. "When everyone is looking to others to act, nothing is ever done."

"I cannot argue with that," the old priest said, looking grim.

Rayden grinned, and the look in her eyes lightened. "But enough of Sereth-Naga for now ... I did not come back here to speak of dire things with you. I came to return the relic ... and bring you something else."

Rayden took a pouch off her belt and gave it to the old priest.

"Here is something to help with the care of those on the streets," Rayden said. "The queen no longer has any need of it."

The priest opened the bulging pouch and stared at the glittering, rare jewels contained within, enough to build a few grand temples if he desired. Rayden had confidence that he would not take that path and would put the wealth to a use that harmonized with the beliefs that he held to heart.

"This is ... a fortune!" the priest gasped, his voice and face conveying sheer astonishment at the sight revealed within the pouch.

"One that has been placed in the right hands," Rayden said. "I know you will take care of those on the streets of Terith-Ka."

The priest nodded and smiled. "Yes, yes, of course I will."

Rayden gazed upon the priest for a moment, fixing the image of the man in her mind. When the world turned dark and brutal, memories of such individuals served as lights in the darkness.

"It is now time for me to go onward," Rayden said. "You have my deepest gratitude and I do hope our paths cross once more."

"If not in this world so full of sorrow and misery, then in another, full of everlasting light and life," the priest said, giving her a slight bow. "May Ahuran-Maz watch over you always."

***

Rayden squatted down next to the old beggar sitting in a stretch of shade on a street leading from the market area. His clay bowl empty, the beggar had been staring toward the ground, an exhausted look upon his face.

Startled at her sudden appearance, his eyes went wide, and he flinched. An exuberant smile dawning upon his face, recognition took hold within his gaze. His eyes brightened, like the sun coming from behind a thick mass of clouds.

"Did I surprise you?" Rayden asked, giving him a wink.

"I knew you were out there, somewhere," he replied.

"I was hoping to find you," Rayden said.

"I am still here," the beggar said. "But the terror has been lifted from the nights. None have vanished or been slain over the past several days."

"I told you that I would fight for you," Rayden said, grinning, and giving him a soft pat on the shoulder. "I have confidence that

General Nassa-Di's rule will be better for all of the people of this city."

"One can never know the minds of those with power," the beggar said. "But I would say there is a good chance from what I hear of him. He is said to have never been a cruel man."

"I saw no wickedness in his eyes," Rayden said.

The beggar's eyes broadened at her statement. "You looked in his eyes? I am sure you have a story to tell."

"One that I do not have the time to tell, right now," Rayden said, a touch of regret in her tone.

"I did not know whether I would see you again," the beggar replied.

"I wanted to see you, before I left Terith-Ka," Rayden said. "My road beckons to me, and another fight lies ahead, I believe."

Tears welled up in the old man's eyes. "I know this city is not your home, but so few have a heart such as yours. When you go, it is a loss to all in this city. I fear that only myself and a few others realize this."

"Maybe I will be back through here one day," Rayden said. She chuckled. "I know that I cannot seem to stay in any one place for long."

"I hope you do find a place where you want to stay," the old man said, a couple tears trickling down his weathered face.

"I do too," Rayden said, in a softer, melancholic voice.

"If anyone deserves to, it is you," he responded. "You put your life at risk for the most powerless, and weakest, of this city. I will pray to Ahuran-Maz for you, each and every day."

Rayden clasped his shoulder and smiled, knowing his words carried the fullest of sincerity. "Thank you, my friend."

"It is the least I can do," the beggar replied. "Thoughts of you will help me endure the days when I encounter only cold hearts and mocking tones."

"Another thing to bring a swift end to," Rayden said, echoing words she had spoken to him before.

"I wish it were possible, but I will not live long enough to see a change in what I have known," he said, giving her a smile that carried a trace of sadness.

"Are you so sure of that?" Rayden asked, a bright grin sprouting on her face.

The beggar looked puzzled at her words, and unsure of what to say.

"Before I go, I have something that I want to give you," Rayden continued, untying another pouch from the belt at her waist. "Set that bowl on the ground."

The beggar did as she instructed, laying the bowl at his side. Rayden then turned her body, so that anyone strolling by could not see what she was doing, and then handed the pouch over to the beggar.

Taking it into his hands, the old man fumbled with the strings for a few moments before opening the pouch. Gazing upon the contents, gleaming coins of pure gold stuffing the inside to capacity, he had an audible intake of breath.

"Keep it in the pouch and go see to getting yourself a place you can call your own," Rayden said. "This will bring you a new day and a swift end to what you have endured here."

Looking upon the gold packed within the pouch, the beggar wept again. "This is beyond any hope I ever had. Why have you chosen to give this to me? Many have suffered on these streets. I cannot take all of this."

"I did not think you would, and that is why I do not fear giving all of this to you," Rayden said. "But you can do little to help others if you do not see to your own strength. Establish a home. Secure your future. Take some comfort. None of those things are wrong. There is enough in that pouch to do that and see to helping others. You wished for light to shine from within me, and now I make the same wish for you, with all of my heart."

"I ... I do not know what to say," the old beggar replied, sobbing, a few of his tears sprinkling the gold.

"Let me escort you to the priest at the temple of Ahuran-Maz," Rayden said. "To make sure none interfere with your use of what is in the pouch or try to take it from you. Then, I must depart. Let us go from here now, and when you return to this place, may it only be to purchase something in the market."

The old man nodded.

After waiting for the beggar to tie the pouch together, Rayden stood up. An act of instinct, the beggar reached for the bowl.

"Leave that here, you will not need it any longer," Rayden said.

The beggar took his hand away from the bowl and smiled at her. "Never did I think that day would come."

"It has come ... this very day," Rayden said, in a gentle, soft voice.

Rayden helped the old beggar up to his feet. With the use of his staff, he hobbled forward at a slow pace.

Shielding him from getting bumped or knocked aside from passersby, Rayden guided him through the crowds in the market. Taking another street leading off the area, she led him to the entrance of the temple grounds.

"May your best days be ahead of you," Rayden said to the old man, when they had reached the waist-high gate in the outer fence.

He looked into her eyes and smiled. "May the light of Ahuran-Maz shine ever brighter from within you, and may you find that place to stay."

Turning he ambled toward the door of the temple.

Thinking upon the beggar's words, Rayden smiled, her eyes misting over at the thought of his second wish for her.

His form disappearing from her view, the beggar entered the temple. Turning, Rayden started down the street, heading for the outer gates of a city that no longer lay shrouded in a nightmare.

Coalescing upon the challenge that loomed before her, Rayden's thoughts settled.

Urian-Na, for all of her power, was just part of a much larger serpent; one that needed its head cut off. What little the priest had shared with her told Rayden all that she needed to know.

Others like Urian-Na held an entire city in thrall.

Those who knew of Sereth-Naga had been looking to others for ages to take action, and none had stepped forward.

It was far beyond time that someone did.

A bright sun reigning in the heavens, Rayden started toward the east.

WINDS
OF
WAR

A RAYDEN VALKYRIE TALE

STEPHEN ZIMMER

WINDS OF WAR

"This enemy will be like a great wave from the ocean," Rayden stated, glaring at the cluster of armed men gathered before her. "It will wash away everything that you are. Yet you continue to fight amongst yourselves. You continue to weaken yourselves. You do not know what is coming!"

Disgust thick in her voice, Rayden found it hard to comprehend the foolishness pervading a land facing an imminent, existential threat. An array of small kingdoms remained divided and at conflict with each other, while a massive empire to the east salivated, preparing to gorge itself upon the morsels spread before it; one by one.

Boggling Rayden's mind further, the men before her would stand with their king in just three days time against the warriors of another while the lands of a kingdom only a week's march away burned and bled in the clutches of eastern swarms.

The fools all believed the eastern emissaries that the sacking of Pargemon was merely a punitive expedition, to punish their king for interference in eastern matters. Having traveled the lands to the east herself, Rayden knew better.

The invasion of Pargemon a pretext, once a foothold had been established the might of the east would pour into the Griacan lands. Exasperated, Rayden could not get the warriors to realize their grave peril.

Only one of the men in the assemblage before her would so much as meet her eyes. A stout warrior of average height, Markos' skill and wit had gained her respect the past few weeks.

Good-humored and spirited, Markos stood well-liked by his comrades. Rayden could also tell that none of them would hesitate for a moment to have him at their side in the most chaotic and dangerous moments of battle.

While stopping in a Thrakkian village for some food and drink, Rayden had witnessed Markos entertaining several of the children living there. Whether engaged in mock sword battles or being chased about in some children's game, Markos displayed a gentle, kind nature with the young boys and girls that gained him even more favor with Rayden.

Eyes that could burn with a great intensity on a field of war sparkled with merriment and good humor among the little ones. Markos had even pulled Rayden into some of the mock battles, evoking laughter from her when a swarm of boisterous children armed with sticks assailed her from all sides.

Now, turning her full attention toward him, Rayden found herself wishing that he stood a king.

"Markos, is there nothing that can be done to bring sense to the rulers of these lands?" Rayden asked, withholding a few more caustic remarks about the kings of the region. Besotted in wealth and power, they had been rendered blind to the starkest of threats. "Is there not a way to bring Thrakkia and Samosia together, to fight the Astrians, who are burning Pargemon even now, as we speak here? If Thrakkia and Samosia meet in battle, it will only spill the blood of both, just in time for your common enemy to march upon you."

"The Astrians claim they will depart, once they punish Pargemon for their interference," Markos said. "But I know you deem that to be a lie."

"A naked lie," Rayden replied, curt in tone. "It is only the beginning of something far worse. You are to be just one part of the fare, for the feast of an emperor ... a tyrant whose appetite is insatiable. The other kingdoms of Griaca will be devoured along with you."

"I believe you," Markos said, looking dour.

"Then how can this madness be stopped?" Rayden asked. "Thrakkia and Samosia must not bleed each other!"

"It is possible to seek a battle of champions," Markos suggested. "But it is doubtful King Cadmenus will agree, for the Samosians have the most renowned warrior in all the Griacan Kingdoms standing with them."

"Desidar ... I have heard much of this one," Rayden said, nodding. The stories reaching her ears claimed that the Samosian warrior stood tall as a mountain and moved as quick as lightning. She doubted both attributes, but she knew that Desidar would have to be of an exceptional nature for a king to hesitate in fielding a champion to fight against him. "It would be far better for all if his blade were set against the eastern hordes coming against you."

"Aye, it would," Markos replied, eyeing Rayden with a rueful expression on his face.

Rayden stared at the Thrakkian warrior for a moment. She could see the agreement with her in Markos' eyes and face, but she knew he would fight for his king in a battle that would see no victor, no matter the outcome.

She understood his predicament. If Rayden had pledged her loyalty to a king, and given an oath, she would do the same.

"What if I can find a way to convince King Cadmenus to choose a battle of champions to resolve the quarrel with Samosia?" Rayden asked, glancing at Markos and sweeping her gaze across the faces of the other warriors.

"Speaking for myself, that would be a very welcome turn of events," Markos replied.

Many of the other men nodded their agreement with him.

"We have been through much together," Rayden said, thinking of the ordeal that they had just been through, rooting out a large band of assassins holed up deep in the mountains. "I have come to have an affinity for these lands, and I do not wish to see them turned into fire and ash."

"What are you thinking of doing, Rayden?" Markos asked in a low voice.

"In this late hour, there is one possibility," Rayden said, forming a plan even as she spoke with the Thrakkian warrior. "But I must leave here at once."

"Do you need any of us to go with you?" Markos asked.

Rayden shook her head. "This can only be done by me ... and me alone."

"Then may the gods keep you in their protection," Markos said

"I will see you on the field when dawn breaks in three days ... there is much I need to do before then," Rayden told him. Deep in thought, she paused for a moment before continuing. "May I have the use of a Thrakkian steed?"

"Of course," Markos said. "You are a friend and ally to the people of Thrakkia. We have bled together, and you have put your life at risk for us. How could we deny you such a request?"

"You have my gratitude," Rayden said.

"You have ours," Markos replied, giving her a slight bow.

Stepping forward, Rayden clasped Markos' forearm and looked him in the eyes. In a whisper, meant only for his ears, she told him, "I will do what I can to find a path to sense for all of these foolish kings. Stay strong and look for me in three days."

***

A resplendent sunset, bountiful in golden hues, had been draped across the western horizon when Rayden set out for the north.

More than once, she turned her head to gaze upon the spectacular view.

Providing a welcome influx of relief after the blazing heat of the day, cooler air flowed over Rayden with the approach of evening. A deeper chill would take root with the rise of the moon, but the current, pleasant sensation would remain for a little while longer.

Rayden kept her steed at a steady pace. A hardy breed, the horses of Thrakkia were a big part of the reason that their vaunted cavalry was deemed the strongest among all the Griacan Kingdoms.

The big stallion that Markos had secured for her to ride had a piebald coat, white fetlocks, and a distinctive star shape in the center of the horse's forehead. More than one of the other warriors remarked that Markos had brought her one the best of the horses available.

Having just been trained as a cavalry mount, the horse was said to have exhibited great speed and a tremendous level of endurance. A warrior named Thetokles, a man well-trusted by Markos who had also been part of the recent mountain expedition, had volunteered the steed for her use.

It did not take long for Rayden to see that the Thrakkians' assessment of the horse's attributes stood accurate. Powerful and sleek, the stallion thundered across the plain. Hooves pounding out a rhythm on the hard ground, the creature handled the accelerated pace with ease, showing no signs of tiring as the leagues passed by.

A long ride loomed ahead of Rayden. She did not want to become too zealous in taking advantage of the stallion's capabilities, but the fate of kingdoms teetered on a precarious edge.

Following the gloaming at day's end, a clear, star-filled sky emerged across the heavens. A bright moon, over three quarters full, climbed into the heights, assuming its dominion over the night.

The lack of clouds enhancing visibility, Rayden stayed to her course, pressing north through a series of low hills. Farther ahead, the approach to a broad river valley beckoned.

Her destination lay within that expansive, fertile valley, but she knew that she would be stopped before reaching it. The low ground would soon funnel into a narrow passage running between the slopes of two steeper hills; The Southern Gate.

The slender stretch of ground served as the only path that any mounted rider coming from the south could take to reach the valley. While no actual gate stood in her way, she knew that the passage would be warded with vigilance.

In truth, Rayden was counting upon it.

Listening to the stallion's hoof beats and the winds coursing through her hair, Rayden settled into the low saddle as best as she could and kept her eyes fixed on the landscape ahead.

***

When the ground tapered leading into a channel between two high hills, Rayden slowed her mount to a walk. Eyeing the shadows, she knew that she had been seen from afar, and could only wait for those warding the Southern Gate to make themselves known.

"Go no further!" a woman's voice commanded out of the night, when Rayden had reached the mouth of the passage.

Pulling her steed up, Rayden raised her hands high in the air with palms open, to show all eyes that she held no weapons.

On the slopes to either side of the narrow passage, within the shadows, several figures stood poised with javelins at hand. Her stallion snorted and stomped on the ground, showing agitation at the presence of the others.

"Who treads upon our lands this late at night?" called the voice from the darkness to the left, again delivered in a forceful, demanding tone. "You are not of Aressenia, and only a fool, an enemy, or one in great need would dare travel in these hills at such an hour ... and we do not suffer fools or enemies."

"I am no fool or enemy, " Rayden answered, keeping her voice at an even tone, firm, but not confrontational. "I am known to those of Aressenia as Rayden Valkyrie, a warrior of lands far to the west and north. I have come on a matter of great importance to Aressenia, and I seek to have an audience with Queen Marsellina."

"On whose behalf do you come here for?" the speaker asked. "You are not of any Griacan kingdom."

"I am here of my own accord," Rayden stated. "I have come on behalf of all Griacan Kingdoms, including Aressenia, who face a common, dangerous threat at this hour. There is little time."

After a short pause, the speaker in the dark said, "Dismount your steed, and come with us."

Swinging a leg around and getting down from the saddle, Rayden took up her horse's tether. Out of the darkness, an escort of eight Aressenian warriors formed, taking positions all around her. Those bearing the javelins remained in their places on the slopes, eyeing the foreigner who had appeared out of the night.

Each of the warriors surrounding Rayden held a long spear and carried a large oval shield, crafted of wood and faced with a thin sheet of bronze. Wedge-shaped markings decorated the center of the shields.

The hilts of blades protruded from sheaths at their left sides. Their summits crowned with forward-curving, thick crests of horsehair bristles, bronze helms fashioned with cheek guards protected their heads.

Other than shield and helm, the warriors had no other armor. Clad in knee-length tunics and high-strapped sandals, each of them wore a long cloak secured at the left shoulder. Long, well-combed locks of hair flowed down their backs from the rear of their helms.

Striding into view, the one who had spoken to Rayden manifested at the forefront of the group. Armed in a similar manner to the others, her helm had a transverse crest, marking the warrior as an officer of higher rank.

All of them women, the nine figures stood Warriors of the Sisterhood of Aressenia.

Along with their counterpart, the Brotherhood of Aressenia, they formed one of the most elite groups of warriors to be found in any corner of the known world.

"We do not ask for your weapons, but do not presume to think of this as a sign of trust," the officer addressed Rayden. "We will not have far to walk. The queen is near, but only because she is leading hunts for Gorgothirs that have been ravaging our southern border areas. The monsters strike both night and day. No place is safe along our borders. We will not take your weapons and cause you to be defenseless, but do not seek to test our resolve."

Rayden understood the threat underlying the words of the Aressenian officer. "I do not seek to cause any trouble, and my weapons shall only be drawn if we find ourselves under attack."

"We now will take you to Queen Marsellina," the officer announced, turning and starting down the passageway between the hills.

Striding along with the Aressenian warriors and leading her horse in the brisk night air, Rayden worked out the soreness that had accumulated during the long, jarring ride in the saddle. Limbering up, she eyed the warriors around her.

All of them held a disciplined silence, and she could tell that the warriors had a great wariness about them. Rayden knew little of Gorgothirs, but the creatures were enough of a threat to instill a high level of caution in warriors known for fearlessness and ferocity.

Rayden's stallion appeared to be at ease, sensing nothing amiss in the scents delivered through the breezes coursing over them. Knowing how hard she had pressed the horse, she determined to get the stalwart creature some fodder and water as soon as possible.

With no one to converse with to pass the time, Rayden turned her thoughts over to the ages-old practices of the renowned kingdom whose lands she now traversed. They had forged the war-driven society and established the rules by which Queen Marsellina had gained her authority.

Brutal, strict, and in many aspects cruel, the ways of the Aressenians both fascinated and abhorred Rayden. Their methods had been adhered to with great dedication and discipline over the centuries, to produce the fiercest, most-skilled warriors possible.

At birth, any Aressenian children deemed sickly or malformed were put to the blade, without hesitation. Those allowed to live and grow into childhood were taken from their parents at seven, and then put through a rigorous training regimen that lasted several years.

Pitted against each other with regularity, and put through an array of extreme hardships, only the most proven among them in feats of arms, endurance, and strength were accepted into the Sisterhood or Brotherhood.

A different fate befell those not chosen.

Men demonstrating solid skill with weapons who had not been selected for the Brotherhood could take up arms in times of war. Otherwise, they were not allowed to own or carry weapons.

These men were tasked with the other needs of the kingdom; forming a body of artisans, craftsmen, messengers, and overseers of slaves. While lower in status than those accepted into the Brotherhood, the designation served as a kind of mercy.

Those who failed to reach that level were assigned to the slave population, most of which were not Aressenian in origin.

Captives taken in war and their progeny comprised the majority of the ill-fated group; a permanent class of laborers, kept in a climate of constant intimidation and subjugation.

It stood another small mercy that none of the Aressenian women passed over for the Sisterhood found themselves condemned to the slave populace. Women not selected for the elite group of warriors were assigned to take care of Aressenia's domestic needs, such as the fashioning of clothing, cooking, and the care of children. Wherever needed, they could make use of slaves in their endeavors.

In addition to holding the highest status within Aressenia, the elite warrior class determined who held the title of king or queen of the land.

Once a year, the warriors of the Sisterhood and Brotherhood came together for a week-long festival known as the Union of Blood and Fire. Anyone other than warriors of the two groups were strictly forbidden from entering the sacred grounds used for the occasion.

The first part of the week featured contests of strength, speed, weapons and other martial skills within each group, until an order was determined among both the male and female warriors.

The Aressenian War Council, comprised of the most veteran members of the Brotherhood and Sisterhood, then declared whether the king or queen could be challenged during that year's festival. For Aressenians, the king or queen was simply the warrior considered the highest in rank, holding the supreme command of the army in a time of war. In most other matters, the War Council and the Council of Ephors wielded authority, though a king or queen could call either council together and address them at any time.

If a king or queen excelled in leadership and commanded widespread respect, the War Council would not allow a challenge during a Union of Blood and Fire. If the competency of a king or queen had fallen into question, or failures in war had occurred, a challenge was allowed.

Anyone of the Brotherhood or Sisterhood could challenge the warrior holding the title of king or queen. If more than one warrior wished to make a challenge, then the order of their finish in the festival's contests determined who possessed the right.

In the case that one from the Sisterhood and the Brotherhood held the same respective rank, they met in combat first. If the victor still desired to challenge for leadership, they were allowed a couple days to recover, before they fought to become king or queen.

Following the final martial contest, the rest of the week entailed a very different nature. The warriors of the Brotherhood and Sisterhood were allowed to co-mingle at will. The ensuing days were given to an excess not allowed at any other time. Full of indulgence and licentiousness, the warriors released tensions and celebrated everything they were with those who shared their status.

Those who finished in the top third of the Brotherhood and Sisterhood who were unmarried earned the right to have a life mate for the procreation of children. Their mates came from the Aressenians not part of the Brotherhood and Sisterhood, for marriage between two warriors could cause a break in the cohesion of a body of equals.

Represented by a narrow golden torque about the neck, the warriors held absolute authority within the new households; including that of life and death. The rest of the household wore torques of silver. The silver and gold used in such a way served as one of the few uses of the valuable metals within the kingdom, where even coins were not possessed or traded.

Duties of a warrior to their fellow warriors still took ultimate priority, but in the case of a Warrior of the Sisterhood becoming pregnant, leave could be taken from martial duties until birth had been given. A male life mate of a Warrior of the Sisterhood who became with child from a Union of Blood and Fire was fully expected to raise the offspring as his own, without any resentment.

Affection and bonds of love, as could be expected, existed primarily between warriors of the two orders, though over time some life mates were known to grow a strong affection for each other.

The ways of the Aressenians were like no other people Rayden had encountered in her widespread travels. Taking no particular issue with most of the things they did and practiced, as every kingdom and land had different ways of living, she could never countenance their embrace of infanticide and slavery.

The two loathsome matters had resulted in some highly contentious interactions between her and the Aressenians before. If not for the urgent need of the moment, Rayden would not have harbored a shred of desire to set foot in their lands.

As things stood, Rayden needed to bring Aressenia into a war involving an existential threat to all the kingdoms of Griaca.

Rayden and the warriors marched onward for a little more than half a league, until they came upon a ring of low, flat-roofed dwellings with a small number of torches and fire pits set about the structures. A cluster of armed sentries confronted them when they drew near. At their recognition of the officer leading the contingent escorting Rayden, they quickly stepped aside and allowed them to proceed.

The array of buildings centered upon a statue of Aressen, the Griacan war god who the kingdom had been named after. A brawny figure in a crested helm, the god held a spear overhead in his right hand, on the verge of striking. Sculpted upon his bearded face, a fierce look that would never waver glowered at some unseen opponent.

The warriors escorting Rayden guided her over to the forefront of the tall statue. To Rayden it looked as if the god stood ready to preside over her fate, his spear already poised if the judgement went against her.

With a quick stride, the officer headed away from the contingent and disappeared among the buildings.

Within a short time of their arrival, the open space around the statue began filling with Warriors of the Sisterhood, all of them armed and ready for combat. The tips of spears and the facings of shields glinted in the flames cast by the torches set around the perimeter of the circular area.

Though all set their eyes upon the blond-haired visitor who had come deep in the night, no one spoke. A few of the warriors then parted aside, forming a channel and allowing a tall figure to pass through their midst.

With the lithe stride and confident posture of a well-honed warrior, the woman approaching Rayden was attired no differently than any of the others, save for a golden headband that held back the long, dark locks cascading over her robust shoulders.

A sword sheathed at her left side, the woman wore no cloak, exhibiting a rippling muscularity throughout her arms and legs. The flowing definition and symmetry made it seem as if a sculptor of great skill had chiseled her body.

Emerging into the firelight, Queen Marsellina looked toward Rayden with a grim expression. Billowing within the depths of her dark, piercing eyes, the flames highlighted a prominent scar running across her right cheek. Her aquiline nose showed slight signs of prior breakage. The traces of former injuries, in their own way, added to the balance of beauty and severity inherent within her appearance. A strong, angular chin line added further to the queen's striking, intense countenance.

Queen Marsellina stood a warrior of great renown, among her own people and across all of Griaca. In her several years as queen, never once had the War Council opened her position to challenge during a Union of Blood and Fire. Even the oldest among Aressenia's elders could not remember a time when a queen or king had held their place for so long without being contested.

"At this late hour, I doubt this is a casual visit, Rayden Valkyrie," the queen stated, breaking the heavy silence in an even tone of voice, neither hostile nor welcoming.

"No, but it is an urgent one," Rayden replied, holding the queen's stern gaze with a strong, unwavering look of her own. "I would not be in your lands if the threat were not dire to all."

"Then do not delay in telling of it," the queen replied. "Speak openly, there is nothing to hide from my Sisters gathered here."

Rayden proceeded to explain everything that caused her to seek the Aressenian queen. She described the predicament concerning the imminent conflict between Thrakkia and Samosia, taking place at the same time that Pargemon burned at the hands of an Astrian invasion force. Striving to convey the greater threat, Rayden shared her perspective on the Astrian Empire and its ultimate aims regarding Griacan lands.

"This is no mere punitive expedition, Queen Marsellina ... it is the beginning of a sweep across all Griacan lands," Rayden said, concluding her account.

"Let the eastern swine come for us, if they wish to die swiftly," the queen said, a hardened expression on her face.

Rayden looked into the other woman's eyes. "There are far too many for any kingdom of Griaca to resist them alone. If they are allowed to conquer Pargemon, multitudes will follow, in numbers like no eye in Griaca has ever witnessed."

Her jaw line growing taut, the queen glared at Rayden. She then replied in a voice indignant, "We are not just any mere kingdom in Griaca. One Aressenian warrior is worth a hundred Astrians. We have overcome enemies holding great advantages in numbers before."

"The greatest warriors in all of Griaca are found here," Rayden said, without the slightest trace of flattery. "But the Astrians can put an army onto the battlefield of a size far, far larger than any Griacan kingdom has ever faced. Enough rain drops can become a flood that washes away everything in its path.

"The Griacan kingdoms must unite and teach the invaders a lesson in blood by destroying the force that has taken Pargemon. Then, their Emperor can look for quarry elsewhere. The division I see now in Griaca draws his eyes toward the west ... and it wets his appetite."

"Let the weaker in Thrakkia and Samosia contend with this, themselves," the queen replied. "Why are you even here, Rayden Valkyrie? It is known by many of us that you do not approve of our ways."

"Not the killing of innocents, or the holding of others in bondage," Rayden said, meeting the queen's eyes with a piercing gaze, and refusing to leave the two matters unspoken. "I make no apologies for that. At another time, we could find ourselves enemies on a field of battle. But all the lands of Griaca could fall into bondage, under an Astrian yoke, if good sense and wisdom does not prevail.

There is no dispute that the strongest fighting force in Griaca is here, in Aressenia. You have the strength to bring sense to the kings of Thrakkia and Samosia ...and you have the strength to destroy the Astrians in Pargemon."

"We are the strongest in all of Griaca because we forge the strongest ... and give authority to the strongest ... within our lands," the queen said, her eyes narrowing. "We do not allow weakness to grow or give influence. We do not suffer fools softened in lives of comfort and leisure. They are chaff in need of burning, and we are wheat worthy of harvest. I say let Pargemon, Thrakkia, and Samosia burn."

"Strength is measured in many ways," Rayden answered the queen, her own eyes narrowing. "One day you may find you have weaknesses that your people have been blind to, because of the path you have taken. Having compassion is no weakness ... but rather one of the greatest of strengths in the world.

"The showing of compassion does not diminish a warrior's skill at arms, or the discipline needed to become the best warriors in all Griacan lands. Instead, the showing of compassion displays strength, and calls upon you to show discipline, courage, and resolve. In having compassion for the people suffering in Pargemon, you are called show yourself to be the strongest. Compassion is shown from a position of strength. Do you not see this?"

"Do not test my patience, or seek to play games of words with me, Rayden Valkyrie, or you will find your strength measured this very night," the queen said, a flare of anger within her voice. "I do not need to justify our ways to anyone. The proof of its value has been demonstrated on countless fields of battle. We have triumphed when any others would have failed. Aressenia stands unconquered, after many centuries."

"I did not come to seek argument with you, or any other in your lands," Rayden said. "I have come to seek the help of Aressenia against the strongest enemy Griacan kingdoms have ever faced. Nothing more."

Rayden paused, looking straight into the queen's eyes. She then continued in a low, resolute timbre, confronting the Aressenian queen with a truth that could not be denied.

"The last time our paths crossed, you gave me an oath," Rayden declared. "You vowed that you would grant me a favor, if ever I had need. I am calling upon that favor now, and demand that you honor it."

The queen frowned at her words. Rayden knew that the queen could not dispute them. Memories of a time of great peril that brought the Aressenian queen and the storied, blond-haired warrior from far to the west together were still vivid within both of their minds. Steeped in bloodshed, dark magic, and horrors out of another world of existence, the threat they had faced together was one they could never forget.

Acting alone in the face of staggering odds, Rayden had saved the queen from what otherwise would have been certain death. In the aftermath, the queen had made a vow, empowered by a sacred oath.

A brooding look upon her face, the queen replied, "I have not forgotten my oath, and nor would I if you were to come twenty years from now. Speak plainly of what you would have me do. As I have told you, I am not here to engage in games of words."

"I ask you to bring an army at haste, when the third dawn from now breaks the horizon, to help me stop the Thrakkians and Samosians from bashing each other's skulls in, right before the Astrians march upon them," Rayden said. "Then, we will destroy the Astrian army now burning Pargemon to cinders and ash."

"And how am I to help you stop the Thrakkians and Samosians from fighting each other?" the queen asked, a hint of amusement woven through her words. "By crushing them both? I am sure you do not wish to see that happen."

"They will accept single combat between champions to resolve their conflict," Rayden said. "I am confident the Aressenians can send a champion against each who will be victorious."

"There are many among us who could stand as champions," the queen said. "But single combat is merely a way used by weaker lands to avoid battle."

"It is also a way the kingdoms can avoid being weakened before the Astrian onslaught," Rayden said. "And it is certain they will bleed each other to a great extent if you do not intervene."

"Why is that so?" the queen asked. "What do you need the warriors of Aressenia for? Could not Thrakkia and Samosia choose to resolve their petty quarrel by single combat?"

"Thrakkia has no champion who they are confident can defeat Desidar, of the Samosians," Rayden said.

"There is a warrior worthy of being in our ranks," the queen said with an air of genuine respect. "No, I doubt the Thrakkians have any who can face him in single combat. But I can think of more than one among us who could prevail against him."

Rayden nodded. "That is what I ask."

"By the rights of single combat, you will be giving Aressenia two kingdoms, all too easily," the queen said, with the hint of a smile on her lips.

"I ask that you do not claim the full rights of a victor," Rayden stated, holding the queen's gaze. "Only that they stand as allies with you, to meet the Astrians in battle."

"Madness has overcome you," the queen responded, her eyes betraying her sheer surprise toward Rayden's declaration. "What is earned in war is ours to keep."

"It would be far more sensible if Aressenians, Samosians, and Thrakkians could simply stand together against a common threat, but what must be done, must be done," Rayden said. "That is my request. Challenge these armies to single combat and then hold them to standing together against the Astrians. You will have plenty of spoils to take when you defeat the invaders."

The queen shook her head slowly. While Marsellina's next words carried a tone of disbelief, Rayden could detect more than a little admiration in the other woman toward her audacity.

"You are like no other, Rayden Valkyrie. Only you could come making demands of Aressenia to spare two kingdoms from their own weakness."

"There is no other way to bring reason to those foolish kings," Rayden said, her voice brimming with anger. It confounded her that the two rulers could not see the obvious for themselves. Between them, the kings had enough strength to confront the Astrian force without the aid of Aressenia.

The queen's gaze swept across those gathered around her. Powerful and brimming with pride, her voice rose into the night.

"My fellow Sisters, it is time to remind the other kingdoms of Aressenian strength! It is time to wage war and spill the blood of enemies. Thrakkia and Samosia will be humbled, and the Astrians' skulls will be dashed against the rocks."

A boisterous cheer erupted from the gathered warriors. Raising their spears toward the skies, they hailed their charismatic, unrivaled queen.

After the acclamation had died down, the Queen Marsellina looked back to Rayden. "Messengers will be sent out at once. The War Council will be called, and our generals summoned. We must be prepared to undertake a hard march the day after tomorrow. You are fortunate I have a large force gathered with me now. A threat in the wilderness brought us here."

"The Gorgothirs I was told about?" Rayden inquired.

"A menace to all things that dwell in our lands," the queen replied. "Several plague the hills of our southern borders. From where they have come, I do not yet know. While my full army is called together, I will still make use of tomorrow to try to hunt one or more of the wretched monsters down."

"I offer my skills for this hunt, if you allow me to join you," Rayden said. "I have faced a great many threats in the wilderness. All manner of wild beasts and monsters. Perhaps I can be of some help, and I would rather not sit idle."

"You may hunt with me," the queen replied.

"Thank you," Rayden said, knowing that the permission to hunt with them was a great sign of respect in the eyes of Aressenians.

The queen turned her attention to the warriors around

her. She called officers forth, designated messengers, and set the Aressenian response into motion. Rayden watched the proceedings with great appreciation, seeing the loyalty and discipline in the eyes of the warriors being given orders.

At Rayden's request, her stallion was taken away to be given fodder, water, and shelter in an Aressenian stable for the rest of the night. Before they parted, Rayden stroked the noble creature's mane and head, while thanking the steed for carrying her.

The horse nuzzled its head against her for a moment, as if in acknowledgment of her words. Watching the big stallion being led off, Rayden knew those who tended the creature would be assiduous.

A culture centered upon war, Aressenia could muster faster than any other kingdom could ever hope to do. Rayden had no doubts that the Thrakkians and Samosians would be in for a surprise when they lined up for battle in three days.

The queen then dismissed the assembled warriors. The officer and eight warriors who had escorted Rayden from the Aressenian Gate marched back into the night, while all the others filtered back among the dwellings.

Before long, Rayden and Marsellina stood alone by the statue of Aressen.

"I did not foresee us standing together again," the queen said, glancing over to Rayden. Her tone and demeanor took on a more casual air. "When last we parted, I did not think you would ever return to Aressenia."

"Neither did I," Rayden admitted. "But there was no other choice than to come to you. I could not stand by and watch these lands fall to the Emperor of Astria."

Without the throng of warriors gathered around them, Rayden looked upon Aressenia's queen in a different light. Marsellina stood a fellow warrior with whom Rayden had a common past.

They had fought shoulder to shoulder, bled together, and depended upon each other, with their lives hanging in the balance. The bond formed between two warriors who had gone through the same perilous experience was something unique, understood only by the two individuals who shared it.

"Fulfilling my oath to you may be the one thing that leads to my first challenge at a Union of Blood and Fire," the queen said, a smirk on her lips.

"Your warriors sounded enthusiastic enough about going to war against the Astrians," Rayden said.

"They would also like to see Thrakkia and Samosia become subservient to us," the queen said. "Few will be happy that we only command them to stand together in war against the Astrians. The Ephors can barely stand to listen to their emissaries in times of peace. All they crave are things, when they should crave becoming as strong and skilled as they can."

"There are many who are soft like you describe," Rayden said. "They give me great disgust, but there are also many among them who do strive to better themselves. Warriors, artisans, others given to things of the mind, and some who just wish to work the land and raise a family."

"Then they should not suffer the weaklings that rule over them," the queen replied.

"I agree, it is a mystery how good people allow the worst among them to hold power over them," Rayden said.

"If their ways were more like ours, they could challenge them," the queen said.

Rayden nodded. "It is one of the things I do like about Aressenia."

The queen stared at her for a moment. "It is a shame we would stand enemies and not Sisters if Astria did not threaten."

"Let us not think upon that now," Rayden said, seeing a hint of affection in the other's face. "You and I have been given a time to stand together once more."

"That gladdens me," the queen said.

"And me as well," Rayden admitted.

"The only thing that remains is to determine who will stand as our second champion," the queen stated. "I hold the right to be the first. I will slay Desidar and end his legend. The other champion can bring an end to the warrior chosen by Thrakkia. There are many who I am confident can do this."

"I have some thoughts on that," Rayden said, again looking the queen in the eyes.

The queen gazed at Rayden and did not reply for several moments. A wisp of amusement glinted within her eyes. "For one who is not an Aressenian, you know far too much about our ways. Why is it that I suspect you will invoke some right of ours?"

With a slight grin, Rayden answered, "You suspect, because you know me."

***

At morning's light, Queen Marsellina, Rayden, and a large force of warriors, the latter all of the Sisterhood of Aressenia, rode into the hills south and east of the village.

Though a little fatigue and a few aches still lingered from the extended ride in the saddle the previous day and night, Rayden greeted the dawn with a refreshed spirit. Having taken another mount for the hunt, after pushing her own steed so hard through the night, she rode upon a hardy mare with a tan coat.

The sun had not ascended too far into the sky when the queen slowed the hunting contingent down. Riding at the lead of the group with the queen, Rayden looked over to her.

"It has been a long time since a Gorgothir has been sighted in our lands," the queen said. "I am not going to have us ride straight into one. We must approach with great caution."

"Where are we going now?" Rayden asked.

"An area where many recent deaths have been reported," the queen answered. "Vines are cultivated on the slopes of many of these hills for our wine. A large number of slaves and citizens of Aressenia labor and live in this area."

"Who have become an easy, plentiful source of prey for this kind of monster," Rayden commented.

The queen nodded. "Groups of men and women have vanished along the pathways and trails winding through the hills ahead. We are fortunate to have a few eye witnesses to confirm that we are facing Gorgothirs."

"I imagine that the people are not traveling their usual paths at this time," Rayden said.

"They have been ordered to stay in their villages and homes," the queen said. "My hope is that their absence will help draw the beasts out in the open when our warriors move though this area."

"We are both bait and hunter then," Rayden said, with a grin.

"You could say that," the queen replied, mirroring the expression.

The queen looked ahead, and she took a deep breath.

"This is as close as we will go on horseback!" Marsellina said in a raised voice, bringing her right fist up. "Dismount! We go on foot from here!"

Behind her, all of the warriors brought their mounts to a halt.

Dismounting and leaving their steeds under guard, the Aressenians divided into several groups. Fanning out, the smaller hunting parties moved forward and began climbing the slopes of the hills ahead.

Rayden accompanied the queen and several of her warriors. Passing close to a few hillsides covered in stakes with vines growing on them, she eyed a small village on a hill farther ahead.

The stone-built structures of the village were clustered

around the summit in a manner that provided the site with some defensive advantages. Rayden did not see any signs of activity within the village, and she hoped that the occupants of the dwellings there had heeded the queen's orders.

Working their way through the low brush on the hill, Rayden and the others worked their way around the rise. They reached a place where a main path leading from the village passed along the base of the hill.

"It is my thought that without the usual groups of men and women traveling the paths in these hills, the Gorgothirs will grow bolder, and draw closer to the sources of their prey," the queen whispered to Rayden. "The Gorgothir are scaled creatures. If they are like a large snake, it is likely they will seek a place where they can ambush their quarry. We should begin our hunt from here."

Moving in silence, the group led by the queen shadowed the main pathway below. Rayden eyed the slopes surrounding the pathway. The craggy, rocky hills, abundant with brush and small trees, afforded a host of viable places for a large predator to conceal itself.

To keep above the pathway, the hunting party had to traverse a low ridge between two summits. The route took them close to a narrow, small ravine formed by a couple of slender spurs running from the slope. Maintaining their higher vantage, the warriors passed the ravine and continued forward, keeping their focus on the area surrounding the pathway.

Thinking upon the queen's speculation, concerning the Gorgothir's scaled nature, Rayden knew that the warriors would have to keep a constant watch about them. If the Gorgothirs hunted in a manner similar to snakes, they would be drawn toward movement and it would be difficult for the passage of a large number of warriors to go unnoticed.

Just ahead, the two warriors at the head of the group

came to a stop and gestured for the others to come up. Walking alongside the queen, Rayden made her way up to where the pair had halted.

All four of the warriors crouched low, using the brush for concealment. Rayden gazed down upon a wider area of ground, where the pathway they had been following intersected with a larger patch of open space set between three hills.

Maintaining a steady composure, Rayden took in the stark, gruesome sight at the base of the hills.

A snake-like monstrosity covered in dark scales extended far across the ground. It would take no less than twelve adult humans, arrayed in a single, continuous line from head to foot, to match the huge creature in length.

Even more astonishing, the serpentine creature had legs. Three pairs of the short, clawed appendages could be seen along the creature's extensive body, the last set of which gave way to a lengthy, tapering tail.

At the moment, a pair of human legs protruded out from the creature's widened jaws. Farther down its body, two pronounced, elongated lumps could be seen. It took little discernment for Rayden to glean what the bulges represented.

A short distance from the creature, the body of a woman in a brown tunic lay upon the ground. The woman did not move, but Rayden could not tell whether she was unconscious or dead.

Aghast at the scene below, Rayden clenched the haft and hilt of her weapons a little tighter.

"Gorging itself, upon our slaves," the queen said to Rayden in a whisper, eyeing the monster with a heated look on her face.

"The bastard will be sluggish and vulnerable," Rayden whispered back. "Let us give it something to fear. Take it with javelins at a distance."

Before the queen could reply, a sharp cry broke out to their right, coming from the area that the warriors had just passed through.

Up and running at once, Rayden, the queen, and the two other warriors hurried toward the sound. They did not have far to go.

An Aressenian warrior lay still on the ground. Looming over her, a Gorgothir was positioning itself close to the top of her head. Jaws unhinging and spreading wide enough to swallow her whole, the creature prepared to ingest its inert prey.

Closing its jaws, the Gorgothir whipped its head up at the approach of Rayden and the others. Lifting its head and the forefront of its body higher, in the manner of a snake poised to strike, the massive creature fixed its gaze upon the warriors.

A crest of thin, deep red spines, running from its head down the middle of its back, flared upright.

"Keep your steps slow, move to the sides, we will strike it together!" the queen called out. In a lower voice meant for Rayden alone, she added, "Stay with me. We will go in to attack behind our shields."

The two warriors with Rayden and the queen split up, one circling with slow, careful steps to the left of the creature and the other moving with great caution to the right. Rayden and the queen stood together at the front of the monster, keeping their weapons at the ready.

Shifting its attention between all of the warriors, the Gorgothir held its place.

"Prepare yourselves to strike!" Marsellina said, positioning her shield in front of her body.

The queen raised her spear above her head with a firm hold on the leather hand grip at the balance point of the long, tapering shaft of ash, the spot set a little back from the center. Austere expressions fixed upon their faces, the other two warriors readied their own spears and shields in a manner similar to the queen.

"Strike!" the queen cried out, surging forward behind her

shield, with Rayden close behind.

Keeping their shields in front of them, the other two warriors closed in fast from the sides.

The Gorgothir responded to the coordinated assault with astounding quickness. Rotating to its right, the creature executed two powerful attacks at once, striking at the warriors rushing upon its sides.

Rear legs anchoring the back portion of its body, the creature lashed out with its tail at the warrior attacking from its left. The charging Aressenian turned just in time to catch the snapping blow solid on the face of her shield, but the force of it knocked the warrior off her feet. Tossed several paces through the air, she hit the ground hard a little to the right of the queen and Rayden.

At the other end of the Gorgothir, the creature's head bolted straight toward the warrior attacking from its right. Batting aside her shield with its snout, the force of the Gorgothir's blow spun the warrior about, causing her to lose her footing and fall to the ground.

Landing face down with her back exposed, she did not see the creature spreading its jaws wide, displaying a fearsome pair of curving, glistening fangs. Head darting down, the creature plunged its fangs deep into her body at the shoulder. An instant later, the Gorgothir retracted its head, pulling the blood-coated fangs out of her flesh.

The warrior trembled all over for a couple of heartbeats and then went still.

An instant later, swinging its head back to the left, the Gorgothir caught the queen just as she began stabbing downward with her spear. Crashing the side of its broad head into her shield, the Gorgothir swept the queen off her feet.

Turning its head fast, the Gorgothir angled back around, orienting upon the prostrate queen. Keeping its head low, the Gorgothir opened its jaws, exposing the sharp pair of fangs once more, and lunged forward.

Its onrush was met by the end of Rayden's sword, thrust with full force from where she had stepped into the space vacated by the queen.

The tip of the blade pierced the creature's flesh on the upper part of its snout. Recoiling from the stinging blow, the Gorgothir closed its jaws and yanked its head far back. Blood trickled out from the wound.

Her sword blade gleaming with the blood of the Gorgothir, Rayden took up a defensive posture by the queen.

"Get back now!" Rayden yelled to Marsellina, while keeping her eyes fixed on the beast.

Managing to hold onto her shield, Marsellina scrambled away from the creature. Facing the Gorgothir, Rayden backed up alongside the queen.

Whirling to the right of Marsellina, the Gorgothir lunged toward the warrior that it had struck with its tail. Dazed from the powerful strike and subsequent collision with the ground, the warrior was still laying on her back when the Gorgothir's head rushed down at her. Trying to shield her face with her arms, she barely got a cry out before the creature's fangs stabbed deep into her torso.

Like her fellow warrior, she trembled in the wake of the bite and then fell still.

Another of the smaller hunting groups, attracted by the sounds of the fierce struggle, then arrived at the scene of the battle. Without hesitation, the newcomers raised their shields and spears, and charged forward.

Whipping its tail about, using its head to bludgeon, and stabbing with its fangs, the Gorgothir took over half of the warriors out of the fighting in a few mere heartbeats.

Warding the queen, Rayden called to the ones still remaining in the fight, "Here! Gather here!"

Responding to her commanding tone, the three warriors hastened over to where Rayden stood. Having regained her feet, the queen lifted her shield and took up a discarded spear from the ground.

Surrounded by the still forms of Aressenian warriors that it had brought down, the Gorgothir turned its head and cast a baleful gaze upon the five warriors. Seeing them standing shoulder to shoulder, it held back from striking.

During the impasse, an idea formed in Rayden's mind. While far from certain, it offered a chance to spare the remaining Aressenians.

"Distract it! Do not attack it! I know how to get above it!" Rayden shouted to Marsellina and the remaining warriors. She slid her blade into its sheath and returned her axe to the loop at her belt.

The others lowered their spears, shifting to underhanded grips, presenting a hedge of sharp iron toward the Gorgothir. Rearing up a little higher, the creature hissed, but still made no move to attack.

Springing into a run, Rayden bounded to the right, keeping a wide berth between herself and the creature. Legs churning with all the strength that she could put into them, she raced uphill. Shifting left and right to avoid clumps of brush, she took herself back in the direction from where they had come.

Rapid movement drawing its gaze, the Gorgothir swiveled its head in Rayden's direction. Homing in upon her, the creature slithered after her, tucking its legs into shallow depressions in its sides.

Well past the creature, Rayden leveled out her course, picking up speed as she raced along the slope. Accelerating faster, she headed down the slope, angling for the low ridge connecting with the other hill.

Seeing the tip of the narrow ravine that she had remembered,

Rayden hurried for the cleft in the ground. Reaching the edge, she eyed the facing of the sides, relieved to see a host of places to set her feet and grip onto with her hands.

Taking care not to become too reckless in her haste, she climbed down into the channel. A short distance above the bottom, she jumped down and started down the confined pathway at a rapid stride.

Looking back over her shoulder, Rayden saw the Gorgothir's head crest the edge of the ravine. Its pupils narrow, vertical slits, the creature eyed her for a moment before starting after her.

Using its legs to brace its body, the Gorgothir descended into the shadows of the rocky passageway. Reaching the bottom, the creature slithered forward, its forked tongue flicking out in an intermittent fashion.

Seeing its pursuit, Rayden broke into a run, putting increasing distance between herself and the Gorgothir. A short distance ahead, the path turned a little to the right. Following the curve, she took a couple of quick glances back to make certain that the creature no longer had her within its eyesight.

Slowing down, Rayden moved over to the right side of the passage and found a couple of handholds above her head. Locating places to set the tips of her feet, she braced and began climbing the rock wall.

The jagged facing, teeming with cracks and shallow depressions, offered an abundance of places for her fingers and feet to gain purchase. Blocking thoughts of the Gorgothir from her mind, Rayden put her entire focus on the climb, scaling the rock in a steady manner.

When she had climbed about halfway up the side of the ravine, Rayden halted. Her feet set, and one hand secure on the edge of a small crevice, she reached down and took her sword from its sheath.

Gripping the sword's hilt with the blade oriented downward,

Rayden turned her head to the right and became still. Holding onto the side of the ravine, she watched for the creature following her to appear.

Making its way down the narrow channel, the Gorgothir drew into sight a few moments later. The width of the ravine just broad enough for the creature to undulate its form without hindrance in the manner of a snake, the Gorgothir glided across the loose soil and rock covering the bottom of the ravine.

Advancing ever closer to the spot where Rayden had climbed upward, the creature's eyes remained on the passage before it. One sudden move on her part would betray her position, leaving her trapped and easy prey for the monstrosity below.

Staying rigid as possible, Rayden estimated the distance remaining until the Gorgothir would be directly underneath her, and she judged her height above the ground. The moment she had anticipated loomed imminent. Drawing in a long, slow breath, Rayden let a warrior's calm settle over her, sharpening her clarity and steadying her nerves, before letting her breath out in a similar, controlled fashion.

The Gorgothir was almost beneath her.

A heartbeat later, she gauged that the time had come.

Rayden let go of the rock facing, twisting and falling the instant that the Gorgothir's snout was poised to enter the space immediately beneath her. Holding her blade with the tip oriented downward, both hands firm upon the hilt, she drove her sword deep into the creature's skull, burying the weapon to the hilt.

Her fall giving her strike momentum, augmented with the burst of strength that she put behind the downward thrust, the blade speared through the upper and lower jaws of the Gorgothir. Skewered, the creature thrashed about, throwing Rayden off its scaled body.

Rayden slammed into the rocky soil, grunting with the hard impact. Shutting the pain out of her mind, she got her feet beneath her and stood up. Reaching down, she grabbed the haft of her axe and yanked it free of the loop at her belt.

The Gorgothir continued to swing its head about, struggling to dislodge the blade. Springing forward, Rayden set her feet beneath the exposed underside of the creature and swung her axe in a wide, overhead arc that carved a deep gash just behind the base of its jaws.

Blood and gore rained down upon Rayden before she shifted to the side, taking her out from beneath the creature. Loosing a war cry, she hacked at the Gorgothir's head in a raging fury. A raw, primal strength flowing into every blow, Rayden laid waste to the creature's skull.

Collapsing to the ground under the torrential assault, the Gorgothir went still, half of its skull chopped to bits and the brain matter beyond pulped into an unrecognizable miasma. Breathing hard, Rayden set her foot upon the end of its snout and pulled her sword free.

Keeping her weapons in hand, Rayden walked around the creature and started back up the ravine. She had not gotten far on the passage when the queen and two warriors trotted into view. Looking at Rayden, coated in the blood and grime of the Gorgothir, their eyes widened in amazement.

"That one is dead," Rayden announced, still catching her breath.

"I am glad to see you have come to no harm," the queen said. "We came as fast as we could. I left one warrior to guard those bitten. I do not know whether they live or not, for there was no time to examine them. I am sorry we did not reach you sooner, but you and the creature were already far down the passage when we climbed down."

"I detest the idea of becoming anything's meal," Rayden stated, before stepping past the queen and warriors. "I do not think the slave girl thinks any differently than me, and we know where another of these bastards can be found. I hope we can return to it in time. Let us go at haste!"

Her breathing settling into a steady rhythm, Rayden quickened her stride. The queen and the other warriors turned about, following Rayden back up the ravine.

***

Using horn signals, the queen had her full hunting group summoned back together, bringing the smaller groups to the site of the first Gorgothir. The creature remained where they had left it, though three extended bulges now showed farther down the length of its body.

To Rayden's great relief, the creature had not yet consumed the body of the woman lying near to it. While she remained inert, showing no signs of having moved since Rayden had last set her eyes upon her, hope for the woman's life remained.

A brief examination of the warriors bitten in the struggle with the other Gorgothir revealed that most were still alive, though all of the survivors remained shallow of breath and still had no command of their limbs or faculties. A couple of the warriors were found dead, but Rayden believed their deaths to be more a result of where they had been punctured by the Gorgothir's lengthy fangs than any effect of the venom injected into their bodies.

The discovery that a great majority of those bitten survived in an immobilized state told Rayden that the Gorgothirs ingested most of their prey alive, a terrible doom for any stricken by their fangs. If the woman on the ground still breathed, Rayden was determined to see that she did not incur the awful fate of her three companions.

With the creature lethargic and gorged, no great risk had to be taken to attack it. Marsellina ordered her warriors into positions lower on the slope, brining them closer to the creature.

Aware of the movements on the slope, and perhaps sensing the looming threat, the Gorgothir lifted its head and began to slither forward.

At the queen's horn signal, a host of javelins were hurled into the air toward the monster.

Sluggish and weighed down with three human bodies inside of it, the Gorgothir could do nothing to evade the hail of javelins. Pelting downward, the storm of javelins riddled the creature's body up and down its extensive length.

The Gorgothir came to a halt and writhed about, breaking several of the shafts protruding out of its body. Another volley of javelins sailed through the air a moment later, showering the thrashing creature from head to tail.

In the wake of the second barrage, the Gorgothir's contortions slowed, and then the creature went still.

Aressenian warriors hurried down from the slopes and advanced toward the Gorgothir. A forest of shafts embedded in its body, the creature showed no reaction to their approach.

Wielding their long spears, the warriors stabbed at its body and head until there remained no question of its death.

Rayden, standing behind the wall of shields and spears, hastened around the creature and made her way over to the woman on the ground. Kneeling at her side, and finding life still within the woman, Rayden breathed out in an extended sigh of relief.

"She lives," Rayden declared, looking back to Marsellina, who stood a few paces away.

"I will have her taken with our warriors and seen to," the queen answered.

At the queen's command, a couple of Aressenian warriors carried the female slave away.

"It remains to be seen how long the venom keeps its hold upon them," Rayden said.

"I imagine that it will take some time for those who survived to recover," the queen remarked.

"They are not out of danger yet ... and neither are we," Rayden said, looking around. "I sense that there is more to uncover about these monsters."

"We must keep a watch for others," the queen said. "The one that attacked us on the slope stalked us, and came up from behind, striking several other warriors before the one whose cry alerted us."

"My intuition tells me that stalking is not the only way these monsters hunt," Rayden said, eyeing the ground and starting forward.

"What are you looking for?" the queen asked, walking with her.

"Stay with me, and I will show you," Rayden said, continuing onward

Searching around the area, Rayden came upon a long channel of loose soil.

"As I expected ... they can bury themselves, and lay in ambush," Rayden declared, seeing that the channel could accommodate the width and length of the slain Gorgothir behind them. "I am guessing this is a path well-traveled by those who live in these hills."

"It is," the queen confirmed.

"With a place like this, the creature did not have to stalk its prey," Rayden said. "It could wait for prey to come to it."

"Then it could use its venom to render many victims helpless," the queen said, a somber look on her face. "And eat them at its own pace."

"This one may seem a glutton," Rayden said, eyeing the javelin-pierced carcass of the Gorgothir, with the three human bodies still inside of it. "But I do not think it was careless. I believe there is a reason for its great hunger. I believe it is the same reason you were confronted with two of these creatures so near to each other."

"What do you mean by this?" the queen asked her.

"The one that stalked and attacked us above had a red crest of spines," Rayden continued, the logic falling into place. "It was not the same as the one down here."

"Speak plainly," the queen replied, with an air of impatience.

"Spread your warriors out, and look for a nest," Rayden said, looking the queen in the eyes. "I believe the one that attacked us above to be a male of its kind, and this one a female. A much greater threat to your lands is near, if I am right."

A flare of concern shone within the face of the queen. Raising her voice, Marsellina gave the order to have the area searched in a thorough manner. The Aressenian warriors fanned out, walking all over the lower ground and bottom portion of the nearby slopes.

Not long after the search had begun, a shout came from one of the warriors, drawing Rayden, Marsellina, and the others to a spot at the base of a thin spur running out from one of the hills.

Wiping away the loose soil covering them, the warrior exposed a cluster of large eggs. Rayden counted over twenty of them nestled within the shallow pit.

"Thank the gods we have found this!" the queen exclaimed, looking over to Rayden.

Her suspicions confirmed, Rayden eyed the batch of eggs. Each one represented a deadly threat to the people of Aressenia.

"Far greater of a threat to your people than the monsters we have slain," Rayden commented. "The beasts invaded your land, and they would have unleashed an even greater nightmare in a short time."

"I do not even want to think about what may have happened," the queen said, staring at the eggs.

"You know what must be done," Rayden said. "Protect your

people."

A resolute look in her eyes, the queen nodded. "Let us not waste a moment longer."

Lifting her spear up and reversing it, the queen positioned the spiked base of the weapon against the soft, leathery surface of one of the eggs. With a swift, downward thrust the queen pierced the pliable shell, crushing the spawn of the Gorgothir curled inside of it.

Raising the spiked base up, she drove the spear down into another egg, repeating the process until not a single egg within the nest remained intact. After probing around for a little longer, to be sure that nothing had been missed, the queen withdrew her spear and wiped the gore from the spike on the edge of the pit.

"We must assume nothing," the queen stated, looking to Rayden and the surrounding warriors. "Set a fire to cleanse this pit, and then let us be sure that no others lurk along the pathway."

***

Staying to the higher ground and navigating the brush, Rayden, Marsellina and the other warriors gave close scrutiny to the low ground most traveled by the Aressenians living in the vicinity. Spread out on both sides of the broad channel below, they kept a constant watch about them.

At least two Aressenian warriors hurled javelins into every possible aberration visible in the surface, along the lower ground. The methodical approach demanded several pauses of the larger group, but it did not risk a single warrior in the instance that a Gorgothir lay submerged within the soil, waiting in ambush.

Again, and again, the javelins thudded into the ground without event. The warriors who threw them trotted down to retrieve them and continued onward.

A little later in the afternoon, when the warriors had almost completed their search along the main pathway, one of the thrown javelins elicited a different result. Dirt and rock exploding out from the surface to reveal a long, wide furrow in the ground, a Gorgothir erupted out of its well-concealed position.

Rayden marveled at the power demonstrated by the creature. Anything close to where it had set its trap would have had no time to flee.

Whipping its head about, a lone javelin sticking out of its back, the Gorgothir found no immediate prey. Raising its head, the creature took in the movements taking place all around it on the nearby slopes.

A hail of javelins already bearing down upon it, the Gorgothir had no time to react to the torrential attack. Twisting and squirming under the barrage of javelins plunging into its body, the beast collapsed heavily to the ground a moment later.

A long, rattling hiss sounded from the creature, and then it went still.

Making their way down from the slopes, several warriors drove their spears into the skull of the Gorgothir, to make certain of its death.

Accompanying them, Rayden walked the length of the scaly creature. Having noticed that it did not have a crest of spines, she examined its body closely.

"Looks like you caught this one early," Rayden said, coming to a stop and pointing with the tip of her sword at a pronounced, bloated area lower on the creature's body.

Pulling her blade from its sheath, one of the Aressenian warriors leaned over and slit open the Gorgothir's carcass, exposing an array of eggs that had not yet been placed into a nest. The warrior's eyes widened at the discovery.

"That would also have become a great problem for the people of this area," Rayden commented. "Make certain there is no chance that it can."

The warrior nodded her understanding. Using her blade,

she hacked the eggs apart.

Striding up, Marsellina observed the destruction of the eggs. After remaining quiet for a few moments, she turned toward Rayden.

"We have truly evaded a disaster this day," the queen said.

"There is something to be learned from all of this, to those who are open to wisdom," Rayden said.

"What lesson is that?" the queen asked.

Rayden stared into the eyes of the queen and spoke in a firm voice. "The three monsters we have slain invaded your territory, but never forget that invaders can bring a greater, longer-lasting threat to your people's future in their wake."

"You speak of the Astrians?" the queen asked.

"Do not allow them to hold Pargemon, or you will face an even greater threat in the future," Rayden stated. "Do not give them time to set their roots, or you will face the monster of the present and the others that would be hatched in time. Do you understand my meaning?"

The queen held Rayden's gaze for a moment, and then nodded slowly. "I do. I see that the gods have been generous to me today. The lesson is clear now, though I may not have seen it if you were not here."

"I am a foreigner in your lands, but we stood together against a threat to us both," Rayden said. "Now do the same on a greater scale and see a looming threat to your lands destroyed."

"Monsters and eggs both," the queen replied, looking back to the cavity in the side of the Gorgothir, where the remnants of a full batch of eggs lay in a shredded, crushed mass.

***

"You brought us some good fortune, Rayden," the queen remarked when they had returned to the village late in the afternoon. "And you guided me to needed wisdom."

"A successful hunt, though I am sorry about the deaths of the warriors and the others who fell victim to those monsters," Rayden said.

"The warriors died honorably, fighting an adversary," the queen said. "It is the way that all Aressenian warriors wish to die. Celebrate them. Do not mourn them."

Rayden held her tongue at the queen's omission of the other deaths, making no comment about the lower status citizens and slaves who had become prey to the Gorgothirs. It was not the time to raise an argument with the queen.

The day's events had opened the queen's eyes to a greater wisdom; one that would enable her to become an even stronger protector of her people. With time, perhaps she would see other things in a different light.

"We shall celebrate them ... dedicated warriors all," Rayden said, after an extended pause.

"Far many more were saved, in finding the nest of eggs, and uncovering the last of the creatures," the queen said. "It also carried a full belly of eggs. Without your insights, we may have overlooked those eggs and faced greater peril in time."

"The Gorgothirs are a primal kind of beast, and the motivations of such beasts are not difficult to understand," Rayden said. "They seek to fill their bellies and give birth to new Gorgothirs, to carry their kind on. Their hunting of humans is not born of any wicked desire ... nor is our hunt to bring them to an end. We do what is most natural in protecting ourselves, and our own kind."

"There is nothing more natural than that," the queen concurred.

"Then never forget that it is just as natural to hunt down an approaching enemy who carries wicked motivations and desires ... to conquer Griacan lands and wipe away the essence of who you are," Rayden said. "What is happening in Pargemon is an attack on Thrakkia, Samosia, Aressenia, and all the Griacan kingdoms."

"I will see that these Astrian dogs are driven back into the sea," the queen responded. "I will not give them the chance to welcome greater numbers arriving in their wake to assail our lands."

"All Griacan rulers must come to understand this," Rayden said with an emphatic edge. "Then you will be able to resist the Emperor, when he hurls all of his might at Griacan shores. That day will come."

"Then we will face that day, when it comes," the queen replied. "But for now, what do you advise regarding these monsters that have plagued our hills? Does anything remain to be done?"

"As I see it, the only thing that remains for you is to be certain whether or not there are any more of the creatures lurking among the hills," Rayden said

The queen's force had completed the scouring of the main pathway, but there were still remote parts of the hills and smaller trails that had not been searched. It stood to reason that a large predator like a Gorgothir would be encountered where an abundance of prey could be found, but Rayden knew that nothing could be overlooked. As she had witnessed time and time again over the years, the things of the world often flew straight in the face of reason.

"We have learned more about the Gorgothirs and how to hunt them today," the queen said. "We shall put that to use, and a search will be made of every hill and pathway in this area, but now we must turn our minds to other tasks."

Rayden nodded, and a slight grin crossed her lips. "I did not forget that we will be marching in a day."

"Join me for some barley cake and black-broth," the queen said. "I have worked up a large appetite traversing the hills today. Let us restore our strength before we go teach lessons to foolish kings and brazen invaders."

"Hunger does tug at me, but we still have one important matter to resolve," Rayden said, casting the queen a knowing look. "I do not think it can wait until tomorrow."

The queen paused, and then nodded. "Yes, we do. Come with me and let us see this matter settled before the last light of day sinks below the horizon. Then we can tend to our hunger and gain some rest."

Side by side, the two warriors walked beyond the edge of the village, looking for an open swathe of flatter ground. A few took notice of the pair striding away, but no one sought to disturb them.

An air of purpose surrounded the two warriors, but no man or woman seeing Rayden and Queen Marsellina could begin to fathom that the fate of Aresenia hung in the balance.

***

When dawn broke, on the third morning after the night Rayden had ridden alone upon a piebald Thrakkian stallion into the lands of Aressenia, two armies on the verge of battle hesitated to advance.

A short time before, the minds of every warrior on both sides had been fixed upon the massed ranks arrayed opposite them, across the broad stretch of flat, rocky ground. Awaiting the braying horn signals that would set them in motion, the warriors of Thrakkia and Samosia had been gripping their weapons and shields tight, while casting glares full of deadly intent toward their opponents.

Now, the warriors of two kingdoms turned their thoughts away from the looming battle.

To their collective astonishment, another army had manifested in the first light of dawn, marching upon them both out of the north.

Helms and spears gleamed in the sunlight. A low rumble rippled through the ground at the steady approach of several thousand warriors.

The black horsehair crests, distinctive types of emblems on the facing of their shields, and crimson tunics identified the newcomers as Aressenians. The recognition unnerved more than a few warriors within the armed masses set in place on either side of the open battleground.

After drawing closer, to a point just beyond the reach of an arrow's flight, the Aressenian ranks drew to a halt and a lull fell across the battlefield. Save for the scattered whinnies and neighs of horses, only the wind dared disturb the tense, heavy silence.

More than one warrior in the ranks of the armies of Thrakkia and Samosia doubted their eyes when two figures strode forth from the Aressenian line. All had expected to see the tall, dark-haired Aressenian queen, Marsellina, whose name had been well-known in their lands for many years.

None had anticipated the blonde-haired warrior who walked at the queen's side.

Queen Marsellina and Rayden Valkyrie approached a central area between the massed armies of Thrakkia and Samosia.

Garbed for battle, the Aressenian, queen wore a pair of bronze greaves to protect her lower legs. Adorned with a transverse horsehair crest, crimson in hue, a helm crafted with cheek guards was cradled underneath her right arm. Unlike most of the Aressenian warriors in the multitude behind her, she wore no cuirass.

The circular shield carried on her left arm had a single Griacan letter painted upon it, representing the war god Aressen. Like the other Aressenians, Queen Marsellina was clad in a crimson tunic that reached down to the middle of her thighs. No boot or shoe covered her feet. The queen carried one weapon, a straight sword of medium length that rested in its sheath at her left side.

Carrying no shield or helm, Rayden's garb was no different than what she had worn the previous day. She wore a short-sleeved tunic of about knee-length, belted at the waist, and a pair of high-strapped sandals.

Sword sheathed, and her axe in its belt loop, Rayden held no weapons.

Rayden had no need for anything else.

She knew that she would not be taking a place within an Aressenian phalanx, a formation drilled into a cohesion that saw it move like a single body. In such a formation, the use of a shield stood indispensable; not just for the one holding it, but also for the protection of the other warriors in the phalanx.

Rather, her battle would take place in the form of one warrior pitted against another; if the offer about to be made was accepted by the kings of Samosia and Thrakkia.

Footsteps crunching upon on the dry ground and eyes fixed forward, Rayden kept her mind clear of all other concerns, centering her thoughts upon the moment at hand. A resolute expression on her face, no worries or anxieties troubled her heart.

She could not control the minds of kings or queens, but Rayden knew that she had done all that she could to steer the Griacans toward a better, wiser path. Whether or not they took that path remained to be seen, but Rayden walked with a clear conscience, no matter the outcome.

Before she reached the center of the battlefield, Rayden caught movements on the edges of her peripheral vision, coming from the other two lines. Turning her head, she took account of the developments.

From the forefront of the Thrakkian ranks, three figures emerged. Approaching the queen and Rayden, two of them wore bronze helms, the apex of which had a low, forward curve to their design. The pair flanked a man of average height, who walked a couple of paces ahead of them.

She recognized the figure in the lead at once: the Thrakkian king, Cadmenus.

A dense, short-cropped beard covered his broad face. Wide of shoulder and robust in build, he stood the image of a warrior as much as he did a king.

A circlet of pure gold ran about his head. Cropped shorter to the ear in the manner of the Thrakkians, his wavy, dark locks carried a lustrous sheen. A bronze cuirass shaped to resemble the contours of a muscular upper body protected his torso, while a pair of greaves defended his lower legs.

Sheathed and suspended from a baldric, a long straight sword at his left side served as his only weapon in view.

Opposite the Thrakkian king, two figures strode out from the Samosian lines and started for the center of the battlefield.

One wore a golden circlet, not unlike that upon the head of the Thrakkian king, though it exhibited a number of figures and designs engraved all along its gleaming surface. A shining cuirass, emblazoned with a scene of a spear-carrying warrior about to strike a lion in mid-leap, protected his upper torso. Each of his knee-high greaves held a depiction of a Samosian warrior standing with spear and shield in hand.

His narrow face and larger nose gave King Oradacer, the Samosian king, a hawk-like countenance; a look reflected further within the piercing stare of his dark eyes.

. The Samosian king had a leaner build than his Thrakkian counterpart. A mix of gray and black hairs, and a few lines of age on his face, marked the king as several years older than either Queen Marsellina or King Cadmenus.

At the Samosian king's right walked a giant of a man. Cradling a horsehair-crested helm under his right arm, the thick-bearded juggernaut stood a full head taller than any warrior on the battlefield.

His cuirass and greaves, though gleaming in the sunlight, had none of the elaborate decoration of King Oradacer's. The bronze facing of his large, round shield carried the image of an eagle with wings outstretched and talons spread wide.

Prominent and craggy, his nose displayed clear evidence of having been broken more than once. A short, bull-like neck sloped into a wide set of shoulders framing a brawny torso. Arms rippling with muscle exhibited a number of scars, their varying sizes, hues, and orientations indicating that the marks had been collected across an array of encounters.

An eagle-headed pommel crowned the hilt of the sword at his left side.

Rayden knew in an instant that she looked upon Desidar.

Eyes that had witnessed multitudes of grisly deaths, meted out in brutal fashion at the feared Samosian warrior's hands, now cast a cold, hard gaze upon Queen Marsellina and Rayden. Though she could not read the warrior's thoughts, Rayden knew the giant measured her as much as she now measured him.

"What is this?" the Thrakkian king asked with a tone of irritation, when all of the parties had converged at the center of the battlefield. "Why have you come here, Queen Marsellina? We have no quarrel with you. Yet your army is positioned to attack."

"Aressenia is prepared to drench this field in the blood of your kingdoms this day," the Queen replied, looking to both of the kings,, her expression ice cold. "What happens depends upon this parley and your responses."

"Then why the parley? And why is she here?" the Samosian king queried, looking more indignant as he set his gaze upon Rayden. "She is a foreigner. She is not Aressenian. Was she not aiding the Thrakkians recently?"

"You are well-informed, but she stands with us," the queen replied, with an air that told the others there would be no further explanation. "I am here to offer single combat to determine the fates of our lands today."

Neither king could disguise the great surprise that echoed in their faces and eyes at the Aressenian queen's pronouncement.

'Single combat?" King Cadmenus asked, regaining his composure. "It is well-known the Aressenians never offer single combat when marching to war."

"My reasons are my own, and do not question them," the queen told the king in a commanding tone.

"There are three kingdoms represented here," King Oradacer said. He looked between the other two rulers. "My dispute is with Thrakkia. Aressenia, it would seem, has come to confront both Thrakkia and Samosia. That presents a dilemma for an offer of single combat, does it not?"

"A champion of Thrakkia shall face a champion of Aressenia ... and a champion of Samosia shall face another champion of Aressenia," the queen said, looking the Samosian king direct in the eyes.

"What if one of your champions prevails and one does not? " King Cadmenus asked, a trace of puzzlement on his face. "And what if neither of your champions prevails? What then of the dispute between Thrakkia and Samosia? Who would become sovereign over Aressenia?"

"If one of Aressenia's champions falls, then the kingdom of the victor will gain the right of sovereignty over two kingdoms," the queen explained. "The defeat of one of our champions would forfeit our other champion's victory, as one of your kingdoms would have claimed dominion of Aressenia through the felling of the other."

Looking between the two kings, Queen Marsellina paused and fell silent. Rayden knew the queen was letting the tantalizing words sink into their minds, to stoke their greed and ambitions.

Each had been offered a path to gaining rule over two

kingdoms, yet the declaration stood logical. If one Aressenian champion prevailed, Aressenia gained the submission of that kingdom, which would all be given over to the kingdom of a champion who managed to triumph over an Aressenian.

"And if no champion of ours prevails?" the queen resumed, a smirk appearing on her lips, showing that she viewed the notion itself absurd. "Then you are free to resolve your dispute in whatever way you choose, with the additional prize of rule over Aressenia awaiting the victor. Spill each other's blood all you want."

Rayden could see the eagerness swelling within the eyes of the two kings. The prospects of gaining rule over two lands, one of them being the legendary Aressenia, loomed before them.

"Intriguing, but it would be unusual to have two sets of champions," King Cadmenus said. "How would the order of combat be determined?"

"They would fight at the same time, set at a distance where they would not interfere with each other," Queen Marsellina said. "This way, no preference is given to either of your kingdoms in the order of the fighting."

A sardonic look crept across the face of King Oradacer. "I agree to this proposal."

"As do I," assented King Cadmenus, a moment later.

"Then all that remains is to declare the champions," Queen Marsellina said.

"Mine stands with me now," King Oradacer stated with an air of supreme confidence, indicating the towering giant at his right shoulder. "Desidar, the Undefeated, will represent Samosia."

"Mekrides will stand for Thrakkia," declared King Cadmenus. "I will have him summoned forth."

"Both of our champions are standing here now," Queen Marsellina declared.

Again, the other two rulers could not mask their surprise.

The wisp of a grin on the queen's face told Rayden that the Aressenian queen relished the kings' astonishment.

"I challenge Mekrides," the queen said, before either of the kings could reply. "And Rayden Valkyrie shall challenge Desidar."

Looking from the queen to Rayden, a rumbling laugh sounded from the mouth of King Oradacer. Smiling, he stated, "Today the gods are with me! I shall possess the lands of Thrakkia and Aressenia. Praise the gods, it is a good day!"

Queen Marsellina made no reply to King Oradacer, though Rayden could see the ire brimming within the ice-cold stare she cast at the Samosian king.

"What man knows what a day may bring?" King Cadmenus responded after a moment, glaring at the other king. "Nothing has been decided yet."

Rayden could sense a burning anger within King Cadmenus toward the pairings. She knew that he deemed the fight between herself and Desidar to be a forgone conclusion, in the favor of the Samosian giant.

The recognition did not bother Rayden at all. She had been underestimated by men and women far greater than King Cadmenus many times before.

"Then let it be decided! Let the clash of our champions begin, without delay," King Oradacer stated, his face betraying that he was all but certain of victory.

"Call your champion forth, Cadmenus," Queen Marsellina said in an even tone.

Continuing to glower in the direction of King Oradacer, the Thrakkian king nodded. "Let it be done."

One of the warriors who had come with King Cadmenus turned and hastened toward the Thrakkian lines. Shortly after he reached their ranks, another warrior stepped forth and started across the battlefield.

Bearing no shield, the advancing warrior carried a two-handed weapon of a type popular among the Thrakkians. Having an extended haft and a narrow, straight, single-edged blade of sword length, it was an effective weapon for both slashing and thrusting movements.

A round-topped bronze helm with cheek and nasal guards protected the warrior's head. Deerskin boots with down-turned flaps at the top covered his feet. A black, sleeveless tunic reached down to his thighs.

Wide of shoulder and narrow of waist, the approaching warrior moved with a cat-like grace that hinted at exceptional agility. While not thick of build, he had a pronounced, sinewy muscularity reflective of considerable physical strength.

When he reached the middle of the battlefield, King Cadmenus introduced the warrior. "Mekrides, who will fight on behalf of Thrakkia."

Mekrides gave a low bow to the king at the mention of his name.

"The four champions are present," King Oradacer said. "Let the places of combat be set, and this contest can begin."

Queen Marsellina and King Cadmenus nodded their assent.

A couple of men were then summoned from the Samosian lines. After putting his helm on, Desidar removed his cuirass and greaves. The men took them from the huge warrior and stepped back, awaiting their king.

In a similar fashion, a pair of Aressenian warriors sprinted from their lines to where Queen Marsellina stood. Removing her greaves, she handed them over to the warriors, who returned at once to the Aressenian lines.

Set far apart, enough that neither pair of combatants would interfere with the other, the four champions positioned themselves for the fight. The two kings and the men with them then withdrew to the forefronts of their respective lines.

Thousands upon thousands of eyes settled upon the center

of the battlefield.

Four warriors would determine the fate of three kingdoms; and perhaps a great many more in the time to come.

***

Measuring their counterparts, both sets of opponents began circling each other.

A few moments later, the first clang of metal pierced the air, erupting from the clash between Queen Marsellina and the Thrakkian champion Mekrides.

While hearing the sound, Rayden could spare no thoughts for the other contest. A fearsome hulk of a warrior bent on her death now stalked her with a blade in hand.

Shifting her stance, Rayden kept her body squared toward Desidar, ready for any charging attack. Everything in her world centered upon the giant, to the exclusion of all else. Instincts, thoughts, and focus merged into an equilibrium that took hold within, guiding her every movement.

With a bellowing roar, Desidar lunged forward and barreled toward Rayden. Anticipating the move, she sidestepped the hulking warrior, moving to his right and striking out with her blade. Iron collided as Desidar caught her slash with the edge of his blade.

Demonstrating quick reflexes, the Samosian turned and advanced on Rayden, pressing a furious attack. Blocking Desidar's vigorous swings, Rayden absorbed the force of the blows, the power from them passing through her body like waves.

Countering with her axe, Rayden forced Desidar to rotate and defend with his shield, preventing him from using it to batter her.

Executing a feint that fooled her opponent to think that she was jumping backward, Rayden got Desidar to hesitate for an instant. The sliver of indecisiveness on his part gave her an opening.

Springing forward, up and to her left, Rayden slashed down along a diagonal slant with her sword, swinging lower with her axe an instant later. Moving fast for his immense size, Desidar caught her blade with his own, but the edge of her axe got through his defenses, cutting a long bleeding gash across the side of his upper thigh.

Grunting in pain and shifting about, Desidar closed off any chance for her to continue the attack.

Rayden bounded forward, putting more space between them and taking her out of his sword range. Squaring toward Desidar, she eyed her opponent.

Though not a serious wound, first blood had been drawn; and not by Desidar. Rivulets of crimson ran down his leg like red streams across a barren landscape.

With a howling war cry and eyes blazing in rage, Desidar rushed at Rayden. Slashing with his blade, and aiming to hammer his shield into her, like a living battering ram, the huge warrior unleashed a torrential assault.

Blocking with axe and sword, and executing lateral movements with great agility, Rayden deflected and evaded the giant's barrage of strikes and blows. All the while, she kept alert for the opening that she needed.

Desidar began to raise his blade for another strike, but before the Samosian could complete his attack Rayden lunged forward.

Her fast, inward maneuver prevented the giant from swinging his blade, but it left Rayden open for a swift, hard blow from Desidar; one that he took full advantage of. Pivoting and crashing the eagle-headed pommel into her left side, Desidar sent a blinding wave of pain rippling through her body.

Desidar moved to grab Rayden, hooking his right arm around to sweep her into him, but his attempt closed on empty air.

Dropping and crouching as low as possible, Rayden shifted to her right and pressed forward. The sudden action taking her just beneath the giant's shield, she vaulted upward.

With a savage vertical thrust of her sword, Rayden caught Desidar in the soft, exposed flesh beneath his chin. Blood gushing down her blade, she drove the weapon in as far as she could.

A sickly noise coming from his throat, sounding like a blend between a gurgle and gag, the giant made no counterattack. Ripping her blade free with a hard, downward yank, Rayden brought a rain of blood upon her face and body.

Without a moment's hesitation, Rayden struck once more. Propelling the blade forward with all the strength that she could muster, she executed another powerful thrust, burrowing the blade deep into Desidar's exposed throat.

The giant swayed in place for a moment. Body slackening, Desidar then fell backward, his momentum almost taking Rayden along with him.

Hitting the ground hard and sword tumbling out of his right hand, the massive warrior lay still. Fixed toward the skies above, in a stare devoid of sight, Desidar's eyes remained open.

Keeping to her feet, and maintaining a firm grip on her sword's hilt, she stood over her fallen opponent. Drops of blood pattering onto the ground from her blade, Rayden gazed down at the dead Samosian champion.

Chest heaving with labored breaths, and grimacing from the thundering blow to her side, Rayden turned to see what had come of the other fight.

Watching Rayden, Queen Marsellina stood a short distance from where the body of Mekrides lay sprawled on the ground; face first.

Blood coated the blade of the sword still gripped in her right hand. Marsellina raised the weapon in a salute to Rayden.

"You have prevailed, Rayden Valkyrie, and total victory is with Aressenia!" the queen exclaimed, with a timbre of pride and elation.

Thousands having witnessed the dual triumph of the Aressenian champions, a deep silence had fallen across the massed ranks of Thrakkia and Samosia. Stunned and subdued, the warriors of the two kingdoms stared toward Rayden and the queen.

Breaking out like a great thunderclap, a zealous roar erupted from the Aressenians. Hailing their victorious champions, the warriors expressed their acclamation in a long, sustained cheer. Queen Marsellina acknowledged them with a raised salute of her blood-coated blade, followed by Rayden a moment later.

Rayden strode toward the queen, leaving the corpse of the defeated Samosian champion behind.

"It looks as if we have gained a few moments to ourselves," Rayden said.

The queen looked between the Thrakkian and Samosian ranks. "It is not the outcome they thought would happen. Fools."

"The greed of kings," Rayden said. "It worked to our advantage."

"Well fought," the queen said in a tone of praise. "I was able to witness how you put an end to Desidar .... you weathered attacks that so very few could endure, and still you found that opening."

"A warrior cannot panic in the heat of the fight," Rayden said.

"Agreed," the queen said.

"Was the Thrakkian difficult?" Rayden asked, looking toward the corpse of Mekrides.

"Trouble enough," the queen said. "The damnable Thrakkian romphaia is a good weapon, and a great weapon in the hands of one such as their champion. He almost had me twice, but I stunned him with a blow from my shield, and then I gutted him."

Rayden nodded, imagining the maneuver within her mind. "And now you wield authority over two kings."

"As I expected I would," the queen replied, the trace of a grin on her lips.

"I expected you would, too," Rayden said, giving the queen a smile. "No matter how invincible they claimed Desidar to be."

Queen Marsellina laughed at Rayden's words before a pained look fell across her face. Wincing, she indicated an area on her right side.

"I still have this to plague me, though, and it did not come from anything the Thrakkian did," the queen said, casting a smirk at Rayden. "I have another to thank for my aching side."

Rayden recalled the heavy blow that she had landed when twilight loomed on the day they had hunted the Gorgothirs. The strike brought an end to the contest between herself and the Aressenian queen.

Her victory over Marsellina in unarmed combat had gained Rayden two rights.

The first was that she could stand as a champion for the Aressenians. The second allowed her to choose the champion that she would fight, between the Thrakkians and Samosians.

"A contest skillful and well-fought," Rayden said with an air of great respect, thinking of how close Marsellina had been to triumph.

"It was," Queen Marsellina agreed. "I am just glad that no ribs were broken, or I would not have been able to take the field against the Thrakkian champion. You have fists like hammers."

"As do you," Rayden said, recalling a few punches she had absorbed during the fight. Grappling and striking, the two had seen the momentum shift more than once before Rayden had landed her crushing bow.

"Mekrides had great skill," the queen said. "But you were a

much more difficult opponent."

"I wish that I had a few moments to witness your fight," Rayden said.

"You did take longer with your opponent," Queen Marsellina chided, with a slight grin. "That is not my doing."

"But victory was seized on both our ends," Rayden replied to the queen with a smile. "And two kingdoms of Griaca may learn to stand together ... perhaps even three."

Queen Marsellina's mirth faded, her face growing somber at Rayden's last words. "Soon enough, we will rout those Astrian dogs. Then I can return to Aressenia and rid myself of soft kings who crave trinkets and stones."

"And I can continue my own journey," Rayden replied. Looking up, she saw small contingents approaching them from the Thrakkian and Samosian lines. Both of the approaching groups had a king walking in their midst. "It looks as if our time together has come to an end."

"The two kings have very different looks on their faces than when we began this," the queen observed, eyeing each of the nearing groups.

Brooding looks reigned upon both of the kings' faces. Humbled and stymied, it would not be easy for either king to accept the rule of the Aressenian queen.

Yet neither king could escape the consequences of their decision. Thousands of Thrakkian and Samosian warriors had been witnesses to the martial contests, and an Aressenian army stood poised to enforce the word of both kings.

With a powerful empire invading Griacan lands, Rayden could only hope that the pair of kings grew in wisdom from the experience.

***

That evening, in the camp of the Aressenians, Rayden consumed a copious amount of the barley-cake and dark broth so prevalent in the fare of the stalwart warriors. Savoring a piece of boar meat, like those distributed to all of the Aressenian warriors, she enjoyed the company of the men and women around her.

All warriors of the Brotherhood or Sisterhood, they mingled together in a genuine spirit of camaraderie. Distinctive with their short beards shaped to a point and upper lips shaven, and hair fixed into eight long, thick braids, the men of the Brotherhood bantered and jested on all manner of topics with the women of the Sisterhood.

Listening to their spirited repartee, Rayden deemed it best to keep their comments about the Thrakkians and Samosians for her own amusement. Though both Mekrides and Desidar had fought well, the fall of the other kingdoms' champions had served only to lessen their status further in the eyes of Aressenia.

Rayden found their attitudes unfortunate, but, no matter what the Aressenians thought of the Thrakkians and Samosians, at least a sensible path would be followed. All three kingdoms were now on course to stand together against the Astrian invaders in Pargemon.

Queen Marsellina joined Rayden later in the evening. A wine cup in hand, the queen took a seat on the ground next to her.

"I think it can be said that the warriors of Aressenia, both the Brotherhood and Sisterhood, accept you as one of their own," she told Rayden. "All agree that your fight against Desidar was a sight to behold. I regret that I only witnessed part of it."

Rayden took the compliments to heart. To be deemed an equal with the Aressenians as a warrior stood a tremendous honor, one far beyond receiving a material reward of gold, silver, or jewels.

"It is a great honor to be measured worthy of the Sisterhood and Brotherhood," Rayden replied, giving a bow of her head to the queen.

"A rare honor," the queen said, her expression growing solemn. "So rare that no one else has been embraced in such a way during my lifetime. Yet you find fault with our ways."

With a grim expression, Rayden stared at the queen for a few heartbeats.

"There is no justifying the killing of infants, or holding others in bondage, against their will," Rayden responded, firm of voice.

"Maintaining the strength and discipline that we have demands hard choices," the queen countered.

"Those choices are weaknesses that could one day prove to be your undoing," Rayden riposted.

"What we do with the young is a mercy," the queen replied, an indignant tone thickening in her voice. "They would have no future. They could not hope to become one of the Brotherhood or Sisterhood. Theirs would be a live of servitude ... and even at that they would never do well at their tasks, given the afflictions they were born with. How can you dare to judge us?"

"How many great minds have been denied to you ... minds that could give guidance and wisdom ... cut off in the dawn of their existence?" Rayden asked. "How many great artisans or weapon makers have you denied Aressenia? You will never know how much stronger Aressenia could have been."

"We have become the strongest kingdom in all Griaca through never straying from our path," the queen responded.

"You have become strong because of the discipline your warriors have, not because you put blades to infants you deem unfit," Rayden said. "How you handle the most innocent and vulnerable among you will testify the loudest in determining whether you are condemned for wickedness one day."

"By what authority?" the queen replied, her incensed tone showing that she scoffed at the idea of Aressenia being held to judgement.

"I do not presume to know the mysteries of the world," Rayden said. "But I would caution you to not persist in such wickedness, in cutting short the lives of innocents. No good at all can come of such darkness. You summon your own destruction."

"I am certain you are of the same mind when it comes to those we hold in bondage," the queen said.

"Those in slavery to you?" Rayden asked, her eyes narrowing. "Yes, I am of the same mind. It reduces you to put others in bondage. If those who labor for you had their own homes, lives, and pieces of land, you would see greater abundance than you can imagine. Men and women thrive when knowing their labor can serve to better their futures. You destroy hope and ambition, and in doing so you reduce Aressenia far more than you realize. Taking the freedom of any man or woman crushes the will. It is of the essence of wickedness."

"You speak of abundance?" the queen asked, looking incredulous. "To become soft and indolent like the other Griacan kingdoms ... craving shiny metals and rocks? Desiring gluttony and drunkenness? No, that is not our way."

"Nor does it ever have to be your way," Rayden said, holding the queen's gaze. "It is simply letting the men and women now in bondage regain possession of their lives again, to be able to enjoy the fruits of their own labor."

"We will never have agreement on this either," the queen replied, a grim look on her face.

"Then we will forever be at odds," Rayden said, casting a hardened gaze at the queen. Her voice then lowered, "That saddens me, as there is so much I admire about Aressenia, and so much others can learn from your dedication and discipline."

"It is unfortunate you choose to be at odds with us," the queen replied, frowning. "I wish it were different. You are a great warrior and the spirit within you is stronger than that of any I have known. I cannot deny that I see you as kindred to me ... a sister of the warrior's path."

Rayden nodded her head to the queen. "I see you in the same way. Perhaps in another time and world, we could be as sisters."

"I would like a time and world such as that," the queen said in a melancholic voice.

Marsellina's face and words exhibited the softest emotion that Rayden had ever witnessed in the Aressenian queen.

"We both know that wishing does little to no good ... this is the world that we have," Rayden said.

"With all of the things that it demands," the queen replied.

"I am afraid that it now demands that I go and get some rest," Rayden declared, getting to her feet. Looking to the queen, the hint of a grin rose upon her lips, and a sanguine lilt infused her voice. "After all, we have an empire to march against, when the sun rises."

"Yes, we do," the queen declared, an iron-hard look returning to her eyes. "Before nightfall, we will tread over the dead, broken bodies of those Astrian dogs."

"It is the fate they chose when they invaded the lands of others, spilled the blood of men, women, and children who were of no threat to them, and put their homes to the torch," Rayden said. Once more, she looked the queen direct in the eyes. "Wickedness invites destruction."

Her dark eyes brimming with vexation and jaws taut, the queen made no reply. Not wanting to provoke the seething queen any more than she had, Rayden said nothing more. Giving the queen a slight bow, Rayden turned and walked away, to seek a little rest before dawn's light arrived to herald the approaching winds of war.

***

The ground rumbling like a simmering thunderstorm, an extensive array of phalanxes advanced in a tight, cohesive order. All along the broad front, bristling with long spears, thousands of Aressenians tread across the open ground, marching toward the teeming ranks of the Astrians; a force much greater in number than their own.

The air booming with the Aressenians' rhythmic chants, the tones of pipes and trumpets sounded from the approaching phalanxes and carried toward the invaders. Circular, bronze-faced shields, displaying the images of serpents, eagles, scorpions, cockerels, boars, and many other creatures, spanned the forefront of the oncoming formations. Forming a resplendent, unified sheen throughout the Aressenian multitude, the sun's golden rays reflected from polished bronze greaves, cuirasses, and crested helms.

A solid wall of Astrian spearmen, bearing tall, rectangular wooden shields, the facings of which displayed patterns and colors aligning with those on the square-topped standards held near to them, stood their ground, protecting a great host of archers behind them. When the Aressenians drew within arrow range, horns sounded from among the Astrians, up and down their massed ranks. At the flurry of signals, the massed archers began unleashing torrential showers of arrows at the approaching phalanxes.

Clad in their distinct, colorful, quilted trousers and tunics, throngs of Astrian cavalry issued from the flanks of the Astrian line. Armed with bows and spears, the mounted warriors tried again and again to gain the edges of the Aressenian flanks, but to no avail. The disciplined Aressenian phalanxes and several bands of cavalry, supported by skirmishing groups of javelin throwers, and slingers, rebuffed every attempt.

Under a relentless hail of arrows, the phalanxes picked up

their gait at a new round of horn and pipe signals, indicating that the final stretch of open ground had been reached. All along the front of the Aressenian line, spears were lowered into place, presenting a host of sharp, well-honed points to the enemy ranks.

The remaining ground between the two forces dwindled fast, until the Aressenians and Astrians came together in a thunderous clash. Continuing to chant and press forward, using their much longer spears and bronze-faced shields, the Aressenians pressed a relentless onslaught.

A trickle at first, then a stream, and soon a flood, Astrian blood began flowing into the parched, Griacan soil.

The heavier, iron-tipped Aressenian spears, able to penetrate the wicker and hide shields of the enemy in a full-force thrust, began breaking apart the wall blocking the attackers from reaching the archers beyond. Wherever a spear broke, embedded in a shield, or was cleaved through by an Astrian blade, Aressenian warriors took up their own blades. At close quarters, the straight and leaf-shaped short swords exacted a high toll upon the Astrians.

It did not take long before the Astrian line began to fall apart. Ruptured in many places from the onslaught of Aressenian spears, the gouges in the Astrian ranks soon became deep fissures, which then began crumbling fast.

Fear swept through the Astrians at the rapid developments, rippling through their masses from front to back. Gripped in a rising panic, archers ceased loosing their arrows and the deadly rain falling upon the Astrians dried up. Some Astrians cast aside their tall shields, seeking speed over protection as they took flight. Turning and running, the enemy warriors paid no heed to the insults hurled at them from the Aressenians, who shook their bloodied spears at the army they had just shattered.

Several thousand Astrians might have survived the day were it not for the combined forces of Thrakkia and Samosia that had come up from behind them. Having taken the beach where the Astrians had landed their fleet triremes, in a bold attack that caught the guarding force unprepared, the forces of the two Griacan kingdoms had undertaken a swift march to the west.

Though weary, the warriors of Thrakkia and Samosia were still in a much better condition than the fleeing, exhausted Astrians, whose headlong flight to their ships had now been closed off. Dismay and dread overwhelmed the thin strands of hope the Astrians had been clinging to. In disarray, and without discipline, they hurled themselves at the living wall sealing their doom.

Standing with Markos and the Thrakkians, Rayden blooded her own weapons many times over before the slaughter came to an end. Calm of mind, in the manner she had been against Desidar, Rayden had little difficulty finding openings to strike at the panicked, terrified men caught in the jaws of three kingdoms.

The common soldiers of Astria fought back with desperation that brought their tiring limbs a little strength, but also spurred more than a little recklessness. Carrying short axes, spears, and swords, they slashed and stabbed with a frantic energy. A large number who had come from deeper in the Astrian ranks carried smaller crescent-shaped or circular wicker shields, and they used them as best they could to defend against the invigorated Thrakkians and Samosians.

Wearing cloth head coverings, winding about their heads turban-like, many of the Astrians had both nose and mouth veiled, but raw terror lay fully exposed within all of their eyes. To a man, all of the Astrians knew that death loomed.

Seeing the blond-haired tempest within their midst, those with their faces uncovered blanched, laying bare their dread. Gouts of blood sprayed outward, spattering the bright, colorful tunics of many Astrians having the ill-fortune of encountering Rayden as she hacked and slashed her way through their withering ranks.

Side-stepping to her right, and evading an overhead strike from a broad, single-edged blade, Rayden hooked her axe head on the top of her assailant's crescent-shield and pulled back hard, exposing the Astrian for a killing blow from her sword. Whirling to the right, she blocked an axe blow from another enemy warrior, bringing her own axe across an instant later to lay open the innards of the enemy warrior.

Her face speckled in blood, Rayden set loose a sonorous cry that caused another Astrian in her path to trip and fall backwards in his haste to get away from her. Springing forward like a great hunting cat ambushing prey, she slew the Astrian with a pair of devastating blows.

With her lips pulled back in a snarling visage, Rayden launched herself at the nearest Astrian that she could find.

Near to Rayden, Markos wielded his sword and shield with grace and power, felling one Astrian after another. Eyes blazing with intensity, he parried and countered enemy attacks with skill and deadly effect. His medium-length blade found its way to strike deep at groins, throats, and guts alike, making for swift kills that eliminated countering blows from the enemy.

When the fighting appeared to be over at last, and the clangs and thuds of weapons ebbed across the battlefield, Markos came to a stop and took a look around him. Setting his shield down and resting it against his left leg, he removed his crested helm and cradled it under his left arm.

Sweat running down his reddened face, catching his breath, he looked over to Rayden. She stood a little distance away, her last opponent lying dead at her feet, bleeding into the soil from gaping wounds to the neck and gut.

Turning her head and surveying the area around her, sword and axe both dripping blood at her sides, Rayden set her piercing blue eyes upon him. Markos grinned wide, lifting his sword in salute to her.

Eyes narrowing, Rayden did not smile back.

Eyes widening, a look of shock took hold on Markos' face as Rayden pivoted fast, hurling her axe along a low plane in his direction. Flashing within a hand-span of Markos' right leg, the head of the weapon buried deep into the neck of an Astrian warrior who had already suffered a mortal wound.

Rayden had seen the dying enemy warrior lifting himself up from the ground, striving to gain one final thrust with his spear at an unaware adversary from behind; the intended victim being Markos.

Now lifeless, the Astrian flopped back to the ground and lay still. Rayden strode over and yanked her axe free, sending a few drops of blood up into Markos' face and her own.

"Always keep your wariness on a battlefield, Markos," Rayden scolded him with a firm timbre, continuing to take an assessment of the Astrian bodies near to them. "Or you will find yourself struck down in the very hour of victory. Celebrate a victory in battle later, when surrounded by your comrades, not the enemy dead."

"A lesson learned," Markos replied in a humbled air, taking in the admonishment and staring at the body of the man Rayden had just slain. "You have my deepest gratitude ... I owe my life to you."

Putting his helm back on, Markos leaned over and took up his shield.

"You would have done no differently, had you seen an enemy poised to strike me," Rayden replied.

"I wish I could throw my sword as you do your axe," Markos responded with a light chuckle.

Rayden smiled, and gazed around the battlefield, continuing to keep her eye out for any signs of movement. Covered with the corpses of Astrians, the place would soon become the site of a grisly feast for hordes of scavengers.

Thrakkian and Samosian warriors moved through the carnage, removing any of their own dead while dispatching any Astrians that they came across with breath still left in them. Other grunts and cries burst out here and there, coming from the lips of wounded Thrakkians and Samosians being aided.

The grim activity would not cease for quite some time. The Astrian dead would be stripped of any useful items and valuables, and the Thrakkian and Samosian dead would be buried near to the battlefield.

A far distance away, Rayden could see the Aressenians, who had marched up to make certain that the Astrians had been destroyed to the last. She knew Queen Marsellina watched the proceedings from somewhere within their ranks.

Rayden doubted the queen respected the Thrakkians and Samosians any more than she had at the beginning of the day. The two kingdoms had merely finished off a broken enemy in Aressenian eyes, but at the least three kingdoms of Griaca had joined together to destroy an invading army.

No matter what role each kingdom had assumed, it would be the seed of a lesson that Rayden hoped would take root, sprout and grow in time. She knew without a doubt that the Astrians would return one day, in an even greater wave that would crash against Griacan shores.

All the kingdoms of Griaca would have to stand together when that time came.

"Where does your road lead now, Rayden Valkyrie?" Markos asked, interrupting her thoughts.

"Who can really say ... myself most of all," Rayden replied, her words carrying a melancholic edge. "I have seen more than enough death to know that each sunrise I witness is a gift, precious and fragile, and never to be taken for granted."

"Enough of death for awhile then," Markos said, eyes

showing a gleam of merriment. "Wine much better than that of the Aressenians awaits you, as does a great feast. It is one area they have no claim upon superiority."

"I must say that Aressenian fare is not counted among my favorites," Rayden said, chuckling. "I would love some Thrakkian wine."

"As much as you can drink then," Markos said, grinning.

"Are you sure that you have that much on hand?" Rayden jested, laughing.

"If we run out, perhaps some Astrian wine can be culled from the vessels we have captured," Markos said, casting a glance to the east.

"That sounds like a wonderful arrangement," Rayden said. "But before then, let us help where we can here. I have regained my breath and rested a little."

"Agreed," Markos replied.

Rayden and Markos joined the Thrakkians and Samosians combing through the battlefield. They assisted with the wounded, a few of which she knew would not survive the night. When night approached, the pair returned to the Thrakkian encampment.

Rayden indulged in Thrakkian wine and food, laughed at the bawdy jokes of Markos and the other warriors, and set her mind free from all concerns for a little while. A cool night breeze soothed her, and the crackling of flames proved relaxing to listen to.

Markos soon had the company of a couple attractive young women, likely servants or camp followers who had come in from the Thrakkian baggage camp. With a mischievous sparkle in his eyes, he bid Rayden a good evening before heading away, his arms wrapped about the waists of the two eager-looking women.

For Rayden's own part, she refrained from pursuing carnal passions for the night, though she could have had her pick of many comely warriors within the jubilant throngs about her.

Content to bask in the moment at hand, she settled in by the firelight and took in the spirited air around her.

Rayden had been through the aftermath of a great many battles. Emotions of all kinds ebbed and flowed within a warrior during such a time, and each aftermath carried its own unique edge.

A powerful, uplifting current coursed through the night at hand. Losses compared to other battles had been light for the Thrakkians. The victory achieved that day had been overwhelming in nature; an entire Astrian army destroyed, and most of their fleet captured. Only a sliver of the host would make it back to the Emperor, to inform him that three Griacan kingdoms had allied to crush the force in Pargemon.

Further, the cause of the battle had been pure. No petty quarrel between two kings, the battle had been fought against a hostile, foreign invader, one bent on imposing dominion across all Griacan soil.

Some would be mourning lost comrades, but most of the Thrakkians had survived and the atmosphere leaned heavily toward a vibrant celebration of victory and life adorned in a righteous cause. Nights such as that did not come all too often in times of war, and Rayden chose to enjoy the revelry for as long as she could.

Wine flowed late into the night, and Rayden partook of more than enough to slake her desire for the Thrakkian variety. Relishing the camaraderie with the other warriors, she did not take leave until mounting fatigue demanded that she seek rest.

Deciding to forgo a tent in favor of sleeping under the open skies, Rayden retrieved her cloak and spread it out on the ground. Stretching her limbs and easing onto her back, she stared upward, letting the starry night sky engulf her gaze until she paid no more heed to the masses of tents, animals, men, and women in the sprawling encampment surrounding her.

As Rayden took in the immeasurable heavens, what appeared to be a small star streaked across the vast firmament, leaving a bright trail in its wake. The sight brought a grin to her face, as she thought of how seers and star gazers alike would scramble to interpret the brief vision.

For her part, Rayden had no thoughts about what the sight portended. Another thread in a great tapestry of mysteries, the ephemeral light crossing the skies served to remind her how enigmatic the world could be.

Though daunting in some ways, cognizance of the world's mysterious nature carried wondrous possibilities along with it. Doomsayers, wicked hearts, and darker powers did not possess knowledge of all eventualities.

Somewhere within the turmoil, strife, and swirling winds of war, something else beckoned, calling in a calm, subtle voice upon those who responded to stay resolute and hold firm to a path of honor. Deep within her heart, Rayden sensed that more than she could begin to imagine remained to be unveiled in time.

The road that Rayden walked was one less-traveled, narrow, and more difficult to tread, but she could not see herself on any other path. The thought gave Rayden comfort as weariness took hold, carrying her into the depths of a restful sleep.

***

Greeting the sunrise, Rayden smiled, welcoming the warm touch of the bright rays upon her face.

A few light, crisp breezes ran through her hair, lifting and caressing a few golden strands with a soft touch. Her axe and sword, both cleaned and honed, rested in their familiar places.

Two pouches were tied to her leather belt. One held a small number of coins. The other, much larger in size, carried within it an assortment of durable foodstuffs for the pending journey.

Clasped at her left shoulder, a dark cloak descended to the

top of the high-strapped sandals she had chosen for the day's trek, one that would be conducted under a hot sun. Her leather boots and a few other items she deemed important enough to take north remained in a small cloth sack looped over her shoulder.

"Where does my road lead?" she whispered into the air, letting the winds carry the words along with them.

No sounds other than the periodic tendrils of breezes came to her ears. After waiting for a few more moments, gazing toward the golden splendor of the eastern horizon, Rayden turned and began walking north.

THE SUN'S CARESS

CARESS

A RAYDEN VALKYRIE TALE

STEPHEN ZIMMER

THE SUN'S CARESS

Soft, white petals, cradled in the arms of gentle breezes, drifted down from the blossoming tree. Sunlight gleaming off her long, golden locks, no lines of concern or worry marred the restful look upon Rayden's face.

Graced with a floral scent, every intake of the cool mountain air cleansed her lungs. Serenading the tranquil, soothing moments, a bird's song danced through the air.

Far down the slope, clustered along the edge of the broad, sheltered bay, a large number of thatch-roofed huts, storage buildings, workshops, and pens marked the presence of a sizeable fishing village. Pulled up along the shoreline, and floating in the water, a wide array of vessels, ranging from small rowing boats to larger sea-going ships, awaited the next time that they would be called into service.

A new day arriving with raiment of golden splendor, the water in the bay sparkled with a crystalline sheen in the embrace of the unsullied morning light.

Seated cross-legged on the ground, sheltered beneath the branches of a magnificent cherry blossom tree, Rayden looked out toward the west. She found it hard to imagine the uncountable leagues that lay between her and the lands of the Gessa, and the other tribes of the northern region where she had first grown into a warrior. Sprawling deserts, rolling seas of grasslands, vast mountain ranges, dense jungles, and much more stood between her and the place where her long journey first began.

For her, a search continued, even if the destination had not yet been fathomed, much less reached. The weight of many long years filled with strife, trials, and encounters with the worst that the world had to offer bore down upon her spirit; but the look in her eyes reflected a quiet, enduring strength that continued to grow.

Her skin displayed a few traces of the increasing years, and marks of battles long since fought, but her body remained well-honed and capable of meeting every task that she asked of it. Heeding the lessons of experience, and striving always to advance her skills, she remained the kind of warrior who met each rising of the sun in a state greater than the day before; but lesser than the next day would see.

"You look as if you are gazing from the edge of the world," a low, gentle-sounding voice interrupted her thoughts. "But I cannot say this place is the edge of it."

Turning her head, Rayden eyed the short, brown-robed figure with the shaved head walking slowly toward her. The sight of Mari-chan brought a smile to her face and filled her heart with gladness.

"It feels as if I am on the edge of the world," Rayden replied, looking back toward the west. Her expression grew more somber as she contemplated for a moment. "It is so far from here to where my path first began. It is hard to imagine there could be more to the world."

"I would have to journey to the lands of the people you grew among, to see if the perspective would be the same for me," Mari-Chan answered. "Maybe one day I shall do so, and I will then cast my gaze to the east."

"I would enjoy your company all the way there," Rayden

remarked, looking to her friend as another smile bloomed upon her lips.

"To think this is just one world, that we are in for a time," Mari-Chan observed, in the reflective manner that she had come to know so well. "This life is such a fragile and precious gift, and so very short in the eyes of eternity."

"So very short?" Rayden asked, a merry laugh coming at his words. "Sometimes it has already felt like an eternity. I have endured single days that have felt like the passage of eons."

"At times it has felt that way for me too," Mari-Chan said, grinning at her words. "But the physical life is a brief one in the eyes of the world, even for those said to have lived for centuries. Do they witness the mountain brought low by wind and rain? All the things of this world change."

Mari-Chan turned his gaze to the west and his face took on a thoughtful mien, an expression well familiar to her.

"So, are you here to talk with me, or am I needed down there?" Rayden queried after a few moments had passed, noticing that her friend remained standing.

"Timiko would like to train at arms now," Mari-Chan replied, keeping his eyes set toward the western horizon. "She did not wish to disturb you, but you implored me to seek you out whenever she desired to spar. I am here as you asked."

"I did ask you, as Timiko offers me a path to advance my skills and keep my body in form," Rayden said.

"You looked so at ease, I almost hesitated to approach you," Mari-Chan said, looking over to her.

Uncrossing her legs, Rayden got up to her feet and grinned at her friend. "I am rested, refreshed, and centered. She had better be ready today."

"I am just the messenger," Mari-Chan replied, chuckling. "But I imagine it will be quite a contest to witness."

Rayden walked out from beneath the boughs of the cherry

blossom tree. Feeling the sun's caress upon her face, she stretched her limbs, while looking forward to another opportunity to grow as a warrior.

"Let the day begin!" Rayden announced in a spirited tone, giving her friend a wink. "Want to walk with me, or do you want to stay here a little longer?"

"Walk with you, of course," Mari-Chan replied. "I do not like to miss even a moment of the sessions between the two of you."

Mari-Chan accompanied Rayden as she started down the narrow trail leading to the fishing village.

***

Her lustrous, straight locks of black hair pulled back and bound around her head with a snow-white cloth band, Tamiko strode into the open ground with a limber step. Gripped in her right hand, she carried a wooden version of her primary weapon, a long, curving blade extending from the end of a lengthy shaft.

A blend of sword and spear, the naginata stood a fearsome weapon. Unlike the round shafts of the spears used by tribes such as the Gessa, the shaft of Timiko's naginata was cut in an oval shape, suited adeptly to executing slashes and chops.

Rayden took up her own pair of wood-carved weapons, both fashioned to closely resemble the axe and sword that she wielded in battle. Stepping forward into the open ground, she eyed the other woman and let her mind settle into the warrior's state that made it seem like time itself had slowed down to a crawl.

The brunt of the bruises and nicks suffered during such sessions had tilted in a significant manner over the long months that Rayden had dwelled among the pirates. When Rayden had first begun training with Timiko, the latter's fighting style and weapon unfamiliar, she had spent many nights enduring the turmoil born from a host of aches and soreness located all over her body.

Now, Rayden took far fewer hits during a session, while Timiko had become the one who spent her nights in great discomfort, recovering from the intense martial exchanges they shared together.

Timiko refused to scale back on the length or intensity of the sessions, even after it became clear to all that Rayden had adapted well to the fighting styles of the far eastern lands. The stalwart pirate leader had insisted upon continuing the regular training sessions, to push her own skills to the limit.

In Timiko, Rayden had discovered a kindred spirit in every way. Unaffected by any petty resentment, or a consuming envy born of pride, Timiko expressed genuine gratitude to Rayden on a regular basis for keeping the sparring sessions in place.

Conducted within the harmony of mutual respect, the two women pushed each other without reservation to discover their own weaknesses, and to advance in skill.

Coming together near the center of the broad span of flat ground, Timiko and Rayden paused. Rendering each other a short bow of salute and respect, they began their latest sparring session.

Both combatants moving with speed and balance, the air filled with the sharp clacks and thuds of wood upon wood. Slashes and thrusts, shifts of stance, blocks and counters, a martial dance unfolded that many of the other pirates watched from nearby in a spirit of wonderment and deep respect. For them, a chance to witness two exceptional warriors, in a land that revered displays of great martial skill, the sparring sessions were an exhilarating delight to behold.

Among the pirates, Mari-Chan observed in silence, with an intent, studious look.

Here and there, Rayden found a brief opening in her opponent's defenses, eliciting a pained grunt whenever her axe or sword got through and landed upon Timiko's body. Though the tally of hits mounted in Rayden's favor, the fighting was not entirely one-sided. During one swirling exchange of blows, Rayden did not react fast enough to a spin by Timiko and found the end of the naginata's shaft planted squarely in her side.

Leaping back and clenching her teeth for a moment from the stabbing pain in her ribs, Rayden grinned at Timiko. Taking a deep breath, she praised the skillful maneuver. "An excellent strike. Well done."

Timiko laughed, and with no hint of jealously replied, "It is just one lone, successful hit, set against the multitude of skillful blows you have been landing upon me this morning. But if I can get a solid hit upon a warrior like you, the easier it will become for me to fell the Great Daimio's best warriors, should they attack me."

"Then let us end today's training on that strike," Rayden said, breathing heavy and keeping her weapons at the ready, just in case Timiko desired to continue. "We have exerted ourselves a lot today."

Timiko nodded, and she lowered her naginata. "We have already sparred much longer than usual. I am sure we have both worked up a good hunger."

"I know that I have, for my part," Rayden replied with a grin, sweat dripping from her brow.

The two warriors smiled, bowing to each other before walking from the open ground. Carrying their sparring weapons at their sides, the pair made their way back into the extended cluster of huts and buildings running along the shoreline of the crescent-shaped bay.

Boundless in energy, several children ran about at play. Rayden and Timiko started to pass through the spirited little throng. Engrossed in their activities, a couple of them bumped into Rayden.

Upon seeing who it was that they had run into, both children looked anxious and hesitant, their eyes going wide and mouths agape in an instant. More than once their gazes darted toward Rayden's wooden weapons, as if expecting a solid whack in response.

Smiling and amused at their reactions, Rayden playfully tousled the hair of one of the startled-looking children, a young boy of six or seven years of age.

"Go on, catch up to your friends!" Rayden encouraged the little fellow, giving him an encouraging pat on the back. "You did not intend to run into me. But it is good to watch where you are running, or you might find yourself falling off the edge of a cliff!"

Seeing that he was not in trouble, a look of sheer relief sprouted across the child's face. A moment later, the young boy smiled and scampered off with his friend to rejoin the others.

Rayden watched the children bounding away for a few heartbeats before continuing forward with Timiko.

"I wish I had that kind of energy," Rayden commented. "I confess that I cannot even remember what having that kind of boundless stamina felt like, when I was a child."

"We could spar all day with the energy those little ones have," Timiko replied, laughing. "That one boy definitely thought he was going to get a good smack from you."

"I am feeling merciful today," Rayden replied with a laugh. "I will save my smacks for the next adversaries that we face together."

"Or our next sparring session," Timiko replied in good humor. "Though I will need to recover a little first."

"As will I," Rayden said, with a broadening smile.

Timiko and Rayden proceeded up the dirt path toward one of the larger homes in the fishing village, a rectangular structure of timber covered with a sloped, straw-thatched roof. Though not anywhere close to being as ornate as the homes of the nobles, higher ranking bushi warriors, and others of status in the lands of Yamatainu, it was the most prominent home in the village.

As the leader of the pirates, and the wife of a slain, revered bushi warrior, Timiko held the highest status and resided there. Rayden and Mari-Chan both stayed in the home as guests of Timiko.

Walking beneath the sheltered entrance, Timiko removed her bearskin shoes before sliding a heavy wooden door panel to the left. Removing her own leather boots at the entrance, Rayden followed Timiko into the home.

Rayden stepped into a room just beyond bordered with walls of rice paper mounted on wood-lattice frames. Scenes of warriors and nature had been painted on the surfaces of the walls in an abundance of vibrant colors. Rayden had studied many of the images close, taking careful regard of details and learning more about the things valued and honored within the lands of Yamatainu.

After proceeding into a side room and putting their sparring weapons away, the two warriors returned and took seats upon floor mats of woven grass and straw.

Futaba, an elderly woman who attended to Timiko, appeared shortly after, ferrying in drinking vessels and bowls placed upon trays crafted with short wooden legs. Finding herself famished after the lengthy sparring session, Rayden welcomed the meal of rice and fish, the latter served in the raw style that she had come to love. Before long, she consumed four bowls of the rice, along with some soup made using a rice and soybean paste prevalent in the region.

Rayden washed the modest fare down with ample draughts of rice wine. The liquid eased her into a more relaxed state, taking some of the edge from the new sores that she had incurred during the training session.

"Many from the west would like a meal like this, very

much," Rayden complimented, appreciative of how the food satisfied while not sitting too heavily upon the stomach.

"One day I will have to try some of the food that you have in your homeland," Timiko remarked.

"I am afraid I trained in weapons, but not at cooking," Rayden responded, laughing. "I fear that I would not give you an accurate impression of what we eat. I would like for you to enjoy it!"

Timiko laughed, and responded, "Your mead does sound like it would be very good."

"That is one thing from the west that I do miss a lot," Rayden said, with a wistful grin. "But I am grateful for this ... your rice wine ... something that cannot be found anywhere in the lands to the far west."

Raising her cup, Rayden took another extended drink of the rice wine.

"It is a great blessing to experience so many different things," Timiko remarked. "I only know the things of my homeland. You have seen and experienced lands that I cannot even imagine."

Rayden nodded in agreement. "It is a blessing, and it is also one of the few comforts of traveling a long, long road. It brings you a perspective that guides you to greater lessons, if you are open to them."

"Different clothes, different ways, different food and drink, different gods ... different words," Timiko stated.

Thinking of all the various lands that her years of travel had brought into her life, Rayden smiled. Relaxed and enjoying the rice wine, a reflective mood came over her

"Yet at heart, the people of the farthest lands to the west have much in common with the people of the farthest lands to the east," Rayden commented to Timiko. "The people of all lands seek to laugh, to love, to find purpose ... to experience joys with family and friends ... to dream and hope for a better life ... and to find that there is something more beyond this world with all of its sorrows, suffering and pain. Yes, the outer things may be very different in nature, and often appearance, but the inner things connect all of us together."

Rayden fell silent, and took another drink of rice wine.

"You have allowed your journeys to bring you great wisdom, Rayden," Timiko said after a few moments, in an air of appreciation.

"Lessons are there to be learned, each and every day," Rayden said. "It our choice to avail ourselves of them or not."

"I would think your journeys have brought you most of what can be learned," Timiko said.

"They have shown me how much more I do not know," Rayden replied, taking another long drink that emptied her cup.

Looking to her left, through the open doorway, she watched Mari-Chan approaching the front of the home. When he reached the threshold of the doorway, he acknowledged Rayden and Timiko with a short bow.

"I was told you would both be here," Mari-Chan said. "I had a brief matter to attend to, after you had concluded your sparring."

"Come inside and join us," Timiko invited. "We are restoring ourselves after that training session."

"Another good contest, I must say," Mari-Chan said, removing his shoes, entering, and taking a seat on the floor with them. "It is a pleasure to watch such a demonstration of skill."

Timiko nodded and smiled. "It was a good contest, and I will have several new bruises to show for it."

"And I will have a very solid one myself," Rayden said, indicating the spot on her side where Timiko had delivered her strike, the site now throbbing with a dull ache.

"Better to have unsharpened wood show you the gaps in your defenses, rather than well-honed metal blades," Mari-Chan replied, giving the two warriors a grin.

Grinning back, Rayden and Timiko both nodded their agreement with him.

Futaba then returned, bringing green tea made from unfermented leaves. Seeing Mari-Chan, she departed to get him a drinking vessel.

"I need to get some training in myself," Mari-Chan said. "I have indulged far too much in the serenity of this place. I do not wish to find myself becoming soft."

"If only the Great Daimio would leave us alone, to live our own lives," Timiko said, a dour look coming to her face. "But such men are not satisfied until all are under their firm control ... and rendering taxes and obedience to them."

"The lust to rule and hold power is insatiable for many," Mari-Chan said, shaking his head.

"An affliction to be found in all lands, from west to east," Rayden said in a grim tone of voice, thinking of a host of examples that she had encountered through the years.

"A regrettable thing indeed," Mari-Chan said. "But the things of darkness cannot abide or tolerate anything that is not under their dominion. These mortal rulers are just a reflection of the deeper darkness that underlies all wickedness."

"We will not make it so easy for them," Timiko responded with a grin, a steely glint in her eyes.

Sharing Timiko's outlook, Rayden stated, "And where we can, we will bring an end to their wicked ambitions. Sometimes in one strike."

"A will to resist wickedness is all that is needed to set other forces in motion," Mari-Chan replied, looking to the other two with an approving air. "The people here are fortunate that there are two such warriors living here among them."

"Three," Rayden corrected her friend in a gentle manner. "You sell yourself a little short at times, Mari-Chan."

"Well, I *am* a shorter man," Mari-Chan replied, chuckling for a moment before returning to a serious tone. "You honor me with your words, but the gods and goddesses of heaven have shined their light upon the both you. Either of you can light the flame in the human heart that illuminates the strength within each of us. The people of this land need that now, more than ever before."

A short, stocky man approaching the entrance to Timiko's dwelling drew Rayden's and the others' attention. In the manner of most of the pirates, his hair had been trimmed back just past the temples, the rest of his locks grown long and pulled back atop his head. A scraggly beard and moustache accented his face.

Upon reaching the doorway, the pirate lowered his eyes and bowed immediately to Timiko.

"What is it, Harumoto?" she asked him, a look of concern growing on her face.

He straightened up at her acknowledgement.

"A large tax grain vessel lumbers up from the south," he announced. "No more than two days sailing from here."

Timiko's mood darkened at the mention of the tax ship. "A poor harvest plagues the land, and yet the Great Daimio takes from those who have little to make certain that those who have plenty do not see any decrease. The tyrant thinks nothing of condemning the very people who worked the land to starvation."

"Such is the way of those who hold great power in this world," Mari-Chan said, echoing the comments of a few moments before.

"And why we do what we must do," Timiko responded in a firm tone, looking back to Mari-Chan.

A nervous edge clung to Harumoto's countenance. After a few moments he said in a low voice, "There is more to report."

Timiko turned back to Harumoto. "Do not delay, tell us everything."

"To the north, one of Fujimara's ships has been sighted," Harumoto proceeded. "Heading toward the Jade Island."

"This far south?" Timiko asked, her voice carrying undercurrents of both dismay and incredulity.

Harumoto nodded and his answer held certainty. "Yes."

"And where there is one of Fujimara's ships, there are bound to be many more," Timiko responded in a somber tone. She looked to Rayden and Mari-Chan. "Those vermin raid in great numbers. Coming this far south, they will plunder as much as they can from the villages found along the shores."

"It looks like a choice stands before you," Mari-Chan responded in an even tone, gazing at Timiko.

Looking at Timiko's face, Rayden could see that a number of heavy thoughts weighed upon her friend's mind. Timiko had good reason to be concerned.

Pirate bands riddled the western islands of Yamatainu. A maze of caves, sheltered bays, coves, and islands afforded concealment and ideal positions from which to launch raids on other areas of Yamatainu's vast archipelago or the mainland to the west, the latter beckoning from a short distance across open seas.

Most pirate bands like Timiko's tended to be smaller in size, but some had grown large and powerful over the years. Fujimara's horde stood as one of the strongest, with a fleet that included warships as large and capable as any in the fleet of the Emperor himself.

Even more worrisome, Fujimara's pirates had a longstanding, widespread reputation for brutality. Any village caught in the path of the feared raiders would be subjected to a storm of horrors.

"I can not think of the grain ship now," Timiko said, looking between the others' faces. "Not when so much blood will be spilled in the area we ply. We will be greatly outnumbered, but we must do what we can to resist Fujimara. If he is coming this far south, we will have to face him sooner or later. I choose to confront his vermin before they ravage these islands."

"I am with you, Timiko," Rayden stated in a calm demeanor. Reading the fatalistic look within Timiko's eyes, she continued. "Numbers do not determine the outcome of a battle. Your knowledge of this area will give you advantages over Fujimara's raiders. Striking when unexpected will give you more. The fact that you will be defending your home region will give you even more."

"I will also go with you, and offer whatever aid I can," Mari-Chan added.

Grim-faced, Timiko nodded to both them, and then turned toward Harumoto.

"Have all of our ships readied at once, and gather our full force together," she told him. "We take to the sea as soon as we are able."

Harumoto gave her a bow, turned, and headed away at a brisk stride.

Watching him leave, Rayden drank the rest of her tea and set the vessel down on the tray before her. Getting to her feet with an unruffled comportment, she made her way from the dining area to the small room where she slept at night. After retrieving her weapons and a cloak, she proceeded to the front of Timiko's dwelling and put her boots back on.

Glancing up the slope of the mountain behind the village, in the direction of the cherry blossom tree that she had spent the early morning beneath, Rayden took a moment to savor the memory of the encompassing harmony that she had experienced there. Inside her heart, she girded herself for the pending sojourn, knowing that the coming days would be anything but tranquil in nature.

A time of blood, war, and trial called. Once more, Rayden did not hesitate to respond.

"We are called to act where there is no other real choice, other than to betray who we are," Mari-Chan observed, joining her in front of Timiko's home. "You and I are not the kind who betray ourselves or anyone else."

Rayden turned toward him. The hint of a smile came to her lips.. "It is good to have a friend at your side during such times. I am glad you are here."

"It is a more natural way," Mari-Chan replied, looking back to her. "We were not meant to walk alone."

The thought brought a full smile to Rayden's face. "Then let us make our way down to the water. The weather is favorable for taking to the seas. Another journey awaits us."

Mari-Chan nodded, and smiled, a thoughtful look upon his face. "A journey within a greater journey."

Side by side, the two of them started down the path, heading toward the sparkling waters of the bay.

***

Having traversed the waters of the surrounding islands for several years, Timiko and her veteran pirates knew every fold and crease in the land concealing an inlet where ships could be hidden from the sight of those unfamiliar with the area. Knowing the movements of the tides, they also knew when certain areas stood perilous and when they could be navigated.

Using her arsenal of knowledge, Timiko took a little used and less known route that threaded a series of smaller islands. The more obscure route lowered the fleet's risk of being detected by others navigating the more common sea routes. The natural maze and ubiquitous hazards lent the fleet further protection in the unlikely instance that they were seen and then pursued by a larger force, of the kind serving the Emperor or Fujimara.

At the end of the labyrinthine route, Timiko led her entire fleet across a short stretch of sea, coming up from the south. In a column of single file, the fleet entered the mouth of a narrow inlet bounded by high cliffs, located near a few villages on the largest island standing in the path of Fujimara's approaching fleet. At the back of the inlet, a great cave with a broad entrance and ample depth beyond provided just enough space for all of the vessels to take shelter inside of it.

A mixture of types, Timiko's fleet included a few mid-size to larger vessels whose original purpose had been for the transportation of merchant cargo. With a spacious hold below the deck, and a sheltered cabin toward the rear, the single or double-mast vessels held a large capacity for people or goods. Raised fighting platforms with railed sides at the stem and stern enhanced their suitability for sea combat.

The rest of the of the fleet contained an assortment of smaller vessels that had little more than a cabin of modest size set near the stern and raised sides for the protection of oarsmen and warriors.

On sails and banners, all of the vessels displayed Timiko's sigil, an image depicting a rare creature known in Yamatainu as a kirin. The four-legged, hoofed creature had a flowing mane and tale, scales over its body, and a pair of antlers crowning a head more lion-like than deer. Rayden had never seen a kirin and, from what she had been told by her, neither had Timiko, but the pirates who had come together under Timiko's leadership had bestowed the symbol upon her long ago.

Joined together in full strength, the fleet Timiko had built over the years conveyed a formidable presence, but it was not so large that it could not take advantage of places where ships could be concealed.

Before the ship carrying them proceeded into the massive cavern, Rayden, Mari-Chan, Timiko, and many of the warriors aboard the fleet's largest vessel disembarked and waded ashore through a short span of shallow water. Once on solid ground, they waited for the small crew left aboard to take the ship into the cavern, board a small landing boat, and return to join them.

After all the other ships had been emptied of their passengers, and the warriors had gathered into a large war band, Timiko gave the order to head inland. Leaving the shoreline behind and entering the forested terrain of the island, Rayden and Mari-Chan walked near the forefront of the well-armed contingent.

Rayden found the environment much to her liking. In the forested hills and mountains, with uncountable possibilities for stealth, ambush, and traps, Timiko's force stood a better chance of confronting Fujimara's great advantage in numbers.

With their scraggly beards, long mustaches, and weathered skin, the men of Timiko's band displayed a rough, hardened appearance well suited for the task at hand. Light in attire, most of the pirates went barefoot. Several wore little more than loincloths, though most had coarse-woven, loose jackets of about knee-length, tied in about the waist. A few pieces of armor were in evidence among them, such as a few lamellar cuirasses, but for the most part the pirates sought to go ashore as unencumbered as possible.

Several of the pirates wore headbands, and a couple had helms crafted in the far eastern style. With iron plates fitted together by rivets to form a low, rounded crown, with a protruding front, the helms had a cascade of connected horizontal strips descending from the lower edge to protect the neck to the back and sides.

Long, straight-bladed spears, naginatas, and swords served as the primary weapons carried by the warriors in Timiko's band. Slung over their right shoulders, quivers bristling with arrows adorned many bearing long bows, the latter strung.

Limbering up fast, and with a spring to her step, Rayden had to be careful to rein in her pace. After being constricted to a ship deck for an extended length of time, she relished the sensation of hard ground underfoot.

Scouts sent farther ahead of the main pirate band returned after a short while, reporting several fires ahead at one of the island's larger coastal villages. Not long after, seeing the first, telltale columns of smoke winding skyward above the tops of the trees, Rayden's heart began filling with anger.

The troubling sight left no doubt that Fujimara's raiders had come ashore.

Picking up their gait, Timiko's pirates headed at once in the direction of the swirling, dark gray pillars. Though they did not have far to go, nightfall would be imminent when Timiko's warriors reached the site of the fires.

"We cannot rush into this fight," Timiko remarked, walking with Rayden and Mari-Chan at the lead of the extended column of warriors.

"We will need to see, and measure, their numbers and positions," Rayden replied, casting her a sideways glance. "I would like to find a higher point where I can observe their placements more completely."

"There will be many possibilities," Timiko said. "The village is ringed with high summits. Find what you can. We will learn what we can from the shadows, at a closer vantage."

"It will not take me long, once I have a view of them from above," Rayden said.

"I intend to see that the woods beyond their fires swallow any that stray while we take account of them," Timiko responded, a sharp glint to her eyes. "Once we have their full measure, we will strike at them. These vermin will be shown no mercy for what they are now doing."

"You are not the usual kind of pirate plying the waters of your seas and rivers," Rayden commented, looking to Timiko. "That is why I fight with you."

"We have been driven by great hardship to our path, to see that men, women, and children do not starve to placate the desires of the powerful," Timiko said. "When we take a grain ship or raid the holdings of a daimio, we simply take back what was taken from us at the threat of force."

"Your raids are not those of a common plunderer," Rayden said. "They are justified. You stand for those who have no voice in deciding what is to be taken from them. You merely take back what was plundered from the defenseless."

"Yet if the daimios ever cease their fighting amongst each other, they will come for me one day in great force," Timiko said, a stoic look coming over her face. "I know I will not survive that day, when it comes. I pray that I am strong enough to not waver and look upon it unblinking. I desire to face the end with honor and show that I am worthy of the Pure Lands."

"I know you are strong enough," Rayden said in a lower, reflective tone, taking in the woman's fatalistic words. "I also know in my heart that you will not waver."

A wisp of a smile crossed Timiko's face. "It is of no use thinking of what may happen. That day is not here yet. There is only the day at hand. For now, we have only Fujimara's murderous beasts to concern ourselves with, and nothing more."

A grim, resolute expression on her face, Rayden nodded. "A hunt is about to begin."

"We will not rest until we have brought down our quarry," Timiko replied, holding Rayden's eyes a moment before looking ahead.

Falling back into silence, they continued through the trees. Dappling the forest floor with patches of light, the late afternoon sunlight filtered through the trees above them. Swaying the boughs, breezes passing through the forest rustled the leaves. The pleasant scents of cedar and pine graced the cool, soothing air.

Flowing in a steady, gleaming cascade, water gurgled about the rocks in a wide, shallow creek. Melodious and uplifting, the songs of birds carried through the trees. The natural odes of water and bird alike lent further to the timeless essence permeating the forest environs.

At moments, Rayden found it hard to believe that a ghastly scene lay just ahead of them.

Serving as beacons, the smoke tendrils clawing for the skies drew nearer, bit by bit. Before much longer, faint cries and shouts began to cut through the tranquil sounds of the forest.

When they neared the village's outskirts, Rayden and Mari-Chan took leave of Timiko and the others. Seeking to engage in reconnaissance from a higher vantage point, Rayden eyed a few possible rises that offered a broader view of the shoreline and land around it.

One summit in particular caught her attention. Setting her mind on the propitious spot, she hastened toward the great hill. Behind Rayden, and falling behind quickly, Mari-Chan had to hurry to catch back up.

***

A shrine complex crowned a sizeable hill overlooking the village now deep in the throes of being plundered and ravaged. The great height of the rise offered Rayden a chance to assess the full strength of the raid, and she carefully made her way around to the base of the slope and headed upward, through the trees.

Coming upon a sinuous dirt path leading directly toward the shrine, Rayden stepped out of the trees and took it. Far behind, fearful, sorrowful cries, braying laughter, and harsh shouts sounded from the direction of the village. Keeping focus on her aims, Rayden pushed the distressing noises to the edge of her thoughts.

The earthen trail came to an end at the shrine complex.

A timber gateway of two high columns supporting a pair of prominent, transverse lintels marked the edge of the shrine's grounds.

Detecting no movements or sounds within the stillness beyond the gateway, Rayden turned back. Taking a few strides in front of the gateway, she returned to where the trail began its descent to the village below. Though the sun now dipped lower on the western horizon, enough daylight remained for Rayden to eye the stricken village and the arrangement of the enemy fleet below.

Several small boats beached along the water's edge, and a few larger floating ones at anchor, an array of vessels were concentrated near the shoreline marking the site of a sizeable fishing village. A couple of the ships at anchor looked to be warships, each with two high masts, a large cabin aft, a small cabin mid-ship; and raised, square fighting platforms set both fore and aft. Both of the imposing vessels were much larger than the greatest ship within Timiko's fleet.

Awash in flame and smoke, the fishing village stood a scene of chaos and despair. Several of the huts and other thatch-roofed, timber structures had been put to the torch, sending great plumes of smoke wafting upward to form the gray columns that had drawn Timiko's band toward the ill-fated village.

A lot of movement could be seen throughout the village. Sorrowful, desperate cries rang out from all over area, interspersed with the coarse shouts and stomach-churning laughter that Rayden knew all too well.

A frenzy of wickedness held most of the village's population in thrall. Rayden had no doubts that a lot of blood had been spilled and many horrors committed. More atrocities awaited captured innocents with the coming of night.

The luckiest of the villagers had escaped into the surrounding forest, but they would find no solace in having survived the main assault. Alone in the dark, the villagers who had fled stood no match for the hardened warriors in Fujimara's pirate band.

The escapees could do nothing for those held captive. The best that they could hope for would be to evade the clutches of the pirates until they finally took to their ships and left the wrecked village behind.

Staring at the numerous fires and listening to the hellish chorus of voices, Rayden's eyes narrowed. Battening down her ire, she knew that she had to glean everything that she could about the pirates from her elevated position, to help give Timiko's band a chance to see that Fujimara's pirates did not return to their ships.

Rayden began calculating the number of ships and general number of warriors that could be expected for each of them. Looking over the village, she noted the positions where it appeared that groups of raiders had gathered, including the places where those unfortunate enough to be taken captive were being held.

A comprehensive grasp of the situation involving the enemy pirates started to take shape within her mind. Judging from the positions of the groups of pirates, they did not expect any challenges or threats from outside the village. With a couple of concentrated, sudden attacks, smaller groups could be overwhelmed before others could respond

Eagerness rose within Rayden to bring the favorable tidings back to Timiko. Another part of her chafed to take the fight to the enemy, draw their blood, and silence their cruel laughter and shouts.

"Rayden, look lower, coming up the slope!" Mari-Chan stated, interrupting her assessment in an emphatic, alarmed tone and pointing down the trail.

Following his gesture, Rayden took in the sight of a large mob of armed figures working their way up the trail, heading toward the shrine. A few moments of focused observation told her that they belonged to Fujimara's raiding band. The last rays of the sun glinted off the blades of their weapons and she had little doubt they had a fair number of bows among them.

"They are Fujimara's," Rayden stated. "They have finished searching through the village, and now they are coming for the plunder of the shrine ... no doubt of that."

She estimated there to be over twenty pirates, possibly as many as thirty, in the group marching steadily up the path. All of them would be skilled fighters.

The throng of smoke columns coiling up behind them testified to their cruelty and rapaciousness. Rayden wanted nothing more than to charge down the trail and leap into their midst, swinging axe and sword, but she could not succumb to recklessness.

Pirates swarmed up the path, drawing nearer to the temple grounds. A choice had to be made.

"Let us conceal ourselves and seek the protection of the deity who dwells here," Mari-Chan said. "A way will be found to strike at them later. Let us not throw our lives away in a vain stand here. It does the villagers and our comrades no good for us to fall now."

"Who says I will fall?" Rayden replied in a simmering voice, a raw fury churning within.

"Even if you fell half of them, the others can remain back and use their bows," Mari-Chan told her.

"I assure you, they will answer in blood for what they have done," Rayden declared, her demeanor not far removed from a feral predator's snarl.

"Come, Rayden, there is no more time," Mari-Chan urged. "I will guide us in the temple."

Tearing her eyes away from the approaching raiders, Rayden fixed her gaze upon her friend. A pair of searing blue flames, Rayden's eyes blazed with intensity.

"Guide me," she told Mari-Chan in a curt manner.

Mari-Chan led Rayden through the gate. Passing by a large water basin set a few paces inside, he took Rayden deeper into the temple grounds.

A few elongated timber structures connected by narrow pathways lay nestled among the trees and foliage. One of the buildings had a small pool of water before it.

Everything about the place, from the buildings to the grounds, had a well-tended look reflecting meticulous care on the part of those who cared for the shrine complex. Of priests or caretakers, no signs could be seen of anyone else being present. Rayden could only hope that they had somehow been able to escape the tragic fate befalling most of the village population.

Mari-Chan headed straight for the most prominent of the constructs occupying the hilltop. Another water basin was set along the section of path approaching the building.

The large square structure ahead of them had an elegant-looking roof that sloped downward and curved up at the corners. A short flight of broad steps led up to the sheltered entrance.

Mari-Chan stopped at the water basin and quickly rinsed his hands and mouth. He then said to Rayden, "In our situation, we cannot observe everything, but we must do what we can."

Rayden emulated his actions, washing her hands off, and then rinsing her mouth.

"That is the main sanctuary, I am guessing," Rayden said, glancing toward the building looming before them. "We are not priests."

"It appears to be a site of worship too," "Mari-Chan replied, looking around. "I see no other building that would indicate a separate worship hall. We will not transgress merely by entering."

"A small reassurance," Rayden said, a dour expression on her face.

"We must have faith that any god or goddess will know that

the ones who truly are transgressing are the ones coming up the path now," Mari-Chan said.

Containing curses and bawdy laughter, voices carried through the air from behind them. Making no attempt at approaching in stealth, the pirates had drawn closer.

"They near the gate," Rayden warned him.

After a glance back, Mari-Chan proceeded toward the main sanctuary building. Rayden stayed a pace behind him, shifting her gaze between the building and the path behind them.

Fortunately, the pirates were not yet within eyesight.

Walking up the steps, Mari-Chan slid the front doorway to the side and entered the shrine. Rayden followed close after him.

She left the doorway open, letting the early eve's moonlight pour into the shrine's dusky interior. Pausing, Rayden allowed her vision to adjust to the dim environs before taking a careful look around.

A large section of open space lay spread before her. Beyond, carved out of wood, several non-human figures with fangs, forked tongues, and horns had been arrayed before a platform with a recessed alcove at the back, containing a golden statue of a heavier-set woman with a beautiful face. Rayden guessed the conspicuous figure to the deity that the shrine was home to, but she could make no sense out of the human-sized figurines set up before the statue.

Containing a pitcher, a few bowls and jars, and other vessels, a couple of narrow shelves fronted the platform. A low wooden altar stood a pace or two in front of the platform.

"This is a shrine of Maso," Mari-Chan whispered to Rayden, gazing upon the statue. "She who watches over the seas and those who travel upon it."

"Who are they?" Rayden asked Mari-Chan in a low voice, looking toward the carved figures.

"The figures displayed before the goddess?" Mari-Chan

asked.

Rayden nodded. "Yes."

"Once demons, who the goddess turned to benevolence," Mari-Chan replied. "It is a story I will share with you at another time."

Mari-Chan then stepped forward, approaching the platform holding the alcove and main statue. Falling to his knees before the elevated statue, he fixed his eyes toward the ground and bowed low, in the manner of a devoted supplicant.

Maintaining a calm demeanor, in such a manner that no eyes looking upon the diminutive man would have had any hint that a horde of rapacious pirates would be upon them in a matter of moments, he began to speak.

"Great Maso, Mother of the Sea, and protector of this village, I come to you in a desperate hour of need," Mari-Chan said aloud, addressing the statue in a low, deferential, humble tone. "A great number of the wicked pursue us and now approach your shrine. They have done great evil to the people of the village. Death will come to us if we do not seek refuge in your shrine. We have no other choice. Please forgive us any trespass and grant us your protection. We place our fates in your hands."

After such a petition, Rayden almost expected a response or at least some kind of movement from the statue representing the female deity. Yet in the aftermath, the shrine remained unchanged, swathed in silence and shadows.

Getting to his feet, Mari-Chan gestured for Rayden to follow him. To her surprise, he climbed up to the surface of the platform.

Bringing her around to the back of the statue, he stooped downward. Lowering into a crouch by Mari-Chan's side, Rayden braced herself, listening to the sounds of voices and footsteps swelling in volume from just outside the front of the structure.

"The goddess will protect us," Mari-Chan told Rayden.

The firm, confident tone of his voice told Rayden that Mari-Chan saw the claim as the simple declaration of a fact and not a statement of hope, born of wishful thinking. In her eyes, whether or not the goddess did anything to help them remained to be seen.

While a goddess intervening on their behalf would be a most welcome development, Rayden tightened her grip on the hilt of her blade and the haft of her axe. Mari-Chan could place his faith in a deity, while she placed hers in sharp, honed iron.

Pirates stormed into the shrine a few moments later. Laughing and cursing, the coarse invaders spread out within the shrine's interior.

A couple of them carried wooden torches. They used them to light unlit ones set on either side of the platform, casting undulating shadows against the walls of the shrine.

Walking through the sanctuary without hesitation, the rogues acted in stark contrast to the reverent behavior Mari-Chan had displayed just moments before. It stood clear that the pirates feared nothing in the shrine.

"It is unfortunate we cannot make a little sport with this sea whore," one of the pirates declared in a loud voice, walking up to the edge of the platform and eyeing the statue. Leaning over and extending his sword, he drew the tip in a light manner across the nether regions of the female likeness.

"You would need a very big sword to play with that fat sea cow," another pirate yelled, drawing a burst of raucous laughter from the others.

"She has these ugly dogs to keep her company," another pirate said, giving a hard shove to one of the wooden figures and toppling it over. The object landed on its side with a heavy thud.

"They can at least stay hard," a man near him announced, guffawing and, shoving another of the carvings over.

"Every woman you have been with wishes you could just get

hard, to begin with," jested another pirate in response, drawing a braying laughter from several of the others.

"Enough of this," another pirate said in a loud, reprimanding voice. "Let us get anything of value from this dung heap. There are women aplenty from the village for us to have our way with. Several beauties too! I do not want to waste time here."

Picking up a clay jug from one of the shelves fronting the platform, he eyed it for a moment before hurling it to shatter in pieces against the side of the shrine.

Remaining in place, Rayden loathed the impudent behavior of the pirates. She did not serve or even believe in the goddess represented by the statue, but she knew the shrine stood at the center of the villagers' lives. Desecrating the shine in such a brazen manner showed the vast emptiness within the hearts of the lawless scoundrels.

Willing to engage in every act of savageness and violation, the pirates had much more in common with rabid animals than they did with humans. Only death could free them from the madness ruling their hearts; and Rayden had no qualms about liberating all of them from their flesh.

The pirates began plucking up anything they perceived to be of value, from small figurines to any implements that appeared to be made of gold or silver. A few more of the carved, humanoid figures were toppled in the process, hitting the timber planks of the shrine's floor in resonant thumps.

One of the rogues clambered onto the platform and began edging nearer to the hiding spot where Rayden and Mari-Chan crouched. A resolute calm settling over her, Rayden eyed the pirate from the shadows, readying to bring him death in one strike.

The miscreant took another step closer, and then another, coming within a stride or two of discovering Rayden's position. She eyed him and remained poised; another step and he would receive a mouthful of iron.

In abrupt fashion, startling Rayden for a moment, the interior of the shrine darkened, and the temperature plunged down to a frigid level. A pungent, sulfuric stench pervaded the air.

Several of the pirates gagged, including the one standing on the platform. His exhalations now visible in icy, ghostly puffs, he turned his back to the statue.

"What foulness is that?" one of the other pirates said. "Did the sea bitch open her legs?"

"What is this?" asked a pirate standing near one of the remaining upright figurines. Taking slow steps, the man backed up a few paces, raising the spear clutched in his hands. Uncertainty and a tinge of fear ran through his words. "What is happening? Look at it! It moves!"

Rayden chanced a look around the edge of her hiding place. Following the wide-eyed gaze of another pirate, she saw that one of the wooden statues appeared to be moving. Solid wood now took on the malleable quality of flesh, as the figure's arms, legs, shoulders, and other areas of its body became animated.

Not trusting her eyes at first, Rayden thought the motion to be an illusion, somehow caused by one of the other pirates and the tricks that shadows cast from firelight sometimes played. She dispelled the notion outright after watching the figure for another moment, seeing that no one stood behind it and that the shadows beyond aligned with its own movements.

Rotating enough that Rayden could see the fullness of its visage, the head of the increasingly supple figure then turned toward one of the invaders. One look upon its face gave Rayden confirmation that the wood-carved figure had taken on a life of its own.

No pirate had eyes of churning flames.

Nor did any pirate have extensive, gleaming fangs.

Nor did any pirate have a pair of short, sharp horns sprouting from the crown of their heads.

Screams tore through the air, some born of pain and others spawned out of a naked, primal fear.

The pirate closest to Rayden rushed one of the living statues. A moment later his feet dangled off the ground.

The supernatural entity held steadfast to the man's throat, raising the hapless pirate higher into the air with one arm. A sharp crack sounded, and the man's head flopped at an awkward angle, a moment before the entity flung the body off to the side. The pirate's corpse landed on the timber floor with a dull thud.

The horned entity turned about and looked directly at Rayden and Mari-Chan. It gnashed its teeth, saliva dripping from its fangs. Loosing a bestial growl from the depths of its throat, the thing made no move to beset them.

Turning away, the menacing creature set after other quarry within the shrine. Rayden remained in place, sensing a purpose underway in the actions of the living statues.

Grating snarls and growls filled the air, intertwining with cries, shouts, and frantic pleas. All along the walls of the shrine, shadows danced and twisted in grotesque fashion, reflecting human forms being contorted and broken in the grips of monstrosities.

Despite her inclinations regarding the horned entities, Rayden kept her weapons at hand, bracing to acquit herself in battle should one of the mysterious creatures assail her. Bodies, and parts of bodies, flew through her field of vision. Men scrambled about, hacking and stabbing with their weapons at the bulky entities tromping after them.

More than once, Rayden locked eyes with one of the creatures. Though she could glean nothing from their fiery, infernal gazes, they continued to leave her and Mari-Chan alone.

Not long afterward, the sounds of the slaughter ebbed and

then ceased. A final, gurgle and low gasp brought the visceral massacre to an end. A weighty silence permeated the sanctuary for several moments that seemed like an age to Rayden.

The deeper gloom that had manifested just prior to the statues coming alive dissipated, raising the luminance within the shrine. Rayden's breaths no longer emerged in grayish bursts, the sharp, freezing edge within the air returning back to the pleasant, cool touch of early night.

A sweet, flowery scent then flooded the air, driving away all vestiges of the awful stench that had filled the shrine only moments before.

After listening for a few moments for any hints of movement or breathing, Rayden emerged from their hiding place, followed close after by Mari-Chan. Looking around with her weapons at the ready, her instincts remained coiled, ready to strike at any inkling of an attack.

Gaze shifting around, Rayden kept her expression still as she took in the stark, bloody scene.

All of the demonic entities had returned to their upright, inert states, only now they were located in positions scattered all over the sanctuary. Around them, blood-soaked carnage blanketed the floor of the temple.

Bits of flesh, limbs, innards, and corpses had been strewn everywhere, and the floor itself stood coated in blood. Not a single pirate still breathed.

Three of the statues were grouped together at the entrance to the temple, blocking the lone exit. Looking upon the stout figures, Rayden knew that none of the rogues who entered the shrine had escaped.

She harbored no pity for them. They had all reaped what they had sown.

Mari-Chan returned to the forefront of the goddess' statue, getting back down to his kneeling position with his eyes toward the floor. Rayden waited in patience, listening as Mari-Chan gave thanks to the goddess for sparing their lives.

A blinding, white light formed in the space before Mari-Chan. Raising her sword hand, Rayden shielded her eyes from the sheer brilliance filling the shrine.

A moment later, the light fell away, revealing a beautiful woman clad in exquisite, flowing robes of pure white. A soft glow limned her entire body.

The woman cradled a small, rectangular object within her hands, wrapped in snow-white cloth.

"I do not shed the blood of those who have not transgressed," the woman announced, her voice like a melodious song to Rayden's ears. "Look up to me, Mari-Chan. Do not fear."

In a slow, deliberate fashion, Mari-Chan raised his eyes.

The woman held the object forth. "Take this and see that it is given to the Guardian. You will know the Guardian when you meet."

"You honor me, great goddess Maso," Mari-Chan said, accepting the wrapped object from her and holding it with great care.

"I know that I can entrust you with this task," Maso replied, giving him a radiant smile. Her expression and voice then took on a somber tone. "But no matter how tempted you may become, do not unwrap this cloth. Do not look upon what is inside. Only the Guardian can set eyes upon the object within."

"I will keep this with me at all times," Mari-Chan replied to her in a low, reverent voice. "I will do all I can to see that it is not opened."

Laying her right hand upon his head, in a gentle fashion, the woman smiled upon him. "Keep strong of heart. The last part of your journey beckons. Heaven awaits you."

Mari-Chan made no reply. A few tears running down his cheeks, Mari-Chan's face shined with a look of joy.

Turning toward Rayden, the smile remained upon Maso's face.

Rayden lowered her eyes and bowed her head, unsure of what to do in response to the goddess' direct attention. Though sensing no hostility, she knew if Maso could see inside her thoughts the goddess would know that Rayden served no deity within the world. How that reality would alter the goddess' disposition toward her remained to be seen.

"You have nothing to fear from me, brave warrior," Maso stated. A hint of humor laced the goddess' next words. "Place your weapons down, you do not need them in hand with me. Clean any blood of the wicked off before you wear them again on your body. For now, speak with me as one woman would to another, and be at ease."

Reminded of the axe and sword still gripped in her hands, Rayden knew that they had no purpose drawn in the presence of a benevolent, supernatural entity. Averting the eyes of the goddess, Rayden leaned over and set the weapons down, upon a drier spot on the floor. Only the blades touched any traces of the blood that had just been spilled. Raising back up, she kept her head bowed in a respectful manner.

"Every man or woman takes an interior journey," Maso continued. "You must choose of your own will in matters involving heavens or hells, and the ones who hold dominions within each. I know you have not chosen to serve any higher power. Yours is the journey of a powerful soul on a long and difficult path of revelation. Tell me, why do you not close your mind like others to the matters of higher powers or life continuing in other realms?"

"Seeing what I have seen in the world, and experiencing what I have experienced, it would be sheer foolishness to say that all there is to the world is what I see with my eyes, or touch with my hands," Rayden replied in a measured tone, keeping her eyes lowered. "I do not possess all the knowledge in the world. How could I ever be certain there is nothing for humans beyond this sorrowful world? I trust that I will learn a little more with each day that I hold true to my heart. But I will not know the answer, truly, until I am faced with the veil of death, a moment that all humans must face alone, no matter if they are sent to it upon a battlefield or in the middle of a night's sleep."

"There is great wisdom in you, brave warrior," the goddess replied, with the air of a compliment. After a pause, Maso told Rayden, "Look into my eyes."

Rayden lifted her head up and met the eyes of the goddess. Maso held Rayden's gaze for a few moments. Within the luminous eyes of the goddess, Rayden stared into depths of light impossible to describe.

The light within the goddess' eyes, though radiant, proved comfortable to look into, if not welcoming to Rayden's eyes, with no need to shield the great brightness. A sensation of refuge and peace pervaded Rayden as she allowed the light to encompass her focus.

A light tingle then passed across Rayden's body. Sensing the presence of powers far beyond her ken, Rayden knew the goddess' sight took in much more than just her and the interior of the temple.

When the goddess spoke again, Rayden could perceive a powerful degree of compassion coursing within her words.

"You have come a very long distance, and there is much that remains in your own journey," Maso told Rayden. "It is not yet time to lay your head down to rest, brave warrior. For now, ward him, for as long as your paths remain together. He has been given an important task that can bring light to all in Yamatainu. A gift of Heaven to all of them must be restored."

"I have never abandoned a friend who is under threat," Rayden replied in a low, respectful voice. "It would not matter to me whether he was on a great task or no task at all. Know that I shall do all that I can to see that no danger comes to him while we share a path in this world."

Rayden then fell silent, and she became hesitant for a moment.

"Speak freely, brave warrior," Maso encouraged her.

Rayden's next words had the air of a confession. "I do not know where my path will take me, or how long Mari-Chan and I will travel together. If you asked me, I could not tell you anything of my destination in this world, and not because of any refusal on my part. After many years, it still remains hidden from me. I journey onward, but I can not tell you where I am going. I have let my heart guide me across these many years, but what lies ahead is as shrouded as it was on the day I first set out on my path."

A kind expression spread across the face of Maso.

"Daughter of Heaven, do not let your heart grow weary or become hardened," the goddess replied in a soft timbre, looking deep into Rayden's eyes. "Know that you have not become lost on your journey. Every time that you have followed the guidance of your heart, you have traveled in the right direction. Stay true to your path and I assure you, brave warrior, that you will find your way home ... the home that is your destination. You will see it one day, brave warrior."

Conveying joy, compassion, and an unconditional love, the smiling expression on the goddess' face appeared to brighten even more.

Shaken inside at Maso's words, Rayden did not know what to make of the ethereal woman's meaning. A cluster of powerful emotions welled up inside, but she did not have a chance to reply, or ask any questions of the goddess, who then vanished from sight into a tremendous brilliance that filled the sanctuary for an instant before dissipating within a cluster of retracting light rays.

Standing in the quiet of the fire-lit sanctuary, Rayden and Mari-Chen did not say a word, or even move, for several moments. To her astonishment, all of the wood-carved figurines had returned to their original places about the raised platform.

Collecting herself following the profound encounter, Rayden looked over to her friend, who now cradled the cloth-wrapped object given to him by the goddess.

"The goddess has looked upon us both with great favor," Mari-Chen said in a voice just above a whisper, breaking the silence at last. "What we experienced is something rare and precious for mortals. We truly gazed upon the light of Heaven. Maso has placed trust in us. We must not fail her."

"I have set my heart to honor what she has asked of me," Rayden said.

"It is all that we can do," Mari-Chan replied. "We are not gods or goddesses, but our limitations are what makes our actions shine all the brighter when we rise to do what is right in this world."

"Every man or woman alive in this world has what they need within them to rise and bring forth light to pierce the darkness," Rayden responded, nodding in agreement with her friend.

"It is unfortunate how few realize that truth," Mari-Chan commented. He looked down at the object in his hands. "I wonder what light this can bring forth."

"Do you know what it is that she has given to you?" Rayden said. She then added, "I know that you cannot look upon it for yourself, but what could it be?"

Mari-Chan shook his head slowly. "I do not know what it is, or what its purpose is. It is not my place to question the wishes of a goddess."

"Nor is it my place," Rayden said. A grin crossed her lips and the firelight gleamed in her eyes. "But it is my place to watch the back of my friend and make sure that he does not find himself in too much trouble. Come, let us get away from here, and rejoin the others."

"There are fewer enemies now to look out for," Mari-Chan said, stepping carefully over the bloody mess on the floor. Looking carefully before taking a step, he added, "It will take long periods of ritual and cleansing to purify this sanctuary and return it back to its intended state."

"I do not envy whoever is given that task," Rayden replied.

"Neither do I," Mari-Chan remarked, navigating his way toward the entrance.

"I will join you in a moment," Rayden told him, remembering the small task that Maso had told her to perform.

Rayden picked her weapons off the ground and cleaned the blades as best as she could, using a few dry segments of clothing on the bodies of dead pirates. The linen and hemp cloth segments she made use of did a satisfactory enough job of wiping the light blood smears off.

In some ways, the wiping of the blades seemed more like a ritual in the moment at hand. Very little blood had been picked up where the metal had touched the floor. In her mind, Rayden wiped off much more than the physical substance. Fulfilling Maso's directive, she saw her actions as ridding the blades of any contamination from the wickedness that had infected the dead pirates.

Once she had finished the cleaning, Rayden slipped the weapons back into their places at her waist. Then, she walked over to the entrance of the shrine and looked out into the night. Nothing stirred on the grounds around the edifice.

"The way looks clear, let us not delay," Rayden said, glancing toward Mari-Chan.

He nodded. "Best to get back as soon as we can."

Moving at a brisk gait, they left the shrine and headed for the gate at the forefront of the temple grounds. Rayden took the lead with Mari-Chen following close behind; an object wrapped in white cloth held tight to his body, under his right arm.

***

"Many women and children, and some of the elderly men, have scattered into the forest," Harumoto said when Rayden and Mari-Chen rejoined a group of Timiko's pirates on a hillside near to the southeastern edge of the sacked village. "We have slain many of the curs who pursued them, but a number of Fujimara's dogs still remain within the village. They are given to drunkenness and cruel amusements."

Rayden told Harumoto of the assessment that she had made of Fujimara's forces before having to take cover in the shrine. Despite the casualties that the enemy pirates had suffered in the temple and making some allowances for further losses involving those who had chased villagers into the surrounding forest, there yet remained a formidable number of warriors to be addressed.

Even so, the losses that the enemy had suffered changed the outlook in a favorable way. Rayden's estimation of the situation facing them appeared to bolster the confidence of Harumoto and the other warriors with him.

Though still outnumbered, Timiko's pirates now stood in a better position to defeat Fujimara's raiders.

"You bring us welcome tidings," Harumoto declared, when she had finished. "We have a greater chance to bring those dogs to heel."

"Then we should take a closer account of the enemy's force still left there, and find a way to finish this," Rayden said, sweeping her gaze across the faces of the warriors around her. Turning to Mari-Chan, she told him with a firm look in her eyes, "When we make our move, lay low, and stay out of this. You know why."

Mari-Chan nodded, clutching the wrapped object that he carried close to his chest.

Rayden, Mari-Chan, and Harumoto then started through the trees down the slope, followed by the other warriors.

An intertwined morass of burning flesh, wood, and other materials, a noxious scent pervaded the air, growing stronger the closer they drew to the village. Channeled within the winds brushing the hillside, a light haze of smoke wafted through the trees, bringing an unwelcome sting to Rayden and the other warrior's eyes.

Closer to the bottom of the slope, the warriors made their way clear of the main direction that the smoke flowed in, opening up their vision and reducing the discomfort to their eyes. A small number of Timiko's warriors emerged out of the shadows, staying their weapons the moment that they recognized Rayden and the others.

"I know there is one group of enemy raiders gathered close to here. How many are left," Rayden asked a warrior named Arakabi, whose naginata was lathered thick in blood.

"Twenty, maybe twenty-five," Arakabi replied. "Several are making a wager now. We are only five here, or we would have stopped them."

"A wager?" Rayden asked, frowning. "What do you mean?"

"Come with me," Arakabi said, turning and leading her toward the village.

Rayden strode after Arakabi and the other warriors fell in with them. The lights of several fires could be seen through the trees ahead.

She knew that nothing good could be taking place within the hellish scene about to unfold before her. Jaws tightening, and eyes narrowing, Rayden set her mind on bringing a proper reward to the perpetrators of the village's doom.

The time to stay her fury had come to an end, at last.

***

Creeping ever closer with silent steps, Rayden and the other warriors peered from within the trees at one of the larger remnants of Fujimara's raiding party. The group of pirates in view displayed a loose, relaxed demeanor, looking unconcerned about the possibility of any outside threats.

Rayden knew at a glance that the rogues had no inkling of what had befallen their ill-fated comrades, those had been slaughtered among the trees and up at the shrine. For all that the enemy warriors knew, the shrine was being looted of its treasures and the village's women were being chased down in a grim night hunt that would see those caught violated for the pleasures and lusts of their captors.

Thoughts of the plight faced by the villagers who had fled into the forest kindled both sadness and anger within Rayden's heart. The villagers who evaded their pursuers and survived the night would have scarce little to console them when dawn arrived.

With their homes reduced to ash, their younger men slaughtered, and many women and children put to the blade, any survivor of the nightmarish raid would find what was their home and community just a mere day before to be a place suited only for the haunt of ghosts.

The wounds suffered by such survivors would have no physical element, but they would be crippling, of the kind that not even a lifetime could heal. In some ways, Rayden found those invisible wounds to be far worse in nature than those that left physical scars on the body. At the least, bleeding would come to an end, sooner or later, with a corporeal wound.

Rayden knew that she could not turn time itself back, but she could do her utmost to bring an end to the evil besetting the surviving villagers. Observing and calculating, Rayden watched the scene before her and prepared to strike.

Her hands and feet bound, a younger woman with a pronounced, rounded belly sat on the ground. Her hair disheveled, and face streaked across from the host of tears that she had shed, the woman looked at the pirates with raw fright shimmering in her eyes.

Several pirates had gathered around her, all looking to be enjoying the spectacle of their terrified victim. One among their number was busy accepting coins from each of the others.

"It is about time to find out what is inside her," the collector of the bets announced to the rest. "Hand over your coins to me, and we will get the answer."

"I say it is a boy in that big belly," one of the pirates said, eyeing the woman with a cruel grin.

"I say it is a girl," another said, shaking his head and laughing as he handed a few coins over to the man collecting them.

"We will find out in a moment, one way or the other," a thick-necked, broad-shouldered pirate declared in a loud voice, chuckling as he held up a long dagger, the blade gleaming in the firelight.

Comprehension hit Rayden. Rage took hold of her.

Sickened at the horrific wager unfolding, Rayden gripped her weapons firm and sprang forward. Charging out of the trees and heading straight toward the group of men and their prisoner, she fixed her burning gaze on the man with the dagger.

The brawny man sauntered over toward the woman, grinning as he lowered his dagger toward the skin of her exposed belly.

"Give me room!" he told the others. "Clear the way!"

The others gathered around backed up a couple of steps to give him a wider berth.

A leering grin frozen upon his face, the man with the dagger toppled over, a hurled axe embedded deep in the back of his skull.

The other pirates turned fast in the direction the axe had

been thrown from, but death was already upon them. Whirling among them in a primal, savage fury, Rayden lashed out with her blade, dealing death in swift fashion to the half-intoxicated pirates.

When Rayden reached the one who had been taking the bets from the others, the wrath reflecting in her eyes surged. "Let us find out what is inside of you!"

A brutal slash of her blade opened the man's guts. Clutching in futility at his innards, now flopping out and falling to the ground, he twisted around and tumbled over. All around him were scattered the coins that he had collected and held from the bets placed just moments before.

After the last rogue involved in the vile wager had fallen, Rayden turned toward the woman on the ground. Blood dripping from her blade, she walked over to the woman's side, keeping her eyes out for other enemy fighters.

The clangs of weapons, shouts, and screams rang out into the night from all directions. Spreading throughout the village and falling upon the enemy, Timiko's pirates entered the fight.

For the moment, nothing threatened Rayden. Setting her sword on the ground, keeping it within easy reach, she kneeled down at the young woman's side.

"You are safe now," Rayden told her in a calm, reassuring tone. "I will not harm you. I am going to free you now ... and then we will get away from here."

The woman cringed a little when Rayden picked her sword back up. With careful hands, moving slow, Rayden then used the sharp edges of the blade to cut through the bindings of the woman.

Wrists and ankles unbound, the woman remained silent, saying nothing in reply. Sitting in place, she continued to sob and shake in the aftershocks of her terror; having been a heartbeat or two away from having her belly sliced wide open to reveal the nature of her baby for the capricious whims of blood-soaked, drunken pirates.

"We cannot stay out here," Rayden told her, keeping the same low, placid tone. "I am going to take you away to others who will protect you. Let me gather up my weapons and we will get out of this place."

Still heaving with sobs, the woman gave Rayden a nod of understanding. After retrieving her axe and wiping it off on the man whose skull it had been lodged in, Rayden put it back in the loop at her belt. Then, she helped the woman up to her feet.

While keeping her sword in one hand, Rayden took great care escorting the crying, pregnant woman from the sacked village. Wary and poised to respond to any sudden attacks, Rayden spoke words of encouragement to the woman in a low, soothing tone. The sharp clang of weapons, shouts, and cries continued through the air, coming from several directions, though none of it sounded close enough to cause any concern for Rayden.

Guiding her ever farther from the scene of carnage, Rayden led the woman into the shadows of the forest. After a short walk, they came to a halt in the general area where Arakabi's small band had been prior to the attack on the village.

Harboring several more of the village's survivors, a few warriors from Timiko's band of pirates appeared soon after. Upon seeing each other's faces, the young woman and the other survivors broke into tears and clutched onto each other.

Sorrowing for all of them, Rayden found the reunion difficult to witness. Each of the beleaguered villagers had lost many that were dear to them and loved at heart, friends and family alike. An established village community such as theirs had roots that spanned generations, and for many the village and its immediate vicinity stood as the entirety of their worlds.

That world had been shattered, irrevocably, in one gruesome day. The surviving villagers now walked into a future containing nothing familiar, other than the survivors themselves.

It would be a long, difficult, and surreal road for all of them. Rayden could do little more than do her part to protect them and offer whatever consolations she could glean from her own experiences.

The distant sounds of fighting finally came to a stop. A couple more groups of Timiko's warriors, accompanied by more survivors, found their way to the place where Rayden and the others waited.

Arakabi and Harumoto were among the new groups of arriving warriors. Rayden was glad to see both of the stalwart fighters, whose grime-covered faces and bloodied weapons testified that they had exacted a heavy toll on Fujimara's rogues.

Timiko, eight of her warriors, and an assortment of villagers that included several younger women and children, an infant, and a few elderly men and women formed the last group to appear. Face coated in blood and soot, Timiko looked almost unrecognizable.

"There are no others, of the villagers or the enemy ... we have gone through the entire village," Timiko announced upon her arrival. She walked into the midst of the group and began looking around at the other warriors and villagers.

Though Timiko's expression remained unchanged, Rayden could see the relief in the pirate leader's eyes as she took account of each of her warriors who survived the battle. When her eyes turned to Rayden, a wisp of a smile touched her lips.

"I think we are both in need or a swim, or long bath," Timiko said to Rayden. "Slaying rabid dogs is one matter. Wearing their blood is another."

"I doubt there is any more of the enemy's blood to spill here," Rayden said. "Our part here is finished."

Timiko nodded. "The fighting is over, and if any of Fujimara's curs live, they took flight into the trees."

"They would be wise to stay hidden," Rayden said, a hard-edge returning to her voice.

Timiko looked around at the warriors and villagers gathered around. "It is time to return to our ships and take to the sea again. This was just a raiding party, and we do not wish to be caught in the cavern if Fujimara's full fleet arrives."

The thought that the large mass of raiders represented just a fraction of Fujimara's force was sobering to ponder. Yet Rayden harbored no surprise at the declaration, as Fujimara wielded the kind of power that could openly confront the naval forces of the Emperor and Great Daimio.

"What about other villagers who may have taken to the trees?" Rayden asked.

"We have swept through the area around the village and found who we could," Timiko said. "We may not have found all who survived, but we cannot tarry here. When dawn arrives, we must return to our fleet."

Rayden understood, but wished that they had more time to do a more thorough scouring of the woods around the village, to turn up any remaining villagers as well as mete out swift justice to any enemy warriors that had somehow evaded them.

"Some may wish to stay," Rayden said.

"The village is in ruins, a heap of ash," Timiko said. "They stand no chance if another pack of Fujimara's dogs put in to shore here, and I do not want to leave them prey to any of the curs who took to hiding."

"Give them the choice, nonetheless," Rayden replied.

Timiko stared into Rayden's eyes for a moment, and then nodded.

After calling for the attention of her warriors and the village survivors, she addressed the latter. Explaining the dangers that they might face if they stayed, Timiko offered the villagers the choice to remain or leave with her warriors.

As Rayden expected, all of them accepted the offer to leave. To some, the offering of a choice would seem a waste of valuable time, but the least that could be done for the distressed villagers was to give them the respect of having a say in their own destiny.

Timiko drew close to Rayden after her speech had concluded.

"What did that gain?" Timiko asked, looking a little confused.

"They leave under their own free exercise of will, under no coercion," Rayden answered. "They can be expected to do their part in the days to come, unlike those taken somewhere against their will."

Timiko grew quiet for a few heartbeats, and then she shook her head. "Are you sure you were not born ages ago in Yamatainu, or that you did not come to us out of the Heavens? I can not say it enough. You do possess a great wisdom."

"Whatever I may have to offer has come at a great cost," Rayden replied.

"We are blessed by the gods and goddesses to have you with us," Timiko stated, giving Rayden a short bow, before turning away and calling for the group to prepare to set out.

As everyone readied to leave, Mari-Chan approached Rayden.

"I thought you might have gone back to the ships," Rayden stated. "I trust that you stayed clear of the fighting."

"I did, though it was not easy to stand by," Mari-Chan answered. He had a saddened look to his eyes as he looked at the cluster of villagers about to go with them. He whispered his next words, for Rayden's ears alone. "So very few of them have survived the bloodshed."

"A nightmare I have witnessed far too often in this world," Rayden commented, with heaviness of heart.

"I know that you have, Rayden," Mari-Chan said with an air of compassion. "Let us see all who have survived home safely.

I hope that what I carry with me can help bring them a better world."

"My hope as well," Rayden said, eyeing the downcast survivors huddled close together.

***

When the first light of dawn crested the trees, Timiko's warriors and the surviving villagers made their way back through the woods and down along the shoreline to where the fleet had been sheltered within the great cavern. Using the small boats left on the shore, several small crews headed into the cavern to bring the ships out.

Not long after, the vessels of Timiko's fleet began emerging from their sanctuary. A few of them drew close to the shore, while the larger ships of the fleet had to remain a little farther out.

After wading through shallow waters and lending help to the children, elderly, and others among the villagers facing difficulties, Rayden, Timiko, and the pirates assisted the survivors aboard the larger ships. Timiko did her best to keep the villagers together, but a crew of adequate size needed to be kept on each of her larger ships, both to operate and defend them, and she had to disperse the survivors among three vessels.

Rayden cradled an infant in her arms as the mother climbed aboard Timiko's main ship. Gazing upon the little, vulnerable life within her hands, Rayden saw the value of everything Timiko's warriors had done in coming to the island and attacking Fujimara's raiders.

When Rayden handed the baby up to the mother, the woman smiled and gave a bow to Rayden. She then clutched the infant to her chest and moved onward, to join her fellow villagers where they were gathering near the center of the ship.

Rayden climbed aboard a short time after. Mari-Chan stood before her, holding the cloth-wrapped object that Maso had given him, in a way that echoed the mother holding the infant.

Timiko's ship would be carrying a precious, invaluable cargo, lives and a sacred object, across the waters.

"It is time to go back," Mari-Chan stated.

"I have seen far enough of this place," Rayden said, glancing back toward the shore. "Enough to put a few more scars on my memories."

Once all had come aboard the ship, the crew set oars to the water and began propelling it from the sheltered bay while others set the masts and sails. Glistening in the morning light, the open sea lay beckoned from ahead.

Soon after, the shoreline and distant smoke from the burned village grew smaller as Timiko's fleet headed into deeper waters. The sun climbing higher into the sky, a steady breeze soon filled the tall, rectangular sails of the ship. With the air currents favorable to sailing, Timiko gave the command to put oars away.

The ship rose and fell, gliding across the low waves. Not acclimating well to the undulating movements of the sea, a few of the villagers grew pale and became sick, heaving the contents of their bellies overboard. Rayden sympathized with them, remembering how queasy she had been when taking her first sea voyage long ago.

Rayden rested her hands on the railing close to the bow of the ship, watching the rolling waves pass by. A few of them shadowing the path of the vessels, gulls soared through the skies above.

Golden locks streaming in the salt-tinged air, she looked forward to returning to Timiko's village. Closing her eyes from time to time, she welcomed the flow of the cool air across her sun-bathed skin.

About midday, shouts erupted on the ships at the front of the long, staggered column of vessels. Hearing the anxiety and alarm in the voices, Rayden headed to the end of the bow, peering at the horizon.

Set across their path in the far distance were the outlines of a large number of ships, including several double-mast vessels as large or greater in size than Timiko's. Rayden did not have to see any banners or sigils to determine who the ships belonged to.

Striding fast, Rayden found Timiko on the raised platform near the bow. Ascending the short flight of steps, Rayden came to a halt at the pirate leader's side. Eyes locked to the horizon, Timiko said nothing at first.

"Now what?" Rayden asked.

"They raid farther to the south, and their fleet blocks our path home," Timiko remarked, staring toward the small, dark shapes dotting the ocean's surface.

"Fujimara's main fleet, right before us," Rayden stated. "Far too many to confront on the open sea."

Timiko nodded. "This is not the time or place for battle against them. We would be throwing our lives away."

"Is there another route homeward?" Rayden asked.

"There is one," Timko replied, looking aside to Rayden. "A way exists that will take us through a group of small islands. It will also be close to impossible for Fujimara to follow, as you must know the behavior of the water in certain places just to get through."

Rayden had traveled just enough on the waters of the great archipelago comprising Yamatainu to appreciate everything Timiko had just said. The movement of the tides created tremendous hazards for vessels in places easily passable at other points of the day.

Only the most experienced of sea navigators could guide a ship safely through a labyrinthine throng of small islands, even on the clearest, calmest of days. If the weather turned hazardous, the chances for a safe voyage dropped precipitously.

Boding well for Timiko's vessels, no angry-looking cloud

masses lurked on the far horizons. With calm weather and armed with her knowledge of the region, Timiko would hold an enormous advantage over Fujimara if a pursuit developed.

Nevertheless, Rayden could see great tension on Timiko's face. She knew the pirate leader well enough to know that the look reflected a deeper concern, involving something beyond Fujimara's vessels.

"You know these waters and islands," Rayden said. "You guided us through a difficult route to reach the cavern at the last island. You can lead the fleet through another difficult route."

"I can, but it is not just the tides and depths of waters around the islands that gives me cause for concern," Timiko said, an unmistakable shadow of worry passing across her face as she peered eastward.

"What do you mean?" Rayden asked. "Tell me, Timiko, what troubles you?"

"If we have to go through the islands, and take this longer route home, we will have to press through the night to make certain we get back to land ahead of Fujimara's fleet," Timiko explained. "Otherwise we may find them blocking our path once more, when we near our village. We will not be able to avoid them, then.

"Make no mistake, Fujimara's pirates on those ships have seen us too, and they know who we are. That removes two choices from consideration. We cannot turn back, nor can we continue along this route. Both would mean certain death for us all."

"Everyone will help and endure, they will understand the urgency," Rayden said. "If the weather holds clear, as it looks now, you can make use of the night."

"There are other dangers at night, ones that no amount of skill at sea or ability at arms can confront," Timiko replied. "We will have to pray for protection and hope that a god or goddess heeds our petition."

Rayden frowned at Timiko's words. "You are not speaking of matters involving tides, weather, our ships, or Fujimara's fleet."

Timiko shook her head. "I am speaking of a strait that passes between two large islands ... a strait that presents no challenge during the day but involves grave risk at night."

"Not a risk from the behavior of the waters," Rayden stated. "I can see that plain enough upon your face."

"A risk from beneath the surface, that no skill at arms or size of fleet can contend with," Timiko said, staring into Rayden's eyes. "Yet it is the one route offering all of us a chance to survive."

"Then that is the route we will have to take," Rayden replied, wondering what mysteries loomed with the fall of night.

**

Under Timiko's guidance, the fleet passed through a series of smaller islands without incident, avoiding hazards and steering around obstacles that would have claimed the vessels of unseasoned navigators. Following a spectacular sunset rife with orange and golden hues, night draped a star-filled canopy across the skies.

Under moon and starlight, the fleet approached a narrow straight flanked by the shores of two prominent islands. The chatter of the crew dissipated as they drew closer to the passage.

Rayden could sense a growing tension among the pirates. More than one had a look of dread. Watching the change coming over them, Rayden knew the danger spoken of by Timiko loomed imminent.

A short time before, when the strait had first come into view, the command had been given to make use of oars, to increase speed through the passage. At a steady cadence, the blades of a solid bank of oars dipped into the sea on both sides, pulling the vessel faster across the surface.

Striding back down the length of the deck, Rayden found

Timiko standing outside the cabin at the rear of the ship. Like the others around them, Timiko had a look of great unease on her face.

"I am guessing that we have reached the place that concerned you, when we spoke earlier," Rayden said.

Timiko nodded. "The passage of this strait is a dangerous one to take at night. Only the foolhardy or desperate chance it. Maybe we are both."

"What is the danger," Rayden asked.

"You will find it hard to believe until you see it," Timiko replied. "It is my hope that we see nothing and pass through."

"What is said to be here?" Rayden pressed.

"Restless spirits," Timiko replied. She paused for a moment, before continuing. "The spirits who dwell in these waters are nothing we can contend with, if they choose to appear and take victims. We risk everything by taking this passage under starlight, but as I have told you, there was no other way."

"The spirits in the water?" Rayden questioned, looking upon the tranquil scene spreading from the edge of the ship to the star-ornamented horizons. She found it hard to believe that any threat could dwell within such beautiful environs.

"Sometimes they are seen, often they are not ... but if they make their presence known, our fates will stand on the thinnest of ice," Timiko said, in a solemn tone of voice. After another pause, she turned to look at Rayden. "Many thousands died here, in a great sea battle long ago, during the scattering of the Three Treasures of Heaven."

"I have not heard that tale," Rayden said.

"A great war was fought to overthrow an Emperor, who was just a child at that time," Timiko said. "The forces loyal to the Emperor were overcome. The final battle took place right here, in the waters that you see before you.

"Three sacred objects, gifts of Heaven that we know as the

Three Treasures, were lost to the seas during the fighting. The warriors who died in the fighting still remain here. I have never witnessed them myself, but I have spoken to more than one seafarer who has witnessed them with their own eyes."

"What do these spirits seek from the living?" Rayden asked, not liking the implications in any way. "Why do they appear to some, but not to others?"

"Who can say?" Timiko responded. "It is a mystery. I only know that the spirits do appear to some ... and it is most perilous to those who witness them, when they do."

Salt-tinged breezes wafted across the deck as Timiko's ship drew closer to the narrowest portion of the straight. In the deep hush encompassing the occupants of the vessel, the lapping of the waters against the sides of the hull and the creaking of wood resonated louder, accompanying the rhythmic measure of the oars driving into the water and pulling through.

Moonlight glimmered upon the dark waters. The silvery light reflecting from their eyes, nervous pirates stared outward, from where they stood about the deck or were arrayed along the rigging for the oars.

Below the deck, in the hold of the ship, the rescued villagers were spared from the trial. After the horrors they had suffered, their ignorance of what transpired above them stood a small mercy in Rayden's eyes.

Bringing an end to the simmering tension, a number of gasps, exclamations and curses broke out among the crew, up and down the vessel.

"Timiko, they rise from the depths!" Harumoto called in a fear-laced voice from mid-ship.

Had the circumstances been otherwise, Rayden would have found the unfolding sight before her eyes to be stunning in its dimension and beauty. Everywhere that she looked, a vast multitude of glowing, bright green lights dotted the surface of the ocean.

Casting ethereal light all about the vessels and shoreline, the luminance continued to grow from beneath, each light expanding in size. Gazing upon the incredible sight, Rayden stood transfixed.

Something of great magnitude and a cryptic nature approached, rising through the depths toward the surface.

A scattered few at first, and then becoming a torrent, a host of translucent specters lifted up from the water and hovered above the low, rolling waters of the straight. Many ascended into the air close to Timiko's ship, a few coming into sight just off the edge of the vessel in the spot where Rayden stood.

Though having transparence, the ghostly figures retained enough clarity in their appearance that their features could be made out with little difficulty. Warriors clad in helms and armor, bearing a variety of weapons, floated in the night before Rayden's eyes.

Death had left its malignant, corrupting touch upon all of them. Each of the apparitions had the look of a corpse long-decayed, their withered, sunken skin grown taut about the bones underneath, giving all of the entities a skeletal appearance.

Gathering into a dense mass, more and more of the spirits converged upon Timiko's vessel. While pressing together in swelling numbers, the otherworldly horde made no move to draw closer to the vessel.

Looking down the side of the ship, Rayden could see that those in the path of the ship parted to make way for its passage. Like their otherworldly comrades, they kept a wide berth from the sides of the craft.

"I am going to see what is happening!" Rayden shouted to Timiko, before heading toward the raised fighting platform at the stern.

Making her way down the cabin's side, Rayden bounded up

the steps of the platform and came to a halt. Casting her gaze toward the other vessels following in the wake of Timiko's ship, she watched the behavior of the spirits.

Having gained a higher vantage, Rayden discovered that the masses of spirits had concentrated their attention entirely on Timiko's ship. The apparitions paid no heed to the other vessels of the pirate fleet, all of which kept rowing at haste to make it to the end of the strait.

Drifting above the water to keep pace, the ghostly army shadowed Timiko's vessel close as it continued forward, gliding across the low, undulating waves. The distinct behavior of the enigmatic horde intrigued Rayden, and she turned her attention away from the ships following in the extended column behind.

Looking at the immediate area around the ship that she stood upon, Rayden soon identified a specific place where the spirits kept pulling back even farther from the side of the vessel. To her surprise, she noticed that Mari-Chan stood at the focal point in the anomalous movement.

"Mari-Chan!" Rayden called out.

The little man looked back to her with a somber expression on his face. The look stood in sharp contrast to the anxiety and fear riddling the faces of the pirates around him.

"Walk to the other side of the ship and stand there!" Rayden shouted. "Trust me!"

A trace of puzzlement crossed his face, but Mari-Chan did as she asked. Crossing over to the other side of the vessel, he came to a stop near one of the oarsmen.

Behind him, the ghosts filled the bulge of open space that Rayden had taken notice of. A new gap within their ranks formed and sustained in the area where Mari-Chan now stood.

Watching the shift in their behavior, Rayden had no doubts that the ghosts were reacting to Mari-Chan. She could not help but look at the wrapped object held within his hands; an item given to him by an otherworldly figure.

The vessel crossed through the end of the strait without a single crew member coming to any harm from the army of spirits. When the pirate fleet turned to follow the coast of the large island to their right, the mass of ghosts halted at the edge marking the end of the waters between the two islands.

Rayden observed that the ghosts kept their gazes turned toward Timiko's vessel, giving no response to the other ships when they altered their course to skirt around the spectral throng. Staying on the fighting platform, Rayden rested her hands on the top of the back side, watching as the last of the vessels in the extended column made it through the strait and passed by the ghostly multitude.

Gradually shrinking as the fleet gained distance from the strait, the ethereal light generated from the specters remained in view for a little while longer. Finally, the sprawling mass of luminance retracted, sinking downward, like a small, greenish sun dipping on the horizon.

Many sighs and expressions of relief broke out among the pirates when no more traces of the numinous light could be seen. The air itself seemed to lighten.

After stepping down from the platform, Rayden made her way past the rear cabin and walked across the ship's deck toward Mari-Chan. A serious expression fixed upon his face, he watched her approach in silence.

"Whatever was given to you in the shrine, it is of great power," Rayden declared, when she had come to a stop at his side. "I also think that it just saved our lives, and the entire fleet's. The spirits sensed what you carried. No mistake about it."

"Those spirits were ravenous, and yet they did nothing," Mari-Chan said, with a hint of astonishment. "To reveal themselves in such numbers and in such a condition ... they did not intend to let us pass. Not a ship should have made it through.

198

We were meant to be their prey."

"My thoughts as well," Rayden agreed, a grim look on her face.

"I have never felt such restlessness, and agitation," Mari-Chan responded. "But there was fear too, among them. A great fear. I saw it in many of their faces when they looked toward me. What I carry in my hands drew them toward me, in an irresistible way, and it also repelled them, with the same kind of strength."

He glanced down at the object in his hands, staring at it for several moments. The caress of a cool, salt-laced breeze attended Rayden's face as she looked at her friend and studied him closely, thinking about the trial he now endured.

Lines of deep concern marked his expression, but in his eyes she could see that he harbored more than a little fear concerning the task that the goddess had entrusted him with. Though Rayden was grateful that she had not ended up the prey of malevolent spirits, she did not envy Mari-Chan in any way.

A massive burden had been placed upon him. An object of such immense power could tilt the course of Yamatainu's history in a much darker, more insidious direction if it fell into the wrong hands. Nothing would consume Mari-Chan more than to think that darkness prevailed across an entire land due to a failure of his.

Rayden knew that her own path in Yamatainu would not last forever, and that one day she would seek the west once more. With everything she had seen and been through, she would see everything there in a new way. Perhaps, before her greater journey came to an end, she could bring something of great value to the people of her blood and those who had accepted her as one of their own.

She missed the great mountains and mist-shrouded forests where her journey had started, but she knew in that moment that the return would have to wait for a little longer. Rayden knew in her heart that she could not leave Mari-Chan alone until he had seen his task through to completion.

In a gentle voice, she told her friend, "I do not know the minds of gods or goddesses, but I know what it is to take on a burden that appears impossible and laden with the worst of consequences. Know that you will not walk alone while you carry that in your hands. I will go with you until your task is finished."

Mari-Chan made no verbal reply, but when he looked up, his eyes had a wet sheen and a crystalline tear slipped from one of them and tricked down his face. He gave her a lower bow, holding his position for a few moments before raising back up.

"I am honored to have you as my friend," Mari-Chan said.

***

Continuing along their return voyage, shortly after the break of day, Timiko's fleet came upon a bountiful prize lumbering through the coastal waters near to their home village. Rectangular sails unfurled upon a towering pair of masts, the bulky vessel plodded through the low waves, heading directly for the extended column of pirate vessels.

An air of elation and anticipation rippled through the crews. The pirates had been hoping to see the huge vessel, the Emperor's grain ship reported by Harumoto before the pirates had taken to the seas to confront Fujimara's raiders.

Unable to maneuver fast and lacking strong winds to propel forward with any considerable speed, the Emperor's grain ship could do little to react when the smaller vessels of Timiko's fleet fanned out and enveloped it.

Far from defenseless, the grain ship carried a well-equipped force of guards and had a much higher freeboard than any of the pirate vessels. Nevertheless, a rain of arrows coming from every direction began claiming many lives aboard the grain ship, allowing for several of Timiko's vessels to draw alongside the massive vessel.

Felled by arrows loosed by the defenders high above them, a few pirates plunged into the sea. Yet to gain an angle on a pirate, the archers on the grain ship exposed their own bodies. Well-targeted arrows released by Timiko's archers from below sent one after another of the Emperor's soldiers plummeting downward, to splash into the waves and disappear below.

Tossing hemp ropes with iron hooks over the sides, many pirates climbed aboard, storming the grain ship from stem to stern. Urgent shouts and the clang of metal resounded along the deck. After a brief flurry of hand to hand combat, everything went still on the great vessel.

Unlike most of the other pirate bands in the region, Timiko's warriors spared the lives of those who surrendered and any other survivors that they found aboard the conquered vessel. The captives were then bound and taken off the grain ship, along with the abundant contents that were found in the hold.

The looting of the grain ship took a long time, given the great capacity of the cargo hold. Bales of rice seized from many starving communities by the Emperor's solders were reclaimed. The sheer volume required that the contents of the grain ship had to be distributed among several pirate vessels.

After setting the grain ship on fire, the pirate fleet continued onward. The plumes of smoke from the burning vessel remained visible for a long time, until they finally faded from view on the far horizon.

***

After returning home to their fishing village, the pirates unloaded the haul that they had gained from the ships of Fujimara and the Emperor. Jars, bales of rice, chests, and even several strings of copper coins, the latter looted from one of Fujimara's ships, were carried ashore. Storage buildings raised off the ground on stout posts were filled with the great bounty.

The villagers who had been rescued from Fujimara's pirates were given shelter and places to sleep in the homes of the pirates. The captives taken from the grain ship were kept together in a pit that had once been dug for such a purpose.

Though cramped and dirty, the soldiers were fortunate to be captured by Timiko's warriors. The men would remain alive, and they not be subjected to cruelties while Timiko determined where they would be taken.

Rayden invited the pregnant woman that she had saved, whose name she had learned was Tomohime, to stay with her. Seeing the look of relief bloom on the woman's face when she asked her gladdened Rayden. She knew that Tomohime still feared being among sea raiders, even if they were not the ones led by Fujimara.

After the trauma that she had been put through, Tomohime would have suffered undue stress being made to live with someone completely unfamiliar. At the least, Tomohime would have the comfort of knowing she would be under the roof of the one who had intervened and protected her from harm.

An atmosphere of celebration reigned across the village at the return of Timiko's fleet. After the ships had been offloaded and goods stored, a sumptuous feast unfolded that lasted deep into the night.

Drums were played, including stout versions set on the ground, the tight skins beaten upon with thick sticks. There were also double-ended types, with narrow mid-sections that were held in the hands.

Above the rhythms, delicate notes rising from the strings of a zither and melodies born from bamboo flutes danced through the air.

Strolling about the village and taking in the jovial ambience, Rayden indulged in rice wine and settled into a light-hearted, relaxed state. Gaining a little time for herself, Rayden took full advantage of it.

Looking weary to the point of absolute exhaustion, Mari-Chan had retired for the night early, taking the object in his care back to Timiko's house. He would not be in need of Rayden's skill at arms or any other assistance for the duration of the night.

Bantering with Harumoto, Arakabi, and the other pirates, Rayden gained a chance to enjoy the company of her seafaring comrades as they regaled the villagers with tales of the encounters and exploits they had just returned from. Eyes wide with fascination stared at the men when they told of the otherworldly host that had come up from the dark, watery depths.

Listening to their tale under a calm, star-filled sky, in the center of a village filled with jubilance, drinking, and eating, Rayden imagined the ethereal sea encounter would be hard to believe for those in the audience that had not witnessed it. Then again, that tended to be the way things went when it came to matters of the otherworldly. Far more often than not, personal experience far outweighed the voices of witnesses.

The pirates spoke of their bewilderment at the restraint of the ghostly horde. A knowing smile came to Rayden's lips.

Only she and Mari-Chin knew the reason why the ships had been spared. For all the others knew, the object that Mari-Chain now carried everywhere with him was just a valued personal item gained on the excursion; and not a heavy burden given to him by a goddess.

A short while after they had concluded the tale, Rayden moved onward, drifting about the village and enjoying the music that continued to float through the air. The night had a silken touch, and as much as the sea held its share of excitement and wonder, the feel of solid ground beneath her feet brought comfort to Rayden.

"You have a relaxed look about you," Timiko's voice emerged

from the shadows.

Timiko stood near a woodcutter's home and workshop situated to the right of the path. Lifted up on robust timber posts, the long, rectangular building was dark and showed no signs of its residents being there. Doubtless, the place's occupants were off enjoying the ongoing festivities with the returned seafarers.

"I figured you would be among the others," Rayden said.

"After being around so many, I wanted to enjoy a little solitude," Timiko replied.

"Then I shall not be the one to disturb you," Rayden responded, in an air of good humor.

Timiko smiled. "Your company is welcome anytime."

"I am honored to know that," Rayden said, giving a nod of her head to acknowledge the compliment.

"Have you had your fill of drink and food tonight?" Timiko asked. "There is no rationing tonight."

Rayden rubbed her belly, and chuckled. "I may have to do a lot of training at arms tomorrow to make sure I do not add any unwanted weight from tonight's celebrations."

"It is good to indulge in the pleasant things of life, at the right times," Timiko said, laughing. "I am afraid I have indulged too."

Timiko's face then grew more somber. Rayden perceived a trace of sadness within her friend's eyes.

"What is the matter, Timiko?" Rayden asked, bothered at her friend's sudden change in mood.

Timiko mustered a smile. "It is nothing, just a passing memory."

"Please, share it with me," Rayden encouraged her. "It is good to give voice to the things that weigh heavy upon us."

Nodding, Timiko replied, "I was just wishing that my husband was here to enjoy this night with me. It has been almost five years since he entered the Pure Lands, but for me the void inside has never left me. Not for a moment."

"He was a great part of you, so a void is understandable," Rayden said. "When we are parted from someone we love or care about, we are separated from a part of ourselves."

"How do we endure over the years, adding more voids as the years pass by?" Timiko asked, looking to Rayden.

"We gain more voids, but the heart also grows, and has no limit when it comes to loving or caring for others," Rayden answered

"It is just so hard for me," Timiko said, her voice echoing a great inner weariness. "I wish that you had the honor of knowing Yoshinaka. He was a good, just man. A great warrior. He would have held you in high esteem. He would also know how to protect the people in these times."

"You know how to protect the people," Rayden said, in a softer tone. "You do just that, each and every day. I have been a witness to this"

Shaking her head, Timiko stared into Rayden's eyes for a few moments. At last, she continued. "The fighting between the daimios has kept them from focusing their power on the villages along this coast and on the nearby islands. Our raids are little more than a nuisance to them, but the Emperor will demand that we are subdued in time. Otherwise, the more powerful daimios may begin to think of acting in a more independent way, as we do here."

"Every community should be able to act in a more independent way," Rayden said, a little irritation flaring in her tone as she thought of the voracious appetites of kings and emperors for the subjugation of their fellow men and women.

"It is not the world we have," Timiko responded. "Sooner or later, the daimios will come for us in force."

"Who knows what may happen between now and that day?" Rayden said, desiring to encourage her friend. "I have learned many things in my travels, and one of them is that nothing is ever permanent. I have seen empires that appeared insurmountable overcome. I have seen many take firm hold of a new day, of the kind that does not shackle them with the fetters of the rich and powerful. Nothing is certain in this world, but do not despair so quickly, Timiko."

"You always have a gift of wisdom for me, at the times I need them," Timiko said, smiling, a little of her normal, lively spark returning back into her eyes.

"I just know what I have seen, experienced, and learned, along many years of taking hits, falling down, and making mistakes," Rayden said.

"It is from the hits that we take that we learn some of our greatest lessons," Timiko said.

"You have learned more than you may realize from the time that you and Yoshinaka shared together," Rayden said.

Timiko fell silent again, but the hint of a smile remained on her lips. "Sometimes it is like he is still with me."

"Maybe he is, who can say for sure?" Rayden said, smiling at her friend.

"I know he would be very happy with our taking of the grain ship, and what we are about to do with what we took from it," Timiko said.

"I have to admit, I am looking forward to our visits with the villages in this area," Rayden said.

"It restores my heart a little when we are able to bring relief to the suffering people throughout these lands," Timiko said. "I just wish I could do more for them. I am not their ruler and I do not seek to be. But I care for them."

"You would make a wonderful daimio ... or even an empress," Rayden said, a grin on her face.

"If only that were possible," Timiko replied. "Such things are accidents of birth."

"Birth should never determine who gains power over others," Rayden said. "Each of us should be sovereign over our own lives."

"That is a most beautiful dream," Timiko replied, a wistful lilt to her tone.

"A dream that could be realized, if people had the will for it," Rayden said, "But most are too ready to concede the dominion of their wills to others. Too many look for others to lead them."

"You and I can still fight for that dream," Timiko said. "No matter what others may choose to do. In a small way, we will be doing that when we set out tomorrow for the other villages."

"Choosing to live according to what is in our hearts and our minds is something that cannot be denied to us ... not by the most powerful daimio or even an emperor," Rayden stated.

A look of contentment arose upon Timiko's face. "Our hearts and minds are our own, for even the poorest among us."

"Maybe one day people will realize the power in that ... to set themselves free," Rayden said.

"Maybe so," Timiko replied.

A relaxed silence clung to the air between the two for a few heartbeats.

A grin then spread wide on Rayden's lips. "Tonight is not a night to be given to things somber or too reflective. We are friends, we are alive, and we have returned from a successful foray. For my part, I am not yet finished drinking that amazing rice wine. Neither should you be!"

Timiko laughed. "Once more, you bring me wisdom, Rayden Valkyrie! Let us go and see what fools our comrades are making of themselves now, and you and I will have a little more to drink."

The two warriors laughed and started down the path, heading for the jovial sounds of men and women gathered in merriment and celebration under the moon and stars.

***

In discreet fashion, using the strings of copper coins taken from Fujimara's ships, one of Timiko's men named Fukei arranged for a large number of packhorses out of the nearest castle town. It took a few days for the train of horses to reach Timiko's village, but once they arrived, the hardy animals were soon laden with straw-lined bales filled with rice.

To quicken the relief to the long-suffering populace, Timiko divided the packhorses, organizing several groups to radiate outward from the village and distribute the rice throughout the villages of the region. Not long afterward, Rayden, Mari-Chan, and Timiko set out to the east, accompanying one of the larger contingents.

Rayden found herself smiling often and light in heart when they came upon other villages. Adult and child alike stared at her in wonder, marveling at the tall, round-eyed Woman with the Hair of Sun Rays walking at the side of the revered Timiko, who had become such a benefactor to all of them in a time of desperate need.

Knowing that the tales spread of Rayden probably had her twice as tall and capable of leaping over mountains with ease, she was not surprised at the looks of astonishment and regular speechlessness that she encountered when beginning to interact with the local residents upon arrival at a village.

Every village that they visited hosted them for the night, though Timiko had to set a watch over the packhorses, lest another few bales of rice found their way to being pilfered in the dark.

Like Timiko, Rayden did her part, taking up one of the shifts in the watch. On two occasions, late at night, she had to stop village men trying to steal a couple more bales.

In both instances, the men tried rushing her at once, to overpower, seize, and subdue her.

The Sun's Caress

Neither warriors, nor experienced in thievery, the men stood no chance in their aims, and their efforts culminated in swift failure. Though firm and decisive, Rayden did not mete out the same level of response that she would have given a true cutthroat or brigand.

Leaving a few minor bruises to teach them a mild lesson, Rayden knew that the agony of watching their families endure the trials of severe hunger drove their rash actions. Their eyes reflecting shame at their attempts to assail her, the men shuffled off into the night after being sent away by Rayden with their lives and no broken bones or lost teeth.

Timiko spoke to Rayden of having a similar experience at another village during her watch. Unlike Rayden, Timiko had almost slain one of the men, saying that she held back at the last instant from removing the man's head with her naginata.

Rayden could understand Timiko's anger, and she did not blame her for harboring it. Some of Timiko's men had died in the attack on the grain ship, and each village was being given enough to help them sustain for awhile. Timiko found it disgraceful to be attacked in the night by those who she had come to help.

The nighttime incidents proved to be the only major blemish on the first part of their mission. The looks of sheer relief in the eyes and faces of gaunt-looking men, women, and children spoke the loudest, regarding the mission that Timiko had undertaken.

***

Rayden walked with Timiko, close to the lead of the extended column of packhorses. A little over half of the rice had been given out, and the next village lay a day's march ahead.

Timiko intended to reach the village by nightfall, but a light rain throughout the morning slowed their progress along the earthen trail. To pass the time, the two warriors conversed about possible scenarios facing Timiko in the future.

"Many provinces war with each other," Rayden commented. "They cannot spare time or warriors to confront you. It could remain that way."

"What happens if this changes?" Timiko asked. "What if a leader arises to subdue this region? What if the Emperor places his attention here?"

"Then you will prepare, in the best way that you can," Rayden said.

"If that day comes, I will worry about it then," Timiko said, nodding, with no sign of concern on her face. "It is like you have said to me before. Nothing is permanent. The only thing we have is now."

"Maybe you will have your own province one day," Rayden said, giving her friend a smile. "I know the people of this village would be glad of that."

"I know that I would make for a different kind of daimio," Timiko replied. "That is for certain."

"And why I hope that such a development comes to pass, somehow," Rayden said.

The column began crossing through a stretch of flatter ground, surrounded by the slopes of small hills. Almost at once, a deep unease came over Rayden, the hackles standing out along her neck.

"Timiko," Rayden whispered, with a sharp edge.

Timiko nodded, turning her head from left to right. With a hand signal, she brought the column to a sudden halt, with the forefront of it about midway through the swathe of open ground.

All of the pirates, up and down the length of the column, took up their weapons.

Rising out of concealment all around them, a multitude of armed warriors manifested out of the brush, high grass, and trees. A pair of pheasant tail feathers affixed to the crown of their helms, the latter were fashioned of riveted plates, with laced horizontal strips descending from the lower edge to protect their necks. All of the warriors had skirted cuirasses of laced scales that reached down to the mid-thigh.

Most of the warriors were armed with naginatas or straight-bladed spears, in addition to daggers sheathed at their waists. The rest had bows in hand with arrows notched, with full quivers at their right sides.

Rayden cast her gaze all around, eyeing the many bows with arrows set and trained upon Timiko's warriors.

An impasse took shape in moments. The warriors accompanying the packhorses remained in place.

It would be sheer folly to charge the much larger force confronting them. Most would die from arrows, well before reaching an opponent.

The lack of an outright ambush told Rayden that the other force did not seek their deaths; at least not yet. Steady of breath and focused, she waited in silence.

After a short span of time passed, an armored warrior on horseback emerged from the trees ahead, followed by a few others garbed in similar attire.

The lead warrior's light brown stallion displayed an impressive set of harnessing. Ringed about with green tassels, the junctures were ornamented with circular, silver emblems that gleamed bright in the sun.

A cuirass of solid, lacquered plates protected his upper torso. Attached to the cuirass, a quartet of armor pieces, each consisting of small, rectangular scales, laced together with leather cording guarded the warrior from the waist to just below the groin. A pair of similar pieces protected each of his shoulders.

Dark greaves adorned with golden bands pulled in his loose-fitting, light blue trousers just below the knees, leaving the upper part bunched up and baggy. A sword and dagger lay within their sheaths at his left side.

A cupped extension supported a crest of colorful blue and red plumes atop the warriors helm, a construct of riveted plates with rectangular pendant extensions of laced scales attached around the lower rim, shielding the sides and back of his neck. The front part of the helm extended a little forward. Beneath, the wary, studious eyes of an experienced warrior regarded Rayden, Timiko, and the others in the column.

The broad-faced warrior had a moustache and beard, the latter cropped to a sharp point beneath his chin.

The mounted warriors rode toward the front of the column at a slow pace.

"If you wish for a chance to live, I advise all of you to put down your weapons," the warrior declared in a deep, commanding voice.

Timiko looked back down the line of packhorses and nodded to her pirates.

Seeing her friend's intimation, Rayden slid her own weapons back into their places at her waist.

"You have strayed from your lands, Oda Sadanobu," Timiko stated in a firm voice when the lead rider had drawn closer. "This land has no master."

"Control will return soon enough to this lawless hinterland," the haughty-looking man replied. "The daimio I serve prepares even now."

"Is not Hojo Moritsuna waging war elsewhere?" Timiko asked him. "Word reaches us by land and sea, and the latest tales we have heard say he has long since marched to war."

"The fighting will soon come to an end," the man replied. "Hojo Moritsuna has his enemy at bay, under siege. When it is over, he will be stronger than ever. No other wars loom on the horizon."

"Those we harvest from at sea may have cause to come against us, but we have not provoked you or Hojo Moritsuna,"

Timiko said. "What brings you here, now?"

"My reasons are my own," Sadanobu responded, in a curt manner.

Sadanobu then looked toward Rayden. She could not read his expression or his intent within the dark pools of his eyes.

"Who is this foreigner?" he asked, his gaze remaining upon Rayden.

"A friend, from lands far to the west," Timiko replied.

The bushi's eyes shifted to Mari-Chan, lingering upon him for several moments. "Another foreigner, from lands not so far to the west."

"It is not a crime to journey to Yamatainu" Timiko replied.

"The company you keep is ... interesting ... Gozen Timiko," Sadanobu stated. "Few come from the west, and I have never set my eyes upon one of the round-eyes until now. You must have something of great importance with you."

Sadanobu's voice trailed off and his eyes lowered. Rayden could tell that the warrior's full attention had turned to the object carried within Mari-Chan's hands.

"We do," Timiko stated. "We are returning what belongs to the people of this land. What they labored for and harvested."

"You sound like your husband," Sadanobu said, in a scoffing tone that raised the ire in Rayden. "Gozen Shosan never could understand the order of things. He did not understand that the low-born were placed here to serve the needs of those anointed by the gods."

"Perhaps it is you, and those you serve, who fail to see the order of things," Timiko riposted, casting the mounted figure an austere gaze.

Her words evoked a laugh from Sadanobu. When the outburst ebbed, he cast an icy gaze upon her. "Perhaps your husband would still be alive if he had not been such a fool. When you take the side of the low-born, you will face defeat by the high-born."

Timiko's face flushed with anger and Rayden knew that it took all the restraint that she had within her to hold back from a violent response. Looking at Sudanobu, Rayden could see that he would welcome a response to his provocation.

"Go ahead, attack me, and every one of you here will be cut down," Sadanobu chided, his lips spreading in a cruel smile. "Then, I will have cause to burn all your villages to the ground. Every last one of them."

Timiko trembled and her eyes gleamed, but no tears slipped from her eyes. "I seek only to continue my journey and bring rice to starving, suffering people. Let us pass. We have nothing you value."

"That depends on the full purpose of this journey," Sadanobu said, dismounting.

Behind him, the other mounted warriors dismounted, before falling in close behind him.

Walking down the line of packhorses, accompanied by his attending warriors, the bushi's eyes never left the object that Mari-Chan carried.

"Did you not think we took notice that the spirits who dwell within the strait allowed you to pass?" Sadanobu asked, taking slow steps. "Why is that? Even the most silken-tongued among you could not talk your way past those spirits. The spirits from the depths choose who will pass and who will not. They made their presence known to all of you.

"It is no mystery. They did not intend to let you pass, yet here you are. No, you were in possession of something ... something that they feared. There is much more than rice being carried along in this column."

"We have nothing else with us!" Timiko declared. She started to take a step in the wake of Sadanobu, but two of his retainers turned and blocked her path.

"Stay where you are, or I will think that you had a part in the deception I am sensing," Sadanobu said, continuing down the line of horses.

Rayden shifted her feet, and she readied to take up her weapons should the bushi show any sign that he would harm Mari-Chen. Sadanobu came to a halt when he reached them, standing directly in front of her friend.

"Give that over to me!" the bushi demanded, indicating the wrapped object held in Mari-Chan's hands.

"I cannot," Mari-Chan said, firm, staring back at Sadanobu. "The great goddess Maso herself gave me this, and I now carry out her wishes. It would not be wise to interfere."

"The words of low-born pirate scum are empty to my ears," the bushi said in a derisive manner. "The goddess Maso choose a foreign scoundrel like you? Make your outlandish claims elsewhere. Seize them!"

The warriors standing just behind Sadanobu surged toward Mari-Chan. Rayden stepped forward, kicking hard with her left foot along an upward trajectory. The ball of her foot landed squarely, driving into the groin of the warrior at the forefront.

The warrior gasped, and his eyes snapped wide open, just in time to view the smashing right fist that landed in the center of his face. Catapulting him backward, the thundering blow sent him crumpling to the ground.

The stricken warrior's comrades rushed her. Rayden landed a couple heavier blows, but quickly found herself immobilized, taken down to the ground with each of her limbs pinned by a warrior.

Mari-Chan kneeled close to her, his nose bloodied, and his arms held fast by two other warriors.

Sadanobu looked upon them both, holding the wrapped object in his hands. Disdain pooled within his eyes.

"I will have you both dealt with in a moment," he announced.

"But you will both live long enough to see me view what you tried to deny me."

"Do not open that!" Mari-Chan told the bushi in an urgent voice. "Not if you value your life!"

"It is just that you do not want me discovering what kind of treasure you have been carrying, you lying foreigner," the bushi responded, laughing, while beginning to unwrap the object.

"Do not look directly upon the object!" Mari-Chan told Rayden, glancing toward her, his tone adamant and filled with warning. "Not a single glance, no matter how tempted you may be!"

Rayden set her gaze upon the bushi's face, watching his reaction when he unveiled the object. Though she did not look at it with full focus, she could tell the object to be circular in shape.

A clammy chill passing over her, Rayden kept her eyes locked on the bushi, resisting the growing temptation to scrutinize the enigmatic object.

A look of disappointment arose on the bushi's face. His voice echoed his expression. "A mirror. Nothing more. Well-crafted, but I do not see why... "

His voice trailed off and the smile faded from his face. A tear of blood formed and dropped from the inner corner of his right eye. Another descended from his left. Blood began trickling from his nose.

Eyes widening, a stunned look took hold of his face just before rivulets of blood poured from nose, eyes, and ears. Clenching his teeth, Sadanobu trembled, before his body underwent a violent shaking all over.

Blood seeping from the pores of his skin and streaming down his face, Sadanobu fell heavily to the ground, while still clutching onto the mirror.

"Away! Run! A curse is loosed!" one of the other warriors cried out, staring wide-eyed at the body of his dead lord.

The pressure on Rayden's limbs released as the men holding her down let go and scrambled to get away. Freed, she got to her feet quickly and looked around.

Sadanobu's warriors fled the slopes and open ground in great haste, running as fast as they could in their armor. Those who had attended to Sadanobu mounted their horses, whirled them about, and galloped away.

In a handful of moments, the large force had vanished from sight.

During the tumult, Timiko and the other pirates had moved a considerable distance from the packhorses. A nervous edge to their expressions, they now stared toward Rayden, Mari-Chan, and the body of the bushi warrior.

Mari-Chan got to his feet and took slow, purposeful steps toward the dead bushi's body. Keeping his eyes closed tight, he felt about for the mirror, clasping it when his fingers touched the edge. After gently tugging it free of the dead Sadanobu's grasp, he wrapped it back up in the cloth.

"A powerful talisman," Rayden said, walking over to him. "And dangerous."

"The mystery is unveiled to us," Mari-Chan stated, looking upon the covered mirror.

"You know what it is?" Rayden asked.

"It is no less than one of the legendary Three Treasures of Heaven, said to be lost forever when Emperor Naramaro's armies plundered these lands," Mari-Chan replied. He paused for a moment, and then looked into Rayden's eyes. "It was an evil, wicked age that extinguished the light of hope for so many. Suffering in this world is unavoidable. But we can still work to alleviate the suffering of others."

"I understand that," Rayden said, nodding. "It is what we are doing here."

"Yes, it is," Mari-Chan concurred.

Rayden looked away from Mari-Chan and signaled for Timiko and the other pirates to approach. "There is nothing to fear. You can approach."

Timiko and the others returned. The leader of the pirate band headed straight for Rayden.

"I am guessing that there is much you need to tell me," Timiko said, a hint of irritation in her countenance. She looked at the cloth-wrapped mirror. "That was not a simple trinket gained on our journey."

Mari-Chan nodded to her. "No deception was intended. The less that know of it, the better."

Timiko glanced around. "All of those here will be fearful and curious about what you carry with you."

"I will explain everything," Mari-Chan said.

"I hope that you will, I did not think you would hide something like this from me," Timiko said. She looked to both Rayden and Mari-Chan, holding her gaze on each of them for a few heartbeats. "It is unfortunate that you do not believe you can place your trust in me."

Rayden caught the undercurrent of disappointment in the warrior's voice. "Truly, I do trust you. It really is like Mari-Chan has said. The fewer that know about what he carries, the better. There is a great danger about it, and I am not talking about what it did to that warrior. It must not fall into the wrong hands."

"Tell me about this later, then, and maybe there is something I can do to help, if you have truly been given a task by a goddess," Timiko said to Mari-Chan. She turned her gaze back to Rayden. Her eyes glistened with sadness. "Who am I to argue with something like that?"

Without another word, she turned and strode off down the line of horses.

"She will understand, when we have a chance to speak with her," Mari-Chan said, looking toward Rayden.

"I hope that she does," Rayden replied in a low voice, a look of concern on her face.

Around them, the rest of the party checked on the packhorses and prepared to resume the journey. Rayden eyed the bales of rice strapped to the backs of the horses, knowing each of them represented longed-for relief in the lives of families weary from toil and struggle.

The recognition brought Rayden a little consolation in the wake of her sorrow at Timiko's hurt.

"What are you thinking of, Rayden?" Mari-Chan asked.

"I am just thinking of how important each bale of rice in this column is," Rayden said.

Mari-Chan nodded. "Stories are told of great warriors and battles, gods and demons, and sorcerers who wield the powers of dark and light ... yet for all of the villagers who will receive this rice ... this is a hero's quest that holds many lives in the balance."

Rayden took in her friend's words and thought about them. The whims of nature had condemned a multitude to starvation. Peasant villagers had nowhere to turn. In a time of extreme privation, one village could do little to nothing to aid in the plight of another.

Nevertheless, powerful daimios in majestic fortresses still exacted the portion they demanded; no matter how little was left over for those who had produced it through their own toil. Sadanobu's view that the low-born existed to serve the high-born explained the callous attitude well enough.

"Men and women should always be able to use, and enjoy, the harvest of their own labor," Rayden commented, her gaze remaining fixed on the line of packhorses.

"A much better age that would be," Mari-Chan said, nodding. "But for now we must bring what we can to the villages and spare the people as much as possible from the hardship they have been afflicted with."

"We can only do what we are able to do," Rayden said. Seeing that the packhorses were in good order, and the rest of the party had regrouped, she continued. "Let us get these bales to the villages. I do not think the bushi's warriors will return anytime soon. They are probably still running."

"Word will spread of what happened here, and what I carry with me," Mari-Chan said, his tone grave. "Warriors will return in time, make no mistake about that. Next time, they will have a single intent ... to take what I carry."

"In time," Rayden agreed. "Which is why we will continue our path and see to it that you complete your task."

Mari-Chan nodded, and tucked the cloth-wrapped mirror under his right arm.

At Timiko's command, the long column of packhorses started forward. Rayden and Mari-Chan fell in with the others; continuing toward the next village in the upcoming group they would be passing through and bringing to each a welcome boon.

***

Rayden found Mari-Chan sitting in a distinctive pose, atop a hill overlooking the last of the farming villages that Timiko's group had visited and given bales of rice. Wrapped and secure, the mirror lay on the ground next to him. Gazing outward, a placid look rested upon his face.

Settling into a cross-legged position near to the man, Rayden put her mind at ease. Letting herself relax, while savoring the tranquil atmosphere, she gazed toward the enchanting splendor of a sunset brimming in rich, lavender hues. Shadows growing longer with the sun dipping on the western horizon, cool breezes rustled the boughs of the trees about them, bringing scents of pine and cedar wafting through the air.

Every breath that Rayden took within soothed her lungs. Little weighed upon her thoughts for the time being. Gratitude filled her heart for the oasis in the midst of the long journey.

"Such great joy to be found in the most simple of things," Mari-Chan remarked after a long while, breaking the silence. Looking over, he smiled at Rayden, an expression of sheer content upon his face. "One only needs to be open to what is there, in front of them. It is a great blessing to witness moments such as this."

Rayden lowered her gaze toward the village, where the distant sounds of music accompanied the approach of evening. The descending sun's rays pained a scene luxuriant in colors and contrasts, from the sparkling water marking the rice fields to the lush greenery ensconcing the thatch-roofed huts of the village.

Another night of celebration loomed, as it had in every village receiving the unexpected bales of rice. Each arrival to a village brought with it a great reward, one that Rayden could never grow tired of.

Seeing the pure joy and relief on the faces of men and women who had been steeped in weariness and anxiety came as a treasure far greater than any sack of gold. So too did the laughter and gaiety of children who would not be going hungry for a long while.

Rayden could not deny that she looked forward to indulging once more in a considerable amount of the rice-wine favored throughout Yamatainu. But that gratification stood as a minor pleasure next to the contentment filling her heart whenever she assisted villagers offloading bales of rice from the packhorses.

"It is a great blessing, Mari-Chan," Rayden replied, in a low voice. After a slight pause, she added, "One I need at times, along the road I walk."

Mari-Chan's eyes held a little sadness when replied to her. "You have walked a road so few could endure. It is my wish and prayer that many blessings come to you in future times."

"You are a true friend, Mari-Chan," Rayden responded,

smiling. "And it is my wish that you find everything you seek."

"I seek only one thing, Rayden Valkyrie," Mari-Chan stated. "To find my way to the Heaven realm, the Pure Lands."

"I wish I could tell you the destination I seek," Rayden said, her words carrying a melancholic undercurrent. "But I have yet to discover it."

A kind smile arose on Mari-Chan's face. A lively spark danced within the older man's eyes. "Perhaps the destination you seek is the same as mine. It is just that you have not realized it yet."

Rayden's smile broadened, echoing the rays of sun still caressing the peaceful, resplendent vision spread before her. Taking in a long, slow breath, and listening to the sounds of music dancing on the winds, she looked down toward the village, draped now in a soft gloaming.

The years fleeing from her, Rayden viewed everything with a child-like wonder, a sensation that she had not experienced in a very long time. A timeless magic infused every gleam of light and pool of shadow.

Thinking of life as a miracle and gift, only one, singular notion filled Rayden's heart and mind in that moment; gratitude.

With that thought, a flicker of clarity, piercing and manifest, resonated throughout her. There, on the summit of a hill at the edge of the world, Rayden had a glimpse of something timeless and pure; a place where no blood could be spilled, no child could go hungry, and where death had no dominion.

The faces of a young man and woman, in the fullness of health and glowing with joy, smiled upon Rayden from within the brilliant inner light.

Love filling every part of her being, she recognized the pair at once.

Gentle and clear, the words of the goddess Maso passed once more through Rayden's mind.

The Sun's Caress

" Stay true to your path and I assure you, brave warrior, that you will find your way home ... the home that is your destination. You will see it one day, brave warrior."

A sparkling jewel graced with the last rays of the setting sun, a single tear of happiness slipped from Rayden's glistening blue eyes, before gliding down her cheek, and tracing around the radiant smile upon her face.

About the Author

Stephen Zimmer is an award-winning author and filmmaker based out of Lexington Kentucky. His works include the Rayden Valkyrie novels and Tales (Sword and Sorcery), the Rising Dawn Saga (Cross Genre), the Fires in Eden Series (Epic Fantasy), the Hellscapes short story collections (Horror), the Chronicles of Ave short story collections (Fantasy), the Harvey and Solomon Tales (Steampunk), The Faraway Saga (YA Dystopian/Cross-Genre) and the Ragnar Stormbringer Tales (Sword and Sorcery).

Stephen's visual work includes the feature film Shadows Light, shorts films such as The Sirens and Swordbearer, and the forthcoming Rayden Valkyrie: Saga of a Lionheart TV Pilot.

Stephen is a proud Kentucky Colonel who also enjoys the realms of music, martial arts, good bourbons, and spending time with family.

Find Stephen online at:

Website: www.stephenzimmer.com

Facebook: www.facebook.com/stephenzimmer7

Twitter: @sgzimmer

Instagram: @stephenzimmer7

HEART OF A LION

Stephen Zimmer

Heart of a Lion
Softcover ISBN: 978-1-941706-21-3
eBook ISBN: 978-1-941706-23-7

Rayden Valkyrie. She walks alone, serving no king, emperor, or master. Forged in the fires of tragedy, she has no place she truly calls home.

A deadly warrior wielding both blade and axe, Rayden is the bane of the wicked and corrupt. To many others, she is the most loyal and dedicated of friends, an ally who is unyielding in the most dangerous of circumstances.

The people of the far southern lands she has just aided claim that she has the heart of a lion. For Rayden, a long journey to the lands of the far northern tribes who adopted her as a child beckons, with an ocean lying in between.

Her path will lead her once more into the center of a maelstrom, one involving a rising empire that is said to be making use of the darkest kinds of sorcery to grow its power. Making new friends and discoveries amid tremendous peril, Rayden makes her way to the north.

Monstrous beasts, supernatural powers, and the bloody specter of war have been a part of her world for a long time and this journey will be no different. Rayden chooses the battles that she will fight, whether she takes up the cause of one individual or an entire people.

Both friends and enemies alike will swiftly learn that the people of the far southern lands spoke truly. Rayden Valkyrie has the heart of a lion.

Thunder Horizon
Softcover ISBN: 978-1-941706-57-2
eBook ISBN: 978-1-941706-56-5

A deadly menace stalks the shadows of the lands to the north, stirring the winds of war. Farther south, the power of the Teveren Empire spreads with every passing day, empowered by dark sorcery. Formidable legions bent on conquest are on the march, slavery and subjugation following in their wake.

Within the rising maelstrom, Rayden Valkyrie has returned to the Gessa, to stand with the tribe that once took her into their care as a child. No amount of jewels or coin can sway her, nor can the great power of her adversaries intimidate her.

With a sword blade in her right hand and axe in her left, Rayden confronts foes both supernatural and of flesh and blood. Horrific revelations and tremendous risks loom; some that will see Rayden's survival in the gravest of peril.

Even if Rayden and the Gessa survive the trials plaguing their lands, the thunder of an even darker storm booms across the far horizon.

Thunder Horizon is the second book in the Dark Sun Dawn Saga.

www.ingramcontent.com/pod-product-compliance
Lightning Source LLC
Chambersburg PA
CBHW030113260626
47156CB00008B/2633